G000069206

The Winter Sniper

James   Mullins

Published By: Longinus Publishing

All rights reserved. This book may not be reproduced in any form, in whole or in part, without written permission from the author.

This is a work of fiction. All characters and events portrayed in this book are either products of the author's imagination or used fictitiously.

©2019 James Mullins First Printed Edition: December 25th

2019

ISBN: 9781675462898

Chapter 1

Karelia Isthmus, Finland November 30th 1939

Hale took a deep breath and let it out slowly. The steam from his warm exhaled air, slowly dissipated in front of him as his ears registered a sound. *Is that them?* He thought. His thumb unconsciously fingered the safety on his SK Nagant M/28-30 bolt action rifle. He could feel a hint of the cold metal through the thick fabric of his gloves.

He looked around at his immediate surroundings. The land was shrouded in a velvety blanket of whiteness broken by a seemingly endless number of trees. The trees, mostly birch, had lost their leaves to fall's chill several months prior. The branches of the trees were all tinged with the white of last night's snow fall. The tree's branches intertwined to form an endless canopy as far as the eye could see. It was a breathtaking sight to behold.

Hale exhaled once more and watched the steam from his breath slowly dissipate in front of him. He felt a dull pain in his posterior, so he shifted his position on the large branch he sat on to relieve it. He sighed contentedly as the pain ebbed. The faint sound continued to buzz in his ear. He asked himself again. *Are they coming?*

He sat in near silence for several more minutes as the faint noise transformed itself into a dull rumble. *This is it. They're coming.* He closed his eyes and imagined where he would be right now if it wasn't for them. Certainly not perched in a tree in the miserable cold of this late November morning, awaiting the invaders.

Reality fell away, and an image began to form in his mind of a blanket wrapped around his shoulders as he sat on the floor in front of a warm fire. He was sipping a cup of hot cocoa, as he let his imagination take over. He could almost feel the hot liquid slide down his throat and fill his insides with its sweet tasting warmth.

He looked around the room. In front of him was a fireplace. Within the fireplace was a pair of logs that were ablaze. A warm flame crackled and occasionally snapped as he absorbed the warm glow. The heat created a ruddy red glow on the pale skin of his face.

From behind, he felt two arms wrap around him. He smiled and turned to see his little sister grinning at him. She was missing one of her front teeth. The tooth had recently fallen out. "Good morning," His sister Aina said.

Hale returned the smile and with a, "Good morning." Of his own. The smell of sizzling meat wafted over them. Turning toward the kitchen Hale added, "Smells like breakfast is almost ready. Would you like some of my hot cocoa?"

Aina's grin broadened into a full smile and she nodded vigorously, "Yes please!"

Hale turned to hand her the cup when a dull clanking noise pulled him back into reality. He opened his eyes and looked to his right at the lonely ribbon of mud and gravel that broke the seemingly endless rows of trees that surrounded him. *Yes, that has to be them.*

Hale removed the mask that kept his face warm and slipped it into his pack. He then set his rifle down gently in his lap and removed his left glove. Stowing it in the pocket of his thick overcoat, he flicked off the safety with his left thumb. Despite the frigid cold, the well-oiled switch clicked into place without resistance. Remembering the day, the rifle was given to him, he thought, *Thanks Dad.* He pulled the glove back onto his left hand and craned his head so that he could see as far up the road to his right as possible.

The dull clanking noise continued to grow in volume. A pair of stags bounded by below him heading away from the noise. He took another deep breath, looked up, and saw several squirrels dashing amongst the branches above him. They too headed away from the noise, *North. Away from the invaders and toward safety.*

Hale began to feel the ground shake as the large Soviet column came into view. A Russian T-28 tank, painted white to blend into the terrain and emblazoned with a large red star on its turret, slowly clanked and groaned as the metal monster made its way up the road. The steel beast belched black smoke out of its hindquarters and spat mud and gravel from its tracks as it chewed up the soil of his homeland, Finland.

The vehicle had tracks on the left and right side with two large wheels at either end, eleven small wheels on the lower half of the track, and three slightly larger wheels that touched the upper track. The two large wheels worked to drive the vehicle forward and the smaller wheels aided in holding the tracks in place.

Atop the tank, sticking out of a hatch in the top of the turret was a man. He wore a green fur cap and a heavy coat. The coat, also a dark green in color, disappeared below his chest into the hatch. His black gloved hands held a pair of binoculars which he used to scan the forest around him as the tank slowly lumbered forward.

As Hale watched, the next vehicle in the column slid into view, it was a GAZ-MM. The GAZ-MM was a truck. The truck had a cab in the front that could hold two people, and a canopy covered rear deck, where soldiers or supplies could be carried. He could see the faint outline of the driver's head through the glass in the door as the vehicle slowly made its way forward behind the T-28. The truck was painted dark green and had a red star of its own emblazoned on the driver's door.

The canopy of the GAZ-MM was the same dark green color as the tank commander's coat. Hale took another deep breath and let it out slowly as he raised his rifle to his shoulder. This time he held his breath as he looked down the length of his rifle and drew a bead on the head of the tank commander with the iron sights.

Hale peered through the first sight which was a half square that stuck up out of the rifle at the base of the barrel just beyond the bolt mechanism. He did this with his right eye as he closed his left. The square had a small notch in it that he lined up with the pip on the end of the rifle. He moved the rifle until both the notch and the pip lined up with the tank commander's head. The head appeared as a small green dot within his gun sight.

He then shifted the rifle slightly forward, so that the head barely showed in the hole of the square on the right side and slowly applied pressure to the trigger of his gun. The rifle belched acrid smoke and flame as it roared to life. The sound of the single shot echoed off the thousands of nearby trees as the bullet traveled nearly instantaneously to the head of the tank commander and hit it.

The bullet carved through the man's fur lined cap, then his skull, next into the fleshy brain beneath, and finally out the other side as it continued its course. Before the bullet ended its journey by striking the trunk of a tree situated somewhere behind the tank commander his lifeless body hunched forward, and the man's chin struck the edge of the turret ring he stood in and blood began to pool on the top of the T-28 contrasting sharply with the white paint. *I have just taken a life. God please forgive me.* Hale thought.

Before the column could react to Hale's shot, he pulled the bolt on his rifle and ejected the first spent bullet. As he slid the bolt back, the second bullet in his five-bullet magazine clicked into place. He then swiveled his rifle to the right, lined up the first truck driver's head in his sights, and squeezed the trigger again. This time his bullet shattered glass the moment before it struck its target. As the driver slumped forward, the bullet, now misshapen from its impact with both the truck's window and the driver's skull, began to tumble as it slammed into the body of the Russian sitting to the right of the truck driver.

The bullet penetrated the man's arm, just above the bone in his left bicep, and entered his chest. As it continued along its path the bullet cleaved the man's heart in two and exited out his right side before coming to rest in the passenger side door of the truck. The column lurched to a stop, as Hale pulled the bolt on his rifle again. A small puff of smoke emerged from the rifle as he did so. Like the first time he operated the rifle's bolt, the spent cartridge was ejected. Hale's eyes followed the steaming brass metal for a moment as it tumbled to the forest floor below. *Stay focused.* He mentally chastised himself as he looked back up at the now halted column.

Several Soviet soldiers emerged from the rear of the canopy covered first truck in line. He drew a bead on the first man to emerge and squeezed the trigger. An instant later the soldier collasped to the snow-covered road. Hale quickly worked the bolt of his rifle twice more dropping the first man's two companions within the space of two heartbeats. Other Soviets who had emerged from the trucks behind the first one, followed the sound of his rifle, and began running toward him. He quickly tabulated the number of soldiers in his head, *Three squads of eight men each. A full platoon. Too many.*

Hale pulled the bolt back on his rifle, opening the chamber. He reached into his right coat pocket and grabbed his next clip full of bullets. With a grunt he slammed it into place, pulled the metal clip free, dropped it in his left pocket, and quickly pushed the bolt on his rifle forward to secure it in place. This action pulled the first bullet in the internal magazine into the rifle's chamber.

Hale took another deep breath as he targeted the first man running toward him in his iron sights. He squeezed the trigger and his rifle roared to life as it bucked against his right shoulder and tried to leap out of his hands. With practice ease he held the rifle in place.

An instant later the lead soldier dropped to the ground. He operated the bolt quickly and expended the four remaining bullets in the rifle. Each shot found its way into the head of one of the oncoming invaders. As more of the invaders emerged from their trucks the guilt he had been experiencing fell away and his heart hardened, *Good riddance.* He thought to himself.

As Hale coldly slapped his third clip of bullets into place, the turret of the T-28 began traversing in his direction. He took a deep breath and held it, as he quickly took aim, and dropped four more of the Soviet invaders with his rifle. The barrel of the T-28 made him nervous as it slowly swung in his direction which caused him to miss a shot.

Dammit, he chastised himself mentally. He pulled the bolt back on the rifle to open the chamber. Next, he reached into his right pocket, grabbed his last loaded clip of bullets, and slapped it into place. A faint click told him that the bullets had slipped into position and locked. He pulled the metal clip free, closed the bolt, and raised his rifle to shoot again. His eyes focused on the black maw of the tank gun now pointed at him.

Time to go, he thought. He slung his rifle onto his left shoulder and leapt onto the trunk of the tree from the branch that he had been perched upon. With his arms wrapped around the trunk he quickly slid to the ground. The moment his feet touched the frigid snow the place where he had been sitting a moment earlier exploded into a ball of flames. The wood of the tree groaned as it shattered into a million splinters and caught fire.

The shock wave from the blast knocked him to the ground face first. The snow helped to soften the blow from the concrete like surface of the frozen ground beneath. As he sat up, he blinked for several moments as stars danced in front of his eyes and his hearing became muted. The crackling flames of the tree branches above him sounded dull, as if he were underneath the surface of a lake.

Hale's mind shifted out of reality back to another time. He stood shivering in the early morning air as he leaned up against a tree trunk. It was snowing. He glanced to his right in the direction that he knew his father stood. Like unmoving statues, they both waited for a moose or a deer to happen by.

Hale heard movement to his left, the sound of several paws striking the snow. He turned to face the sound and shivered as he met the steely gaze of a wolf running toward him. The beast's coat was a dappled mixture of white and gray. As it drew near, the creature curled its lips into a snarl, revealing two sharp fangs, and dozens of smaller pointy white teeth.

Hale raised his single shot rifle up to fire; it had been his grandfather's. Frightened, he closed his eyes and squeezed the trigger. As his Grandfather's gun spat fire, the memory faded, and he snapped back into reality. Hale shook the cobwebs out of his head and slowly made his way to his feet.

Nearby, he heard a branch snap. He pulled his rifle off his shoulder as he whirled around toward the sound. He caught sight of an enemy soldier topping the ridge a hundred meters from him. Like the wolf, as he caught sight of Hale, the man curled his lips to reveal his not so white teeth. The soldier's fur cap had a large red star emblazoned on it. As he saw Hale a hundred paces in front of him, he raised his rifle and squeezed off a quick shot.

The poorly aimed gunshot slammed into the trunk of the burning tree to Hale's left. Hale raised his own rifle and returned fire. He didn't miss. The next four Soviets to top the ridge quickly suffered the same fate as the first.

Hale slung his rifle over his shoulder again and glanced at the ground. He instantly spotted what he was looking for. *My skis.* He placed his booted feet into the skis and hurriedly strapped them in. As he drove his ski poles into the snow and started moving forward the sound from three rifles discharing washed over him. A moment later three bullets impacted into the snow around his feet. The impact caused the snow to leap from the ground for a moment before falling back to earth.

As Hale built up speed, a group of Soviet's standing atop the same ridge where he dropped several of their companions, moments before, fired their rifles at Hale's retreating zigzagging form. As Hale made his way up the opposite ridgeline bullets flew past him, some near enough that he could hear a faint buzzing sound and felt a wisp of wind as they passed.

As soon as Hale topped the ridge and disappeared from the sight of the oncoming soldiers, he changed direction to the south. He continued in this direction for several minutes. He fell into a familiar rhythm as he made his way across the countryside. Right pole, right leg forward, left leg pushing, then left leg forward, and left pole to propel him.

Hale had gone several hundred meters before he heard the voices of several Soviet soldiers behind him. Unable to understand what they were saying, he imagined their confusion as he wasn't in sight. *It won't be long before they see my tracks and figure it out.* He thought.

He slipped back over the ridge in the direction of the road. Finding a large oak tree amongst the birch. He came to a stop and placed the trunk of the tree between him and his trail. He then knelt and opened his overcoat. Underneath the coat and over his shirt, he wore two belts that held dozens of 7.62 x 53R rounds for his SK Nagant.

Hale took his gloves off, dropped them into his lap, and then reached into his left pocket to grab one of the empty magazine clips. He wore his ammo belts inside his coat to keep the bullets warm. This enabled him to do this barehanded reload quickly. He slipped the end of the first bullet into the clip he held, then the second, the third, fourth and finally the fifth.

Task complete, he pulled the bolt open on his rifle and pushed the clip into the rifle's breech. Feeling the telltale click of the bullets sliding into place, he quickly pulled the clip out, and slid the bolt forward closing the breech. He dropped the empty metal clip into his lap, where it landed on top of his gloves. He quickly reloaded each of the clips until his right pocket bulged with the weight of fifteen bullets.

As Hale completed loading, the sounds of footsteps crunching in the snow on the other side of the ridge behind him could be heard. He slipped his gloves on, and then quickly ensured that his rifle was ready to fire. Preparations complete he quietly stood up.

Hale heard the voice of the first soldier on top of the ridge line. The man said, "Syuda." The voice sounded young like his own. *Such a waste. We should all be inside by a warm fire, not trying to kill each other.* He thought.

He peeked around the tree trunk he hid behind and quickly stole a glance at the enemy. The young Soviet soldier, who missed Hale's quick glance, looked much like the rest of the soldiers he had killed. Green fur cap, with a red star emblazoned on it, black leather boots and gloves, with a dark green overcoat that stretched down to the man's knees. A small lock of blond hair was visible hanging down from the hat, *Same color as mine.* Hale thought.

As Hale stepped out from the protection of the oak tree, the Russian soldier was looking back at his companions on the other side of the ridge. Hale quickly raised his rifle, took aim, and squeezed the trigger. The bullet slammed into the back of the young man's head with a dull smack and he fell backwards. His green cap and body fell separately, as they disappeared and tumbled down the hill. As the corpse came to rest at the bottom of the gorge, another senseless and nameless victim of Stalin's aggression, the loose lock of blond hair became matted in the young man's blood.

Hale quickly retreated behind the trunk of the tree to wait. He heard the voices of the man's companions as they talked hurriedly in Russian. After chattering excitedly for several moments, they came to a consensus on what to do next. Silent now, they began to creep forward toward the top of the ridgeline that separated them from Hale.

Hale heard the men crawling forward and then stop, *What are they doing? Do they know where I'm at?* He thought.

Before he could decide on his next course of action, the men rose to their feet with a roar and began charging down the hill toward Hale's oak tree. Not knowing what else to do, Hale sat down so that he would blend in with the snow, slung his rifle over his shoulder, and pulled out his Lahti pistol. Next, he removed his gloves and checked the pistol's magazine to ensure all was in order. The metal of the gun felt cold against his skin. Task complete, he held it with the barrel pointed skyward and his right index finger on the trigger.

Without warning, the squad of Russians barreled past him as they ran down the hill. As they rushed past, they seemed heedless of him as his white overcoat and pants helped him blend in with the snow on the ground. Hale stood and stole a glance around the oak tree, back in the direction the Russians had just come from. There were two more of them standing on the ridgeline, *I'm surrounded.* He thought in dismay.

Not knowing what else to do, Hale raised his pistol and took aim at the Russian that was furthest away from him as the man charged down the hill and squeezed the trigger of his pistol. The Lahti bucked in Hale's hand as the bullet found the back of the Soviet's neck. The unfortunate, fell face forward into the snow and slid for several feet before coming to a stop.

The seven other members of the squad dropped to the ground in reaction, as the single shot rang out. Hale managed to put a bullet into another of the green clad soldiers as they dove for the earth. The forest became silent save for the injured man's cries of pain.

The two Russian's behind him on the ridgeline conversed hurriedly in their native tongue, *Trying to figure out where the shot came from.* Hale thought.

Coming to a consensus, the two enemy soldiers started slowly creeping forward toward Hale. Panic ensued as the reality of the situation set in. *What do I do now? I'm trapped between two groups and it won't be long before they figure out exactly where I'm at.* Hale thought.

Hale's thoughts slipped away from reality as he remembered back to a time when he was in a similar situation. He glanced down at the cold water he stood in and shivered, *Must stay quiet or they will find me.*

He had sat in the cold creek for what had seemed like hours as two older boys hunted him. Hale had made them look like fools in front of the other children at recess earlier that day in school and now they aimed to even the score. The sound of the trickling water from the creek reminded him that his bladder was full. The gurgling, bubbly, frothing water tormented him as he continued to try and out wait the boys that hunted him. He gritted his teeth as he resisted the urge to let it go. *I'd never hear the end of it, if they found me, beat me up, and I pissed myself.*

As one of the larger boys drew near, Hale crouched down further into the creek bed trying to make himself invisible. It didn't work. Without warning, two large hands painfully grasped his shoulders and jerked him to his feet as the voice behind those hands said, "I've found the little worm!"

Hale shuddered as his thoughts snapped back into reality. A Russian, another young man like himself, stood over him and yelled, "Bot Oh!"

As the Soviet's rifle swung upward, Hale took aim with his Lahti, and put a bullet in the man's head. The soldier, slain, fell backwards as his rifle tumbled to the ground. Hale, hearing movement directly behind him, swung his pistol toward the noise and fired.

Another man, his eyes wide as his faced filled with a look that was one-part horror and one-part shock, was a mere three feet from his own. The man's stunned look and wispy hints of his first beard would forever be seared into Hale's memory. As a scarlet spray exploded from the Soviet's neck. He stumbled back a step and tried to place his left hand over the wound to staunch the bleeding. It didn't work. *Must have hit an artery.* Hale thought.

Without warning a pair of arms grasped him from behind forcing him to drop his pistol. *Oh God not again!* The thought exploded into Hale's mind as anxiety took over.

At the same time, the dying enemy soldier in front of him staggered forward and raised his right hand to grasp him. Hale grabbed the knife from the bleeding man's belt with his left hand and thrust it over his right shoulder. The arms around him slackened and fell away without a sound. He then kicked the dying man in front of him in the stomach. The breath knocked out of him; the man Hale had shot tumbled down the hill. As he rolled, he tried to warn his comrades but all that came out of his mouth were red bubbles and a hiss as his lungs filled with blood.

Hale dropped to the ground to retrieve his pistol. He glanced to the right to confirm that the man he had stabbed wouldn't be a threat. The man would never be a threat to anyone ever again, as Hale's desperate thrust had put the knife right through the man's left eye. Hale glanced around and shuddered at the gruesome sight. The snow around him had turned red from the blood of his enemies.

He felt a pang of guilt before his heart hardened and his thoughts shifted to rage. *The soil of my homeland will feast upon the blood of every last one of these filthy invaders.*

A few shots rang out from the group that had ran past Hale in his general direction. He heard a few of the bullets slam into the trunks of nearby birch trees. Hale crouched down, careful not to get any of the blood on his white pants and great coat. He searched the body of the soldier he had slain with the knife. As he searched, his hand wrapped around the cool metal cylinder he was hoping to find, a grenade. The word *Bingo* flashed through his mind.

Hale took the grenade and twisted the cap, so that it was armed. He wrapped the fingers of his right hand around the wooden shaft and threw it down the hill toward the origin of the poorly aimed gunfire. Moments later an explosion erupted, and the gunfire ceased. The grenade created a large fireball that expanded and reached up toward the heavens.

Using the grenade explosion as a distraction, Hale immediately stood up and began using his ski poles to pull himself toward the top of the hill. Moments before he reached the ridge a rifle was fired. Hale felt a huge crushing weight slam into his back which caused him to topple over the top of the ridge just in front of him. He lost his balance and tumbled down the hillside. Just before he reached the bottom of the gully, he crashed into a tree. Pain now wracked both the front and back of his body.

He took a few moments to take stock of the situation through his pain-addled mind. *I'm hit!* He thought, his inner voice laced with panic as fear exploded in his mind.

Hale took a deep breath and removed his rifle from his shoulder. The pain in his back shifted to a dull throb. *I thought being shot would feel worse than this.*

He reached around with his left hand and felt the place on his back that throbbed. He brought his hand back around and stared at it for a moment, *No blood?*

Surprised, Hale then looked at his rifle. Just below the bolt, and right where the metal section joined with the wooden stock, was a faint indention on the metal. He breathed in silent relief and looked up at the sky, *Thank you God.*

His moment of reverie was abruptly ended by the voices of several Russians. They had returned to the top of the ridgeline that he had just tumbled from. The Soviets were hunting for him. As they gazed down the hillside, they saw his movement, raised their rifles, and simultaneously fired three shots in his direction. The bullets impacted the ground around him and kicked up snow. Hale stayed low, and quickly checked his rifle to ensure it was in working order.

When Hale was done with his rifle, he looked up at the source of the gunfire. He saw three enemy soldiers. Their green forms were silhouetted by the gray sky behind them. He raised his rifle in the direction of the middle one and took aim. He pulled the trigger and felt his Mosin Nagant kick against his shoulder as it roared and sent death on its way. Nearly an instant later, all three men dropped to the ground seeking cover. One of them would never rise again.

Hale pulled the bolt on his rifle ejecting the spent bullet. Two more shots rang out. This time the bullets were nowhere near him, *Just trying to keep me down. They can't see me now that they are on the ground.* He thought.

Hale released his boots from his skis and crawled around to the other side of the tree to put it between himself and the enemy. As he did so several more shots rang out. They were all too high, *The cowards are scared to rise and take aim.* Hale thought in amusement.

Given a moment of reprieve, his mind slipped back to that day he hid in the creek bed. The two larger boys, one with red hair, the other with black, had pushed him up against a large elm tree. The largest, a boy of perhaps fourteen who had been far too fond of sweets, grinned at Hale and said, "Did you think you were going to get away with that little worm?"

Hale's eyes narrowed as he glared back at the fat boy and struggled against the arms that grasped him from behind before smiling and saying, "Of course, everyone knows you're the dumbest boy in the school."

The larger boy's plump cheeks flushed until they matched the color of his hair. Enraged, he let out a scream and slammed his fist into Hale's abdomen. Hale gasped as pain exploded in his stomach. The red-haired boy's freckled face contorted into a menacing grin as he said, "I hope you enjoyed that you little shit. There is more to come. Much more."

The fat boy's voice trailed off as Hale looked down at the bully's shoes. He could see his reflection in their black well-polished leather. The reflection of his face taunted him. He looked back up at the red headed boy, smiled, and spat in his face.

Enraged at Hale's defiance, the overweight bully screamed, and threw punch after punch at Hale. Hale's mind exploded in anguish at the pain of that day as the memory faded and his thoughts returned to reality as another volley of bullets zipped by overhead.

Hale stood up and took a quick glance around the tree trunk. The attempt was awarded with a shot and a bullet that whistled by where his head had been a moment before. *They've figured out my exact location.* Hale looked at the forest around him. He sighed as he saw no avenue of escape, that left one option, *I've got to take them down before they get me.*

Hale pondered the situation for a moment. As he did so, another bullet slammed into the tree he was using as a shield between himself and the Soviet soldiers. *I need a distraction.* Hale took stock of everything he had with him, his rifle, pistol, magazines, clothing, and coat. Everything he wore was the color of snow. Then his eyes shifted to the fur lined cap on his head and he grinned. *Worth a shot, I guess. Maybe two.* He silently chuckled at his own pun.

Hale raised his rifle up with his left hand and rested the stock on his shoulder. With his right, he removed his hat, and then reached around the tree and threw it toward the two soldiers on the top of the hill. Two shots immediately reverberated through the trees as Hale dropped his own rifle into place and took aim at one of the figures sitting on the ridgeline. He took a deep breath and held it. Both men operated the bolts on their own rifles as they glanced nervously down at Hale's form taking aim at them.

As they started to raise their rifles, Hale fired his rifle. His target's green cap flew off his head as his bullet found its mark and he crumpled to the ground. The other man quickly returned fire at Hale. He missed. Unphased by the return fire, Hale quickly operated the bolt on his rifle as the hastily fired shot sailed past him. He took aim on the second man as he frantically operated the bolt on his rifle to drop another bullet into the chamber.

The rifle jammed, and the man's resolve broke. He stood to flee down the hillside behind him. He didn't make it. Hale crouched back down behind the tree he used to hide from the slain soldiers and listened. The only sounds that filled his ears were those of the woodland. Snowflakes striking the earth, and the sound of tree branches creaking in the wind. Gone was the sound of voices, footsteps, and gunfire. He was alone.

He sat there for several minutes just listening to the frantic beat of his heart as it thundered in his ears. When it finally slowed, he gathered up his skis and slowly made his way toward the corpses of his enemies. The first one he found nearby at the bottom of the hill in front of him. He searched it and found two things of interest to him, a bottle of vodka, and a grenade.

Hale slipped the grenade into his belt and stood. He unscrewed the cap off the vodka and took a sip. As the vodka burned its way down his throat, he heard a rifle shot to his north. He smiled and thought, *The day was young and there were many more invaders that needed killing.*

Chapter 2

Karelia Isthmus, Finland November 30th 1939

Hale's knuckles turned white as he clenched the steering wheel in front of him. Beads of sweat slid down his forehead as he drove the truck along the gravel road. As he glanced to his left, trees whipped by in a blur as his foot kept the accelerator pressed to the floor.

As the sweat started dripping into his eyes, he released his left hand from its death grip upon the steering wheel. He glanced at his hand, as he raised it up to his forehead to wipe away the beads of sweat, it was shaking. Sighing deeply, he glimpsed to his right at the empty cab. The other seat in the cab was unoccupied except for the hand grenade that rolled around upon it.

How much longer? Hale wondered nervously. Despite his anxiety, the tree speckled white lands outside the truck's windows dulled his senses and his thoughts began to drift into the past.

"Hale! Press the clutch down to shift the gear!" Sergeant Kivi barked into his ear gruffly.

As Hale attempted to shift into second gear the engine began to stall, "See-saw dammit!" Roared Kivi.

Hale nodded as he attempted to push down on the accelerator. At the same time, he kept his left foot on the clutch. Despite his best efforts, the truck, a Sisu sputtered and stalled, "Goddam it!" Roared Sergeant Kivi, "I told you to see-saw!"

Hale visibility shrank into his seat and said, "I'm sorry Sergeant."

"You goddammed right you'll be sorry! Screw this up again, and I'll bury my boot so far up your ass, you'll have to open your mouth, so I can scratch my toes!" Sergeant Kivi bellowed. He took a deep breath, let it out slowly, then added in a normal tone of voice, "Start the motor and try again."

Hale nodded, shifted the gear back to neutral, pressed in the clutch, and turned the key on the ignition. Starting with a string of sputters, and coughs, the truck roared to life, "Now try again. Shift it into first gear, gently release the clutch, and slowly press down on the accelerator."

Hale nodded as he said, "Yes sir."

Hale reached out and grabbed the knob on the end of the shifter and tugged it downward and to the left, "Now give it some gas and start letting up on the clutch." Sergeant Kivi advised.

Hale let up off the clutch while simultaneously pressing

down on the accelerator. With a lurch the Sisu began moving forward. Sergeant Kivi smiled, "That's it, you're doing it!"

Hale continued to slowly press down on the truck's accelerator as he let up off the clutch. He watched as the speedometer on the dashboard in front of him slowly ticked up to 15 kph. As the truck passed 15 kph the engine began to roar, "It's time to shift to second." Sergeant Kivi advised.

Hale swallowed hard, as he nervously nodded in acknowledgement to the order. Holding his breath, he pushed down on the clutch with his left foot, grabbed the shifter, and moved it toward the dashboard in a straight line. With a lurch, the truck shifted into second gear, and the loud roar of the engine immediately died down to a dull hum.

He gave the truck some gas and started letting up off the clutch. Sergeant Kivi slapped him on the back, smiled and said, "You got it. Take us up to 30 kph and level off. You need to practice keeping the truck on the road. Once you get the hang of that, we'll let you practice on a gravel road. If you ever have to drive, it will likely be on a gravel or dirt road."

Hale's thoughts faded back into the present, off in the distance, on the road ahead, he saw a blurry black dot. *That has to be the column.* Gritting his teeth and clenching the wheel, he kept the accelerator mashed to the floor as he quickly closed the distance between himself and the vehicle ahead. The engine of his Gaz-MM truck roared in his ears as the trees whizzed by.

The vehicle slowly morphed from a black shadow on the horizon into an olive drab green twin of the Gaz-MM truck he drove. Underneath the canopy that covered the truck's bed, he could see a squad of Russian soldiers huddling together for warmth. One of them glanced in his direction. After a moment, the Soviet man smiled and waved. The truck bed and the men along with it, would occasionally bounce upward as the wheels struck a pothole in the gravel road.

Hale returned the smile and saluted in the Russian fashion. He continued to close the distance to the last truck in the column. As he brought his vehicle within twenty feet of the canopied rear of the truck ahead of him, he reached over with his left hand and started rolling down the window. Finishing, he raised his right knee up to hold the steering wheel in place as he reached over and grabbed the cast iron RGD 33 hand grenade rolling and bouncing around on the bench next to him.

As his fingers clutched around it, he reached over with his left hand and twisted the top to arm it. The Soviet soldier that had smiled at him only a few moments ago forehead creased in worry, as he frowned at Hale's continuing approach. Switching the grenade to his left hand, Hale reached out of the window and tossed it toward the opening in the rear of the Soviet truck. Which was now only a few feet ahead of the front bumper on his own vehicle.

Hale's eyes followed the grenade as it lazily arced into the canopy covered rear of the truck in front of him. The man, who had been watching him carefully, eyes widened in shock. Reacting quickly, the man dropped to his knees. He frantically tried to grasp the grenade as precious seconds ticked by. Stubbornly the metal cylinder rolled around on the floor just out of his reach.

Mission accomplished, Hale, slammed on the breaks of his Gaz-MM. As the metal discs of the breaks screamed in protest, his wheels began to skid on the loose gravel.

Trying to maintain control, he clutched the steering wheel as hard as he could. The truck fought him as it attempted to turn the steering wheel of its own accord and wrench it out of his hands.

As the rear wheels of his own truck began to skid to the side, and the front of his truck started to turn to the left, the Soviet truck, now some hundred feet or so in front of him, exploded into a hail of shrapnel. A moment later, a piece of smoldering metal penetrated the gas tank of the burning truck. The rear of the truck lifted off the ground as the gas tank exploded into a reddish orange fireball.

The shockwave from the explosion caused Hale to lose what little control of his own truck he had, and the vehicle turned completely sideways as it skidded down the roadway. The Gaz-MM's center of gravity was hopelessly compromised as the vehicle rolled onto its side and began sliding down the road. This continued for nearly a hundred meters as Hale's truck came to rest just a few short meters from the smoldering remains of the enemy truck he had destroyed.

He rubbed his head and groaned. At some point during the chaos, his head had smashed into the steering wheel. *How did I get here?* Hale asked himself with his inner voice.

Fighting to stay conscious, the memory of the afternoon's event came flooding back to him. After he had broken contact with the Russians that pursued him that morning, he had used his skis to try and keep pace with the Soviet column on the road as they resumed their northward journey. For two hours he pushed his body as hard as he could to try and keep up.

His arms and legs became leaden with fatigue as his breath came in increasingly ragged gasps. The cold air burned the walls of his lungs as he was forced to breathe deeply of the frigid air to keep the pace. With no other choice, given the physical limitations of his body, he was forced to slow down.

Despite the freezing temperature, beads of sweat ran down his back beneath his great coat. *This heat is miserable, but if I open my coat to cool myself off, I'll make myself sick, and then I won't be able to fight. Finland needs every last one of us to hold the line against these damned invaders. They are so many, and we are so few.* His eyes shifted to a steely gaze as he continued his thought. *Despite their numbers, they will learn what it means to earn the ire of a Fin.*

As the sound of the column drifted away to the north, the air was filled with complete silence. It was as if all the forest denizens somehow knew of the invading army and tried to remain as quiet as possible, so as not to attract the invader's attention. Hale decided to angel toward the road. *Perhaps one of the bastards will break down, and I can use their truck to catch up with the column.*

He held onto this hope for nearly two hours as he slowly made his way northward over the snow. As kilometer after kilometer slid by, he began to completely lose hope. Finally, his eyes caught a dark shadow up ahead on the roadway. He quickened his pace to close the distance to the strange shadow and discern what it was. *Could it be?* Hale thought.

He lost sight of the, whatever it was, as he dipped into a gully that lay across his path. As he emerged on the other side, the Gaz-MM, slid into view. Hale dropped to the ground immediately so as not to attract any attention. Laying in the cold snow, he slowly removed his ski's, strapped them to his back, and began to slowly crawl forward.

He crawled on hands and knees for several minutes until he was two hundred meters from the truck. As he got close enough to pick out individual figures around the truck, he saw that the hood was raised, and someone's rump was sticking out of the opening as they worked under the hood, *Just as I had hoped a breakdown.* Hale thought.

Hale pulled his SK Nagant M/28-30 off of its resting place on his shoulder and slowly took aim at the posterior of the would-be mechanic. Satisfied he could make the shot; he moved his iron sight over to another man slowly pacing around the stranded truck with a rifle in his hands. *That would be the unlucky bastard who drew the short straw and therefore guard duty. There must be at least seven more men underneath the canopy out of sight.*

Hale sat and waited. He watched as the guard continued his slow route around the truck. He could tell by the way the guard carried himself, that the man was bored and oblivious. Occasionally, he would catch a wisp of the mechanic's voice, and the guard would scurry over to a toolbox on the ground, rummage around in it for several moments, and pull out a tool. He would then hand it to the grasping hand of the mechanic sticking out from under the hood.

As Hale grew bored, he let his mind drift to a memory of a similar wait long ago. Hale took a deep breath and let it out slowly. The deer he was watching a few hundred feet away, cried out in pain. It had slipped on the edge of a gully and plunged down the side. As it came to rest on the bottom of the trench, it somehow broke its leg. Now it lay on the ground, unable to stand up, and blinded by pain.

Hale's Grandfather had taught him that opportunities should never be wasted. He remembered the old man telling him on one of his first hunts, 'If you come across an animal that can't move, don't kill it. Though an easy dinner is assured, you can use the beast to draw in a predator or a scavenger and double your good fortune.'

Hale had listened to his Grandfather's words and taken the lesson to heart. Thinking about it didn't make the wait any more interesting. He yawned as he fought to stay awake. As the minutes slowly ticked by and the ever present cold began to creep into his bones, he waited for the down on its luck deer to attract some interest from a hungry predator.

Hale's eyes snapped open, *How long had I been asleep?* Anxious that he had lost his deer, he quickly located the poor animal, it was still alive. As the wait dragged on, snow began to fall. The snow shrouded the Sun in clouds, as the orb drew close to the western horizon.

The snow eventually petered out, and the clouds moved off to the south. The Sun came out and cast its rays about as it touched the western horizon. It was at this moment that Hale noticed the two eyes staring at the deer. They glowed yellow, reflecting the fading rays of sunlight. The rest of the animal was shrouded in shadows. *A wolf. There is rarely just one wolf. Are the others near?* Hale thought. Nervous, he checked the bolt on his rifle to make sure all was at the ready.

Hale slid the bolt back on his rifle and saw the bullet within. Letting out his breath slowly, he raised the rifle and took aim at the yellow eyes. Before he had the opportunity to complete his aiming process, the wolf sprang from the underbrush and dashed for the deer. Hale followed the movement of the wolf as the animal dashed across the frozen earth. Unwilling to take the difficult shot, he waited until the wolf reached the dear. Sharp teeth were exposed as the wolf opened its mouth and tore into the deer's neck.

The deer cried out in agony as the skin on its neck was shredded by the sharp teeth of the vicious predator, and then fell forever silent. With the wolf relatively motionless, Hale completed aiming, took a deep breath and held it. Confident, he squeezed the trigger of his old Lee-Enfield rifle. The ancient firearm, a relic from the Boer War, roared as it flung the bullet in its chamber toward the wolf.

A moment later the bullet struck the wolf in the side of its head. The round penetrated the wolf's skull and entered the animal's brain. The unfortunate beast died instantly. Slain, the once mighty predator's corpse collapsed onto the deer it had just killed. Blood from the two slain animals intermingled upon the snow-covered ground.

Hale quickly worked the bolt on his rifle and another round popped into the chamber. *There was always more than one wolf.* His grandfather's words echoed in his head. He heard the undergrowth rustle to his right. Turning toward the noise he began raising his rifle just as a shadowy figure launched itself at Hale's chest. Hale, desperate and unable to get a shot off, raised his rifle to block the incoming animal. The wolf, a large bitch, surprised by the rifle, bit down upon the wood and metal, instead of the soft flesh of Hale's neck.

The momentum of the beast slamming into his chest, sent Hale falling backwards. As he landed on his back, the wolf opened its mouth to free its teeth from the rifle and lunged at Hale's now unprotected neck. Hale could feel the warm breath of the animal upon his neck as it drew close. His nose registered the fetid odor emanating from the creature's mouth as its sharp teeth drew within an inch of his neck.

It was at that moment that Hale, plunged his knife into the skull of the wolf. The thick bone refused to yield to his desperate thrust and slid downward along the side of the skull. Luckily, the blade sank into the wolf's ear canal and plunged into the exposed flesh beyond killing the wolf. With his heart thundering in his chest from reliving such an intense memory, Hale's awareness slipped back into reality. *We ate well that night.*

Hale reached up and placed the palm of his left hand, where underneath his great coat, sweater, shirt, and undershirt, the right paw of that first wolf kill lay. It was attached to a leather cord which hung from his neck. Touching the paw of his first predator kill gave him comfort, *These woods are filled with so many predators.* Hale thought nervously. He sat for another hour, shivering in the ever present cold, as his heart rate slowly returned to normal.

Having lain on the frozen earth for too long, he began to shiver as his body fought to maintain its internal temperature. After what seemed like an eternity to Hale, the mechanic clambered from underneath the hood, climbed into the truck, and cranked the engine. The Gaz-MM, stubborn in its unwillingness to start in these temperatures, sputtered and coughed for at least thirty seconds before the mechanic gave it more gas and the engine roared to life. *Good, they fixed it finally.* Hale thought.

The mechanic hopped out of the cab of the Gaz-MM, gathered up his tools, and slammed the hood of the truck shut. With a loud thump, the hood caught the latch and closed. The guard, grateful that his duty was finally completed, took the toolbox from the mechanic, walked to the opening in the canopy covered rear, and passed the toolbox off to someone inside. He then slung his rifle onto his shoulder and pulled himself up into the back using the handholds built into the tailgate.

The mechanic, who was apparently also the driver, put the truck into gear and gave it some gas. As the vehicle slowly lurched forward, Hale raised up his rifle and took aim at the left rear tire. He took a deep breath and held it, as he lined up the shot. The truck continued to accelerate away from him. Satisfied he had the shot; he squeezed the trigger and his rifle roared to life.

A moment later, the rear left tire on the Soviet truck exploded in a burst of flying debris. The rubber of the disintegrating tire was flung in all directions as the truck skidded to a halt. Hale heard the driver exclaiming loudly, "Chert poberi!" As the truck slowed to a stop.

As soon as the truck stopped moving, the driver flung his door open and jumped out of the cab. As his booted feet struck the snow-covered surface of the road, he looked to his left and saw the source of his problem, the disintegrated tire. Letting out what must have been another loud curse, he put his hands on his hips. Whatever he said attracted the attention of one of the men underneath the canopy. The man threw a leg over the tailgate and began to make his way down to the ground.

As the driver stood and waited, Hale raised his rifle up and took aim at the man's head. He worked to line up the shot despite his shaking arms. He took a deep breath and let it out slowly. This helped him to relax and still his uncooperative appendages. He took another deep breath and held it. Satisfied the shot would hit, he squeezed the trigger. The rifle barked and slapped his shoulder with the force of the recoil.

A moment later, Hale's 7.62mm bullet struck the man's forehead. As the bullet smashed through the bone of his skull, it was deflected and bounced around inside the unfortunate's head. Outwardly, the driver's uncovered head appeared to explode like a melon smashed by a giant fist.

Before the driver's body hit the ground, Hale worked the bolt on his rifle, took quick aim at the other soldier, and squeezed the trigger. The driver's corpse gained a companion. A Soviet soldier inside the canopy covered rear deck of the truck, stuck his rifle out from behind the canopy and fired a shot. As soon as he pulled the trigger, another man jumped to the ground. Losing his balance as he leaped, the man's fur covered cap came off his head as he struck the frozen ground. Thinking quickly, he rolled to absorb the impact.

Hale waited patiently for the man to sort himself out and stand up. As the man reached his feet, someone from within the canopy covered area, tossed him a rifle. The man turned toward the movement, as Hale took aim, he saw a skin tone that he was unfamiliar with. The man's coloration was darker than anyone he had ever seen in the frozen tundra of his Finnish homeland. *Where is this guy from?* Hale thought. *Could he be one of those China men I read about?*

Not wasting any more time to think about what he was seeing; Hale pulled the trigger of his rifle. The bullet penetrated the left eye of his target, causing his luckless victim to drop the rifle he had just caught. The man wavered for a moment, then dropped to his knees and fell face forward into the snow.

Hale was forced to duck, as a shot was fired from the back of the truck. He quickly worked the bolt on his rifle and crawled over to the nearest tree. Using the tree's trunk as a shield, he stood up, raised his rifle, and peeked out from behind the tree. He nearly ate a bullet as the sound of a Soviet rifle rang out and the bullet struck the tree mere inches from his head. *This one has some skill.*

Hale tried to take a moment to identify the shooter from the shadowy interior of the truck. Not wanting to linger as his unseen assailant worked the bolt on his rifle, Hale squeezed the trigger. His rifle barked and he heard a Russian yell out in pain as his bullet found flesh. As he started to grin, a second rifle report rang out and the bark of the tree he was leaning against fractured less than an inch from his face showering him with splinters.

Apparently, the shooter is still alive and well. I must have hit someone else. Hale worked his bolt quickly and fired his fifth and last round into the opening in the canopy. This time he did not hear anyone cry out in pain. *A miss. Worth a shot, especially with that enemy sniper in the back.* Hale grinned at himself over the use of a pun in his internal monologue.

Hale ducked back behind his tree, removed his thick gloves, and pulled the bolt back. caught it with his left hand as it fell toward the ground. He reached into his right pocket for the reload clip. His fingers closed around the cold metal of the bullets. Pulling it out, he slapped the clip into place on his rifle. The clip of five bullets easily slipped into position with a click and he pulled the now bullet free metal clip from the rifle's chamber.

He heard several voices and what was likely the sound of boots hitting the snow-covered road. *If I stick my head out, that Soviet bastard will likely take it off.* Sighing deeply, Hale slipped his gloves back on, slung his rifle onto his shoulder, dropped to the ground, and began crawling to the south.

As Hale slowly worked his way along on the ground, the surviving members of the Soviet Squad cautiously made their way toward his last known position. Hale would occasionally pause his own movements, to listen for the Soviets. Each time he heard their boots crunching in the snow, still at a distance, he continued crawling.

After about two hundred feet of crawling across the frozen ground, Hale decided that he had put enough distance between his original position and his current location. Remaining prone on the ground, he slowly worked his way around until he was facing in the direction of his former position. He took the rifle from his back and checked it to make sure there was a round was in the chamber. Satisfied, he took aim at the position he recently occupied as he dealt death to the Russian invaders.

The Soviets, moving cautiously, took another ten minutes or so to reach the location that Hale had slain half their number from. It took them only a moment to spot his trail, and one of them pointed in his general direction. It was the last act he would ever take in this life. The other two men dropped to the ground, as Hale worked the bolt on his rifle to chamber another round.

Hale raised his rifle back to his shoulder and attempted to take aim at his two surviving opponents. From his position on the ground, Hale could not see them. Deciding to take a chance, he crawled forward and stood up behind a tree trunk. From somewhere off to his right, a rifle fired. He felt the warm breeze of the bullet travel closely by the back of his neck.

Not wanting to wait around for a second shot, Hale threw himself on the ground. It saved his life. Two more shots came from the soldiers in front of him. As soon as he dropped to the ground, they stood and took careful aim at him, *They have me in a crossfire!*

The sound of Hale's heartbeat thundered in his ears and his body flooded with adrenaline. Trying not to panic, he followed his training and remained still. As he did so, his mind slipped back to his training. "If the bastards know where you are, but don't have a shot, remain calm. If you panic, your blood will be feeding the trees." Sergeant Kivi said.

Hale made eye contact with the Sergeant's pale blue eyes as he continued to speak, "Be patient and sit still. This will buy you time, and most importantly make the enemy nervous. A nervous enemy makes mistakes. Especially half trained Soviet farm boys who can't wipe their own ass without permission from their political officer." Sergeant Kivi said.

"How do you know so much about the Soviets?" Dal, a private standing a few feet away from Hale asked.

Sergeant Kivi, unconsciously raised his hand to his face and fingered the jagged scar on his left cheek before replying, "I volunteered to fight the communist in Spain. Over the course of the war, the Nationalist's International Brigade, which was made up of volunteers from every country that wasn't Germany or Italy, had several engagements. Several of those engagements were with a brigade of Soviets fighting for the Republicans. None of the Spanish Nationalists could go toe to toe with the Soviets, so we got ordered into their path frequently."

"How did they perform?" Hale asked.

"They were well equipped with the best the Soviet Army had to offer at the time. As a group, they fought much more ably than the Spanish peasants did."

"And individually?" A private named Leo asked.

Sergeant Kivi laughed for several moments before replying, "Individually, they are as dumb as a fence post. They haven't been trained to think for themselves you see."

"Why does that matter?" Dal asked.

"Because private, if you don't have a sergeant to direct your inexperienced ass when it's time to shoot the enemy, or seek cover, you'll just stand there with a dumb look on your face." Sergeant Kivi replied.

"So, the Soviets are at their worst, if we can break them down into small groups?" Hale asked.

Sergeant Kivi smiled and said, "Well I can see that at least one of you isn't an idiot. Yes, that's correct Hale."

The memory faded from Hale's mind as he drifted back into the present. The recollection of that warm fall day, a few short months ago, was much more pleasant than the frigid cold of his current reality. Hale continued to lay on the icy earth waiting for the Russians to lose their patience and make a mistake. He sat still and listened. For an hour all he heard was the sound of the faint wind pushing the smallest of the tree branches about overhead. The stiff branches, frozen from the extreme cold, made noise as they stiffly moved about.

Finally, his ears registered a sound that didn't belong. Off to his right he could faintly hear boots crunching in the snow, *The sniper.*

Hale slowly used his right hand to reach the holster on his right hip. He unsnapped the flap and drew out his pistol. *If I remain still and silent, I can surprise him.*

The sounds of the crunching snow disappeared for a time as Hale sat wondering. *Was I hearing things?*

Hale's doubts slipped away, as the sniper began slowly moving forward again. The sound of the crunching snow under the man's boots grew ever closer. Every few minutes the sniper would pause and listen. When the man was satisfied, he would start moving forward again.

As the Soviet Sniper drew closer, the passage of time seemed to slow to a crawl in Hale's mind, *Where is he?* Hale thought for the hundredth time in the last twenty minutes. The sniper paused again and grew silent. By Hale's reckoning he was maybe twenty feet off to the right.

Hale began to sweat despite the bitter cold. *Did the bastard see me somehow?*

Finally, after what had felt like an eternity to Hale, the man started moving forward again. Careful to not make a sound, Hale unbuckled the strap of leather that secured his knife to his left hip. The knife sheath, like the pistol holster, rested on his hip. Step by step the man drew closer, until he was just on the other side of the large tree trunk that concealed Hale from his sight.

The sniper chose that moment to stop and listen, *Oh come on! Just one more step and I'll have you.* Hale lamented.

The seconds slowly ticked by as Hale did his utmost to remain still and not make a sound that would give away his position. He wrapped the fingers of his right hand around his knife, planning to stand up and stick it in the man's chest as soon as he rounded the tree in front of Hale.

The Soviet Sniper, satisfied that no one was near, finally took that step. Unfortunately for Hale, the man chose to walk around the back side of the tree, and immediately spotted Hale's legs laying in the snow. As the Russian brought his rifle up to put a bullet in Hale's posterior, Hale released his hold on the holstered knife, rolled over, and slapped the sniper's rifle away with his free hand.

The enemy soldier's rifle thundered in Hale's ear as the man put a bullet into the ground a mere inch from Hale's right knee. *If I hadn't let go of the knife and spoiled his aim, I'd be dead now.* Hale thought.

The young Fin scrambled to his feet and moved around the front side of the tree, pistol in hand. The man took a step back and frantically worked the bolt on his rifle to chamber another round so he could take another shot. Before the Soviet Sniper could finish, Hale emerged from the other side of the tree with his pistol raised.

The sniper met Hale's eyes with his own, they were hazel, and gave him a faint smile. He dropped his rifle and raised his hands up and said, "Sdacha."

What am I supposed to do with him? They never told us anything about prisoners. Hale thought. A shot was fired, it must have come from the other two Soviets nearby to the north. A moment later the Soviet sniper clutched his chest and collapsed to the ground.

Hale threw himself to the earth, as a second shot quickly followed the first, *The other Russians. I forgot about them!* A moment later the bullet slammed into the tree that Hale had been hiding behind earlier. *Was I seen, or was the second rifleman just taking a guess?* Hale asked himself.

Fueled by a shot of adrenaline from his near death, the sound of his heart sounded like a runaway freight train in his ears as his blood pressure increased. Trying to calm his frayed nerves, he took a deep breath and let it out slowly. Quieting the drum in his ears, he sat perfectly still for a minute and listened intently for the Soviets. The only thing he heard was the sound of silence.

Satisfied that the two men weren't rushing him, he crawled over to the twitching corpse of the sniper. Searching him, he found a small bottle of vodka, a grenade, and a picture of the man's sweetheart. Hale placed the bottle and grenade into his pack. *With this much vodka, I'll be very warm tonight.*

He took another moment to listen for the other two Russians. Once again, his ears were greeted with silence. Satisfied, he looked down at the picture. The woman, slender in appearance, with high cheekbones, and a small nose looked back at him from whatever moment in time the photograph was taken. She wore a floral printed dress that showed off her figure, which bulged and curved in all the right places. *I guess you'll be in the market for a new man soon.*

The picture reminded him of a happier moment and Hale's thoughts slipped away from the present back to his last day at home. Germany had invaded Poland and thanks to the Molotov-Ribbentrop pact the Soviet Union was given a free hand in Eastern Europe which included Finland. To prepare, Finland had mobilized its small army and called for volunteers. Hale had heeded the call.

It was a bright and warm early September afternoon. His last full day at home before he boarded the train that took him to the army. Looking up he saw his beloved Nea walk into the barn, "What are you doing?" She asked.

He put down the shovel he was using to muck out the cow's stall, and met the gaze of her green eyes, *A man could get lost in those eyes forever.* "Mucking out the barn." Hale replied.

"This is your last day before you have to leave for the army. Shouldn't you be doing something a bit more fun than shoveling cow dung?" Nea asked.

Hale took his gloves off and turned to face her, "Probably. Did you have something in mind?"

"How about a walk? The leaves are starting to turn." Nea replied.

Hale nodded and took her hand. They walked out of the barn and quickly found their way onto a nearby path that led into the forest. Hale marveled at how closely Nea's red hair matched the color of many of the turning leaves. As they walked, his eyes slowly traced the lines of her creamy colored neck as her skin disappeared into the folds of her dress.

As his eyes continued to trace the lines of her body beneath her dress, she stopped walking, and turned to face him. Surprised by her sudden stop, he jerked his eyes upward as she met his gaze. *Too late.* He thought.

"Getting an eyeful?" Nea asked.

Hale smiled down at her sheepishly and nodded feeling dumb. Still holding his hand, she tugged him to her. She looked up into his eyes as Hale used his left hand to brush away her crimson bangs. *Oh God, there's those eyes again! A man could swim forever in those emerald orbs, and she smells so good.*

He heard the sound of his heart pounding in his ears as he desperately thought, *What do I say?*

Nea, ended his conundrum by tilting her head upward and pressing forward with her lips. He lowered his own chin, and their lips met. They kissed briefly, and both of their cheeks took on a scarlet hue as the two stepped back and averted their eyes from each other.

Recovering quickly, Nea smiled up at him reassuringly and said, "Hale, it's ok."

She took a step forward and without hesitation he wrapped his arms around her slender frame and pulled her close. His lips sought hers and they kissed. This time the kiss was more insistent. It seemed to go on forever as they explored each other with their tongues. Breathless, they finally broke the contact.

Nea, threw him a smile and dropped her eyes to his waistline and took in the growing bulge beneath his pants. Smiling, she took him by the hand and led him into the trees. Hale's thoughts snapped back into reality. He was still holding the picture of the unknown woman in his hands. Sighing he looked down at it. Unable to gaze upon the woman anymore he flipped the picture over, on the back was a name and an address. *I can tell her what happened.* He thought. *At least this one wasn't my fault.*

Hale slipped the picture into a coat pocket just as his ears registered the sound of snow crunching. Listening, he was able to discern two sets of boots as they made their way through the snow toward him, *They think I'm shot.* He surmised.

The edges of his lips turned up slightly as he thought, *They are going to pay dearly for their mistake.* He crawled around the base of the tree until he was positive that the trunk was between him and the two approaching men. He then stood slowly to maintain his silence.

He peeked out from behind the tree and spotted the two Russians. They were perhaps thirty feet away from him. They kept walking toward him without breaking stride, *They didn't see me.*

Hale brought his rifle up and rounded the tree opposite to the Russians. As the two Soviets registered his presence, he put a bullet in the face of the soldier on his right. Horrified, the other man stood there with a dumb look on his face as Hale worked the bolt on his rifle.

Snapping out of his shock, the man started to raise his own rifle up to take aim at Hale. He never got the chance. The silence of the forest was pierced for a second time as Hale pulled the trigger on his rifle. At this range Hale couldn't miss, and the unfortunate dropped to his knees and then toppled sideways over onto the body of his slain comrade.

Hale approached the two men and quickly searched them. Unfortunately, they lacked both grenades and vodka. *Poor bastards.* Quickly forgetting about his victims, he started walking quickly towards the truck, *I hope it won't take too long to change that tire. . .*

Chapter 3

Karelia Istumus Afternoon November 30th 1939

Hale awoke. His head throbbed as he rolled over and wondered. *Where am I?*

Steeling himself for reality, he opened his eyes. His vision filled with a brown padded bench seat overhead. Groaning, he closed his eyes as a wave of nausea passed over him. Fighting the urge to vomit, he steeled himself and opened his eyes again. The first thing he noticed was the light. It was dim. *The sun must be setting for the light to be so low.*

A shiver ran through his body from the intense cold. As he struggled to keep his eyes open, his vision blurred, and another wave of nausea hit him. He clinched his eyes shut and tried to will the demon in his gut to remain silent. This time he failed and narrowly avoided making a mess of his white overcoat. As he leaned forward, the contents of his stomach burst forth from his mouth. Finished, he sighed in relief as the nausea dissipated.

Seeing spots, Hale blinked his eyes several times trying to clear the stubborn dots from his vision as he removed a glove. He reached up with his hand and rubbed his temple trying to relieve the pain he felt in his head. Despite the pain, he was finally able to focus his mind enough to once again ask, *Where am I?*

He closed his eyes and took a deep breath. Opening them, his vision finally sharpened enough to register where he was, the cab of a truck. Looking down at his chest, which was covered in shattered glass, he asked himself, *How did I get here? I don't remember what happened.*

Before he could search his mind for an answer to his question, he heard the roar of an engine. The noise drew his eyes to the back window of the truck. Spots danced in his eyes as he was blinded by the dull yellow glow of twin beams. The light caused his vision to swim and his mind drifted. Losing consciousness again, the next thing he remembers is looking up into the barrel of an SVT-38, "Pokazhi mne svoi ruki." A voice barked.

Hale's addled mind raced as he drifted back to his brief lesson in the Russian language given to him by the Army. "Repeat after me." Oda, his instructor, a stern looking woman of around thirty-five said, "Ya podchinyauys. I surrender."

Along with the rest of the class, Hale's tongue stumbled over the unfamiliar syllables of the Russian language. The strange words were so very different from his native Finnish.

From the back of the classroom Sergeant Kivi roared, "You sound like a bunch of drooling simpletons!"

Oda, their Russian language instructor, cast the class a stern look from behind her horn-rimmed glasses, slapped a ruler onto her desk and said, "Focus! Again, repeat after me. Ya pochinyauys. I surrender."

Hale dutifully repeated the words. When they finished Sergeant Kivi nodded, "Better, but you still sound like a donkey with a tree branch up your ass."

Oda's forehead creased as she cast an irritated glare at Sergeant Kivi. "Repeat after me, Ya pochinyauys, I surrender."

This time the class uttered the phrase in near unison, "That's better. Maybe you fools aren't as stupid as you look." Sergeant Kivi said.

From somewhere in front of Hale a voice said, "No sir. We are plenty stupid. Otherwise we wouldn't be here training to fight a foe that outnumbers us ten to one."

Oda snorted, trying to stifle a laugh at the words. Sergeant Kivi's cheeks turned a deep crimson as he leaped to his feet and roared, "Who said that?"

The enraged Sergeant was met with silence as he stormed up and down the aisles of the simple classroom. Stopping next to Hale, he pulled on his shoulder, spun him around in his chair to face him, and bellowed, "Was it you?"

Hale barely succeeded in fighting down the urge to urinate upon himself at the sight of the enraged Sergeant. It was his second day of training and he hadn't figured out if the Sergeant was God Almighty or a Demon sent from the foulest bits of hell to torment him. He looked up at Sergeant Kivi's with wide eyed fear etched on his face as the big man loomed over him. The Sergeant's scarlet hued face crinkled in rage as his blue eyes bored into Hale's hazel irises. *It's as if he is looking into my very soul.* Sweat began to glisten on the Sergeant's forehead as he roared, "I asked you a question, soldier. Was it you?"

Hale wiped Kivi's saliva from his face with his left sleeve as he replied, "No sir!"

Sergeant Kivi's eyes narrowed, and his nostrils flared as he glared at Hale. The younger man could almost see puffs of flame emerging from the Sergeant's nostrils. After several long moments, the Sergeant turned and walked up the aisle. Finding another victim, he bellowed the same question. Hale took a deep breath and slowly let it out. Relieved that the Sergeant was gone, and that he didn't piss himself before he turned his attention elsewhere.

Oda, met Hale's relieved gaze and gave him a faint smile of encouragement before she turned back to the class and said, "One more time, repeat after me, Ya pochinyauys, I surrender."

The class dutifully repeated the words as Sergeant Kivi spun another hapless victim around and yelled, "Was it you?"

The older man, his faded blond locks turning to gray and his face etched by many years of exposure to the sun and the wind, smiled up at Sergeant Kivi and said, "Yes it was me."

Sergeant Kivi glanced down at the nametag on the man's uniform and said, "Corporal Pekka, I trust that you will stop disrupting the class so that my privates can focus on their lessons."

Corporal Pekka reared back in laughter and said, "If you'd stop being such an ass from the back of the room, perhaps they could focus."

Sergeant Kivi grabbed Corporal Pekka by his uniform

shirt and pulled him up out of the chair as a voice from the doorway barked, "That's enough Sergeant, Corporal Pekka with me." Lieutenant Riku said.

Corporal Pekka threw Sergeant Kivi another smile and gently removed the Sergeant's hands from his uniform. The Sergeant's hands dropped wistfully to his sides as Corporal Pekka made eye contact with Lieutenant Riku and said, "At once sir."

"Class, I think you have this one. Let's move on to the next phrase." Oda said.

The remaining members of the class, all privates under the guiding hand of Sergeant Kivi said in unison, "Yes ma'am."

Oda smiled, "Good, now repeat after me, "Pokazhi mne svoi ruki. Put your hands up."

Hale's mind slipped back into the present as the voice on the other side of the gun yelled again, "Pokazhi mne svoi ruki!"

Obeying the command, Hale slowly raised his hands up. The man holding the gun took a step back and another set of hands reached in and unceremoniously pulled Hale from the cab. The man with the SVT-38 gestured upward with the gun barrel as he said, "Vstavat."

Getting the message, Hale nodded and slowly came to his feet. As he reached his full height, his head swam, causing him to stagger. The same arms that had pulled him from the truck reached out and steadied him.

"Nazovite sebya!" Barked the Russian with the two triangles on his coat collar that indicated his rank of Sergeant.

I guess angry and loud sergeants are universal. Hale thought.

The Soviet Sergeant took a step forward and punched Hale in the gut with his right hand and yelled, "Nazovite sebya!"

Hale, surprised by the blow, crumpled, and dropped to his knees. *What does he want?* Hale desperately wondered. His mind tried to go back to his brief half day lesson in Russian, but before he could, the Sergeant slapped Hale in the side of the face with his open palm. The blow caused stars to explode into Hale's vision and he toppled sideways striking the ground.

As the cold embrace of the frozen snow greeted him, his foggy mind thought, *The cold feels good.*

The Sergeant took another step forward. He loomed over Hale, leaned down over him, while placing his hands on his knees, and once again yelled, "Nazovite sebya!"

The Russian raised his gloved hand to strike Hale again. Bracing himself for the blow, Hale closed his eyes. Before the enraged Sergeant could land the blow, another voice barked, "Dovol'no"

After several seconds and no blow came, Hale opened his eyes to see what was happening. A hand was wrapped around the Sergeant's raised arm. Like the Sergeant, the newcomer wore a dark green overcoat with a fur lined cap.

The Soviet caps Hale had seen thus far sported a Red Star of varying size, made from cheap red thread. This man's cap had a shiny red star fashioned out of metal and painted a bright cheerful red. In addition to the difference in the Red Star, instead of an enlisted man's triangles, the man's collar sported three red squares, *An officer!* Hale thought, *I'm really in the shit now.*

Surprisingly the newcomer addressed Hale in his own language, "You'll have to forgive the Sergeant's enthusiasm. Like most men of the Soviet Union, he is a simple peasant who doesn't understand any language other than force. What's your name?"

Hale made eye contact with the man's pale blue eyes which were much like his own and said, "Hale."

"I'd say it's nice to meet you Hale, but I believe you have some explaining to do. Let's start with why you are in a wrecked truck belonging to Mother Russia." The officer asked.

Ignoring the question Hale asked several of his own, "Who are you and what are you going to do with me?"

The officer signaled to two nearby men who unceremoniously pulled Hale to his feet. The Soviet took a step forward and leaned in until their faces were a few inches apart. He smiled wickedly and said, "You appear to be in possession of Soviet property. I'd say you are a spy and you deserve to be shot for your crimes against the revolution."

As he said the last words, he leaned in close so that their faces were a mere inch apart. Hale could smell his foul breath which reeked of garlic, tobacco smoke, and vodka. Fighting back the darkness that threatened to engulf him as his head swam, Hale said, "You're in Finland. That makes the truck mine."

The Soviet officer tilted his head back and laughed heartily. Finishing, he met Hale's look of defiance with amusement and gestured to the Sergeant with a slight nod of his head. The Sergeant smiled malevolently as he reared back with his arm and punched Hale in the side with all the force he could muster.

Hale nearly bit his tongue as the blow took him by surprise. His knees gave out and he began to topple to the ground. Two firm sets of hands reached out and prevented his collapse, "I will ask you this once. You will start giving me answers, or I will let the Sergeant have his way with you. I imagine you would want to avoid being beaten to death, yes?"

Hale nodded, "Good. Now tell me are you a Finnish soldier?" The Officer asked.

"Yes."

"Now that wasn't so hard, was it Hale?" The Russian replied. His inflection on the H made it sound more like he said Whale.

"How did you learn to speak my language?" Hale asked.

"My mother was Finnish." The Officer replied.

Hale opened his mouth to speak again but the Officer slapped him across the face with a glove, "Enough! I ask the questions here. You provide the answers."

"How did you gain possession of this truck?" The Soviet asked.

"I found it abandoned on the side of the road." Hale replied.

The man looked skyward and let out a hearty laugh, "You found it abandoned on the road." The man paused to laugh again. Once he was able to bring his mirth under control he asked, "And how many warriors of the revolution did you slay in the vicinity of this truck?"

Hale tried to take on a countenance of mirth himself as

he said, "Warriors you say? I don't recall there being any warriors around this truck. Just illegal invaders trespassing on Finnish soil."

Enraged by Hale's flippant tone, the Sergeant moved to slap Hale across the face. Before he could strike, the Officer reached out with his hand and stopped the assault, "Dovol'no!"

The Sergeant threw the Officer a glare before nodding curtly and stepping back. Using his loose black leather glove, the Officer once again slapped Hale in the face with it. The stiff leather caused a sharp prickly pain to erupt in Hale's cheek. Starting to enjoy the anger he was evoking, Hale fought down the urge to cry out and remained silent.

"Day mne vintovku." The officer snapped.

From somewhere behind him, a soldier passed Hale's rifle to the officer. The man turned to Hale, held up his rifle and said, "Judging by this rifle I'd said you are a cuckoo. I imagine many sons of Mother Russia have perished from this instrument of cowardice."

"Bird's don't use rifles." Hale replied.

"There is another word for it." The man closed his eyes and his face crinkled as he slipped deep into thought. Finally, he opened his eyes, met Hale's gaze, and said, "I believe the word in your language is sniper."

Hale met the Russian's gaze impassively and tried to look disinterested. He failed. The officer smiled, thrust Hale's rifle into his face and asked, "How many soldiers of the Revolution did you slay with this to gain possession of this truck?" The Commissar asked.

"Sadly, not all of them." Hale replied with a smile.

Turning to the Sergeant the Soviet officer gestured at Hale and said, "Komik. Zastaqvit' yego krovotochit' nae tot raz."

The Sergeant nodded curtly and said, "Da"

Turning to Hale, the Sergeant smiled malevolently, cocked his arm back and punched him in the face with all his strength. Hale's nose exploded in a gout of crimson, as it crumpled under the mighty blow. His mind swam, and spots appeared in his eyes as the intense pain radiated from his nose. He tried to fight back the light headedness he was feeling. Failing, the edges of his vision grew dark and then faded altogether. Giving in to his overwhelming sense of fatigue, he lost consciousness.

The Commissar sighed in disgust, turned to the Sergeant, and said in Russian, "Idiot, you hit him too hard." He paused for a moment to register the darkness and the blocked roadway, before adding, "The sun has set, let's set up camp here, we can unblock the road in the morning. Ensure that he is tied up and placed in a dark tent. I want him to be disoriented when he wakes."

The Sergeant stiffened to attention, saluted, and said, "Yes comrade Commissar!"

An indeterminate amount of time later Hale awoke. Keeping his eyes closed he listened. His ears picked up the faint sound of the wind rustling through the stiff tree branches of the Karelian forest above. He focused on that sound for several minutes thinking back to the moment it was last this quiet, *The hours before the Russians came.*

His reverie was destroyed by the sound of a man starting to snore. *Even in slumber they assail my ears with their endless racket.* As Hale became fully aware, he felt the harsh sting of the rope against his bound wrists as he began to struggle against them, *They have tied me up!*

Attempting to choke off the panicked thoughts flooding his mind, he tried to move his legs. Like his hands, they were bound up. *How did I get here?* Hale's mind raced as his desperate thoughts overwhelmed him. *Must escape!*

Adrenaline exploded into Hale's veins as he grew frantic. The sound of his heartbeat thundered in his ears as the adrenaline released into his bloodstream gave him strength and clarity. For the first time since he was captured, the fuzziness in his mind melted away. With strength born of desperation, he tugged at the ropes that bound him. *I can't get out!*

After several minutes of fruitless struggle, Hale was no better off than when he had started. In fact, he was lucky that the Russians had tied the rope over his white overcoat. Otherwise, his wrist and legs would be bleeding from his fruitless efforts to escape.

He sat there for several more minutes. His breath, fueled by his panic, whistled, and rasped shallowly from his lungs. After what seemed like an eternity to him, lying there alone in the darkness, his mind quieted and a wave of fatigue pulled him into unconsciousness.

He awoke sometime later in the darkness. The sound of men snoring and occasionally making wind filled his ears. Hale listened for a time and picked out the individual voices within the chorus of slumber. There were four different men that he could discern snoring. What must have been a large man nearby, probably that brute of a Sergeant, sounded as if he was drawing all the air of the forest in. When he finished, it burst out with such volume, it's a wonder they didn't hear him all the way in Helsinki.

A bit further away, the other three men, seemingly clustered together, pierced the night with their own, lesser versions of this racket. As Hale listened to the disharmony piercing the forest outside of his tent, his mind slipped back to a past memory. His thoughts left the tent and the cacophony of Soviet snoring and returned to the barracks he occupied during his special operations training in the fall.

Hale awoke in the middle of the night. He had thrown his blanket off at some point, probably during a bad dream, as he was covered in sweat. The chill air of the unheated cabin that he lay in, along with forty other men had caused him to start shivering, which woke him. He pulled the coarse wool blanket over himself up to his neck, and curled up into a ball, trying to warm up. As he slowly stopped shivering and warmth crept back into his limbs, he was struck by how loud a room full of forty men were, when they were asleep.

The silence of the night was pierced by a disharmony of sounds erupting from the denizens of this cabin. Snores, coughs, and often other noises that would result in smells that made one's eyes water would erupt from the slumbering men. In between these noises, the steps of the guard could be heard as he slowly made his way back and forth across the room, watching over the sleeping men.

As Hale warmed up, his thoughts turned to the day ahead. *Sergeant Kivi.* The Sergeant had singled Hale out and humiliated him in front of the other men of the unit. *Why does he have it in for me?* Hale thought.

Before Hale could explore the memory further, he was brought back to awareness. He registered the faint sound of fabric tearing nearby. Curious, he focused his senses on the sound. *It's coming from behind me.*

He quietly shifted his position to turn his head in the direction of the sound. As a result of his movement, the sound paused for several moments, before it resumed. The impenetrable darkness of Hale's prison shifted slightly as a sliver of faint light appeared. Hale studied the growing shard as the tearing sound continued. Over the course of several minutes the hole slowly grew larger.

From time to time, he noticed the edge of a blade as it slowly sawed away at the fabric. *Who's on the other side? Are they here to rescue me?* Hale's thoughts began to race as he considered the possibilities. For the first time since he awoke, despair gave way to hope.

The sound abruptly stopped. From somewhere outside, Hale heard the telltale crunch of boots on frozen snow as someone approached the tent from the opposite side of the growing hole. A few feet away from the tent the man came to a stop and listened. *Please God, don't let him notice the hole, and whoever is making it.*

The seconds slowly ticked by. For Hale each one seemed like an anxiety filled eternity in which his benefactor might be noticed. The Soviet guard took another step forward toward Hale's tent. This time the impact of the man's booted foot upon the snow was much quieter than it had been, *He must have heard something and become suspicious.* Hale thought.

Suddenly the darkness was broken, as the guard threw back the tent flap and peered into Hale's prison. The light of the full moon shone into the tent. Hale squinted and blinked in reaction, as his eyes adjusted to the unexpected glare. Over several seconds Hale's eyes adjusted and he met the gaze of the guard glaring at him.

As he stood in the tent's entrance, the man's shape was silhouetted by the light of the moon. Seeing Hale's eyes upon his own, the man smiled, revealing several missing teeth. Those that were still present were a mixture of yellow often speckled with black marks.

Hale, hoping the man would just go away, met the Soviet's gaze impassively, trying not to attract any further attention. He failed. The man lowered his head and stepped into the tent with Hale. The enemy soldier reeked of stale tobacco smoke and a hint of something else. *Vodka? Are these Russians ever sober?* Hale wondered.

Before he could further contemplate the state of sobriety amongst soldiers of the Soviet Union, the man fell to his knees in front of Hale. He began roughly pawing at Hale. Reaching into his pocket he found the picture of the woman that Hale had taken from the Russian Sniper.

Raising it up into the light, the man smiled and whistled softly as he gazed upon the attractive woman in the picture. He reached down to touch himself as his growing admiration for the woman's form manifested itself. His musing was interrupted, as a shadow cut off the moonlight from somewhere behind him. Surprised, the man started to turn as a puukko was slowly drawn across his neck. Simultaneously, before the hapless guard could cry out, a hand was placed over his mouth.

Following the slight snick sound of the blade being stowed in a metal holster, another arm appeared and wrapped itself around the soldier's torso as he struggled against it. The Russian tried desperately to break the grasp of the man that had slit his throat. This went on for about a minute as Soviet's efforts became weaker and weaker. Finally, the light left the guard's eyes and what remained of him was quietly lowered to the ground.

Behind the guard, was a slender form dressed much like Hale in white overcoat and trousers. Recognition dawned on Hale's features, as he looked at the man in the silvery moon light. Hale whispered, "Corporal Pekka?"

The Corporal's well lined and weathered face crinkled as it broke into a smile, "Keep quiet, there are perhaps a half dozen Russian within ear shot. Can you walk?"

"I think so." Hale replied.

Corporal Pekka nodded in response. He paused for a moment to clean the blood of his puukko using the slain guard's coat and then set about sawing at the rope around Hale's wrists. The snoring outside the tent continued unabated as the Corporal finished up freeing Hale's arms. With a faint snap, the ropes around his wrists loosened and fell away.

The Corporal handed Hale the puukko and said, "Take care of your legs. I'm going to search this fool. Do you know where they have your weapons?"

Hale shook his head, "No. When I awoke, I was in this tent."

Pekka sighed deeply, "It's almost daylight, so we don't have time to search the camp for them."

The Corporal quietly pulled the slain guard's rifle from the man's back and passed it over to Hale, "Here, you can use this one."

"Thanks." Hale said as he looked down at the gun. It was a Mosin-Nagant carbine style weapon.

Corporal Pekka continued searching the corpse. He smiled as he pulled out a metal flask and opened the cap, "This will help keep us warm." As he sniffed the contents inside the flask, he frowned at the odor coming from inside, "Why don't these bastards ever get the nice vodka?

Why is it always the crap?"

Hale shrugged his shoulders in response. Finishing his task, the Corporal said, "Here take these, you'll need them."

A faint smile flashed across Hale's face as he took the 7.62mm bullet clips from Pekka's hand, three in all. "Did he have any bullets on him?" Hale asked.

"No, all he had was the vodka and these full clips." Pekka replied.

Hale quietly slung the rifle onto his shoulder and reached down into the darkness. He pawed around the slain Soviet's corpse until he found the man's hands. He pried the right one open until it loosened and revealed the picture of the Russian woman. He slipped the picture into a pocket.

"What's that?" Pekka asked.

"A picture of a woman I got from a sniper's body." Hale replied.

"Are you hoping to have a nice time with yourself later over that?" Pekka snapped, his gaze accusatory.

"No, it has an address on it. I was going to send it back to the address along with a note of how he was slain." Hale replied.

"That's overly nice of you. You a choir boy or something?" As Hale opened his mouth to answer, the Corporal held up his hand and said, "Never mind. Let's stop wasting time and go. The horizon is already turning gray."

Hale wordlessly nodded and quietly stood up. Corporal

Pekka turned and silently slipped out of the tent. Hale, right behind him, paused for a moment as they emerged and looked up at the moon. *The moon is almost full. The wolves will sing tonight after the sun sets.*

Corporal Pekka turned to Hale and whispered, "There's no time to daydream, we've got to get out of this camp." He pointed at the ribbon of gray light on the eastern horizon and added, "It will be daylight soon."

"What time is it?" Hale asked.

"Nearly Eight AM. The Soviets made a late night of it because of you, so they are sleeping in." Pekka replied.

Hale nodded and followed the Corporal. The pair of men very slowly and silently crept through the trees away from the camp. After about two hundred feet, the grizzled veteran held up a clenched right fist. The signal to stop. He turned and looked at a large birch tree off to their left. The immense old tree had thick branches that could support a man's weight. As Hale's eyes followed the trunk upward, he noticed that the topmost branches of the tree were shrouded in the golden light of the rising sun.

"This will do." Pekka said.

"What did you have in mind?" Hale asked.

"We need to get your gear back. You're not much good with that crappy little carbine we lifted from the Russian corpse." Pekka said.

Hale grinned, "The bastards took my puukko. My grandfather gave me that knife, and my father gave me my rifle. What's your plan?"

"There's only eight of them left. Six men, the Sergeant, and the Commissar. As soon as they start moving around,

I'm going to start putting bullets in them." Pekka replied.

"That's going to draw them here. You won't have long, we're only two hundred meters or so outside of their camp." Hale replied.

The Corporal smiled knowingly, "Indeed, that is where you come in. You'll be down on the ground ready to ambush them with your little pea shooter there."

Hale frowned and cast a disdainful glance at the Russian made carbine. "I won't be able to hold them off with this piece of crap." Hale replied.

Pekka pursed his lips as he contemplated the dilemma. Arriving at an idea, he smiled faintly and started rummaging through his pack, "Here. I was saving this for a special occasion."

Hale took the item by its wooden handle and smiled, "Where did you get a German grenade?"

Pekka smiled as he winked at Hale, "Do you expect me to give up all my secrets on our first date?"

Hale's mouth dropped open as he cast Pekka a look of confusion, "This isn't a date."

Pekka laughed, "Sure it is. It's our first date killing Soviet swine together. Isn't that romantic?"

Hale's confusion deepened at the Corporal's statement. Pekka let out another faint chuckle and said, "Never mind. I guess the joke is lost on you. Kivi seems to have drummed all the humor out of you." He paused for a moment and pointed back at the Soviet camp, "Once I start killing them, they'll come straight at me. Set yourself up for an ambush well forward of my position and surprise the bastards. With luck, we'll be eating their breakfast soon."

Hale nodded in response. He thought about telling the Corporal his experience with the tree in his first engagement, and how using one for a firing position wasn't a good idea. Hale decided not to question the man who had just rescued him. As he turned away from the corporal to follow his instructions, he could hear the faint sound of the older man grunting as he pulled himself up into the birch tree. Hale carefully crept forward looking for an ideal spot from which to spring an ambush. He found it in the form of a thick trunked oak tree about halfway back to the Russian camp.

He put the tree between the camp and himself. Leaning up against it with his back, he slid downward to a sitting position on the frozen earth. His mouth watered as the smell of sizzling pork from the Russian camp washed over him. Taking the carbine off his back, he laid it across his lap. He then watched patiently as the reflection of light grew in the metal of the weapon. Every time he exhaled the weapon momentarily disappeared as the steam from his breath shrouded the weapon in a blanket of gray.

As his thoughts began to drift, he was jerked back into the present by the crack of Pekka's rifle as the weapon spat forth death. The faint voices he could hear from the camp stopped and turned to shouting. A moment later, the sound of Pekka's rifle once again pierced the forest. Within the camp, the sounds of confusion intensified.

Several shots boomed out from the enemy camp in random directions, *The bastards haven't figured out where he is yet.* Hale thought.

Several minutes passed as Hale watched the golden light of the sun slowly make its way lower and lower down the birch tree in front of him. Cold from sitting in the snow, he shivered as his mind began to slip into a memory of a warm summer day. His day dreaming was interrupted as another shot rang out from Pekka's direction.

Back in the Soviet camp excited voices erupted. A moment later they returned fire. All the shots went in the direction of Pekka. *They've figured out where he's at.* Hale thought. The gunfire, a mixture of single shot bolt action rifles and a higher pitched automatic, reached a crescendo, then fell silent, *They'll be coming soon.*

Silence once again descended upon the forest as the two opposing groups reached a stalemate. Hale shivered as he waited patiently for the Russians to work up the nerve to charge Pekka's position. He didn't have to wait long.

Suddenly, a wave of automatic weapon's fire erupted from the Soviet camp and a handful of screams pierced the silence. Pekka responded to the wall of lead with a single shot. As the guns fell silent for a moment Hale could hear the enemy soldier's boots crunching in the snow moving toward him. He took the carbine from its spot resting on his knees, ensured a round was chambered, and made ready.

Another round of automatic gunfire erupted from the camp in the direction of Pekka. This time there was no response, *Did they get him?* Hale wondered.

Before he had a chance to do anything, three soldiers of the Soviet Union rushed past his position. The group was so focused on reaching Pekka, they failed to see him as they ran by. *There should be at least one more man out there. The one with the machine gun, is he still in the camp?* Hale wondered.

Despite the sinking feeling in his stomach over the missing man, Hale was forced to act. He stood and carefully took aim at the back of the soldier closest to Pekka. Satisfied that his shot would fly true, he held his breath and squeezed the trigger. He was startled as the carbine exploded to life a moment before his own rifle would have. Despite the surprise, Hale's aim was good enough. The man closest to Pekka toppled forward, face first, into the frozen earth.

The other two men dove for the ground as Pekka fired his rifle. Hale saw some snow spring up from the ground next to one of the prone Soviets. *Pekka missed!* The two Soviets were gazing in the direction of Pekka. *My gambit of shooting the lead man worked. They think my shot came from Pekka!*

Hale took careful aim at one of the Russians who was unaware that he lurked behind them. He carefully drew a bead on the back of the man's head with the iron sights of his carbine. Satisfied he had a good shot, he held his breath and started to squeeze the trigger. He was interrupted as two large hands grabbed him by the shoulders and spun him around.

Before Hale could bring his carbine up to shoot this interloper, a large fist smashed into his face. Momentarily stunned, he staggered back and dropped his weapon. As the carbine hit the snow packed earth, he looked at the grinning face of the Soviet Sergeant. Hale dove for the weapon. Before his hands could reach the gun, the Sergeant grabbed him by the scruff of the neck and punched him in the face again.

Hale's head swam as he staggered back. The Sergeant, with a look of pure delight on his face, stepped forward, snatched up Hale's rifle, and threw it away.

"What the hell?" Hale muttered.

The Sergeant held both of his hands up in front of his body and gestured with his fingers for Hale to come toward him with a smile and said, "Srazis' so mnoy!"

Hale, wanting to avoid a fair fight reached for the pukko in the sheath on his belt. It wasn't there. The Russian grinned at him, pulled the pukko from his own belt and said, "Ishchu eto?"

Hale, not knowing what the Sergeant just said, seethed with rage, as the Russian held the blade his Grandfather had given him for his thirteenth birthday. Two more shots behind him thundered across the forest. They were of a slightly different pitch than Pekka's gun. *Pekka must be alive! The two soldiers just tried to kill him.*

Losing his patience with Hale, the Sergeant stepped forward and tried to stab Hale with the knife in his right hand. Anticipating the move, Hale dropped to one knee, as he simultaneously slapped the side of the Russian's arm with his left hand sending the pukko thrust just past his left ear. He then rolled to his right side and came up on his feet. The Sergeant turned and faced Hale as two men started circling each other warily searching for an opening.

Without warning, the Sergeant lunged at Hale. Surprised, Hale failed to avoid the Soviet's grasping left arm as it swept him up and pulled him close. Hale attempted to break the grip of the stronger man and failed. He caught a whiff of the Sergeant's foul breath as the man grinned down at him.

Hale saw his own death in the man's eyes as the Sergeant raised the pukko blade to deliver a killing blow. Hale managed to wiggle one of his arms loose and tried to break the grasp of the Russian. It didn't work. As the blade began to descend towards Hale's face a single shot rang out. A spot of red blossomed on the large man's forehead and he collapsed to the ground dragging Hale with him.

Another shot pierced the silence and slammed into the oak tree behind Hale, missing him by an inch. It was one of the soldiers that had charged past him. As the man worked the bolt on his rifle, Hale grabbed a pistol out of the dead Sergeant's holster and shot the enemy. The other Soviet had turned to face Hale and was taking aim with his rifle.

Hale wouldn't be able to bring his pistol up before the man fired a shot. Fortunately for Hale, a bullet slammed into the back of the man's head. This sent him toppling forward as he fell to the earth. Hale saw that the back of his head was a misshapen reddish goo. *Thank you Pekka.* Hale thought.

Out of danger, Hale took his pukko from the dead Sergeant's hand and slipped it into his belt sheath. He then searched the corpse. He found the expected bottle of vodka, a wad of rubel bank notes, and a pair of dice. Curious, he cast the dice on the ground and they both landed with the six-side facing up. *A lucky throw.* Hale thought. Deciding to try his luck again with the dead man's dice, he cast them one more time. He rolled another double six. *Now I understand why you have so many banknotes.*

Pekka looked down his nose at Hale on his knees amusing himself with the dice, "If your done fucking around. We still have one more of the bastards to kill, the officer cowering in the camp with the SVT-38."

"That's the automatic weapons fire we heard as the soldiers charged?" Hale asked.

"You go to the head of the class." Pekka replied

"I'm famished, let's go get some breakfast." Hale replied.

The two Finns crept warily forward toward the Soviet encampment. As they drew close to the Russian tents, they quickly fell into a rhythm. One man would silently creep forward, while the other man covered him. In this way they were able to cover each other as they slowly advanced. Much to their surprise, they reached the camp unopposed.

"Where did the Commissar go?" Hale asked.

Pekka didn't answer. Instead he circled around the camp until he settled on a pair of footprints, "Look here at these prints. They are the only ones that leave the camp in a different direction."

"Back toward Russia." Hale said.

"I guess the cowardly bastard has had his fill of Finland." Pekka replied.

"Perhaps. He told me last night, in Finnish, that he was half Finn and half Russian." Hale replied.

"I hope the bastard has enjoyed his homecoming so far. Hopefully he'll freeze to death before he reaches the border." Pekka replied.

Hale walked over to the dying fire in the middle of the camp. Sitting over the smoldering flames was an iron pot with a lid upon it. Steam leaked out of the lid's edges and slowly wafted up into the sky. Hale, with his gloved hand, grabbed the handle on the top of the pot and raised it. A pleasant smell of boiling pork, rice, and vegetables filled his nose, "They made stew for us."

"Let's take the pot and go. I don't want to risk that

cowardly Commissar getting the drop on us." Pekka said.

"I wouldn't worry about that, he's a bully. He wouldn't try anything without at least a squad of soldiers between us to keep him safe." Hale argued.

"Let's at least use the truck to pull the wreck out of the way so we are clear to make our escape should the Commissar find friends."

"Then after that?" Hale asked.

Pekka looked up the road to the north, then back at the dark green Gaz-MM emblazoned with the red star of the Soviet Union, thought about the possibilities, and smiled, "I'll drive."

Chapter 4

Morning Karelia Finland, December 1st, 1939

Hale let out a belch, "That was good."

Pekka nodded in agreement, "I wonder which one of them was the cook?"

"I'm sure it wasn't the Commissar." Hale replied.

"What makes you say that?" Pekka inquired.

"He seemed too much of an arrogant ass to actually get his hands dirty doing anything." Hale said.

Pekka pulled up the sleeve of his white overcoat and glanced at his watch, "We'd better get moving before another Soviet column shows up here and wonders why two Finns are sitting in the middle of a camp surrounded by their dead comrades."

"What did you have in mind?" Hale asked.

Pekka looked off to the north as he pondered Hale's question for several moments, "How's your Russian?"

Hale laughed at the question, "We were in the same basic Russian class with Oda. What do you think?"

"Pretty shitty." Pekka replied.

"Exactly." Hale said.

"We can at least look the part. Let's get ourselves into two of their green overcoats and hats." Pekka said.

"Won't our own people mistake us for Russians and try to kill us?" Hale asked.

"Maybe, but the odds of us running into one of our folks out here is pretty slim. There's just a handful of us trying to delay their advance. General Mannerheim has a nice surprise cooked up for them a bit further north." Pekka replied.

Pekka stood up and walked over to the tent where Hale had been held prisoner the previous night. He disappeared for several moments before emerging with a green overcoat and hat in his hands, "This one is pretty clean." He started to remove his white overcoat. As he did so, he pointed to another Russian body nearby, "I shot that one in the head. Why don't you roll him over and see if he bled any on his coat?"

Hale did as he was instructed. He rolled the corpse of the slain enemy soldier over and said, "The coat looks good, but the hat is a bloody mess. I shot one in the back out in the woods. I bet you his hat is just fine."

"After you collect your weapons, why don't you go and get it. I'll see about starting this truck." Pekka said.

"I want to check these other tents first." Hale said.

There were two more tents in the camp. Hale started

with the larger of the two, assuming that is where the Commissar spent the night. He lifted the two folds of the dark green fabric and secured them to two hooks sewn into the fabric for the specific purpose of holding the entry flaps open. This shed enough light into the dark interior that Hale was able to make out contents.

In addition to two cots, Hale saw his gear neatly stacked in the back of the tent. He collected his rifle and pack. Checking through it to make sure all was well, he quickly noticed that the vodka he'd looted the previous day from several enemy soldiers was missing, "Bastards." Hale muttered under his breath in disgust.

A moment after he spoke the word, a loud noise came from the direction of the truck. It sounded like one-part grinding gears, and one-part shrieking banshee. The screeching element of the noise, similar to the effect of dragging fingernails across a chalkboard, sent a shiver up his spine. After several long moments of this, the sound abated, and the truck began sputtering to life. Several long seconds later, with a great belch of black smoke from the tailpipe, the engine started.

Hale inspected his rifle as he walked through the forest. When he was satisfied that his rifle was in working order. He pulled the leather shoulder strap that secured the Russian carbine to his shoulder and without a second look dropped the Soviet weapon into the snow. With a faint smile on his face, he slipped the SK Nagant M/28-30 that his father had given him onto his shoulder.

The familiar weight of the weapon gave him comfort, as he trudged through the frozen forest. As he searched for the enemy he had slain earlier, his mind slipped back to the day his father had given him the rifle. "Happy birthday!" His family, which included, his grandparents, parents, and little sister said in unison as his mom walked out of the kitchen with a chocolate cake. Included in the small gathering was Nea the daughter of the couple that owned the neighboring farm.

They were clustered around a simple battered wooden table. The room, barely large enough to hold them all, was decorated with colorful streamers. His mother brought the cake to the head of the table and tilted it slightly so that everyone could get a good look at it before she met Hale's gaze and said, "German chocolate." She paused for a moment as the smile spread across Hale's face before adding, "You're favorite!"

Unlike a regular chocolate cake, the icing on this masterpiece of home cooking, was more of a caramel color than the dark brown typical of chocolate. The smell of the freshly baked cake filled the small room. Hale's mother set the cake down on the table. Working with Hale's Grandmother, the two women carefully slipped thirteen candles into the icing. As the two ladies finished and stepped back, Hale's father struck a match and began to light the candles one by one.

The candles blazed atop the cake as Hale's family began to sing Happy Birthday to You, in unison. At the conclusion of the song, his mother said, "Blow out the candles honey and make a wish!"

Hale inhaled deeply and blew for all he was worth. The candles winked out quickly. As the wicks of the candles began to smolder and send rings of smoke lazily into the air, Hale's family clapped in approval. Aina said cheerfully, "Now you get to open your gifts!"

Hale looked down at his sister, she was barely more than a toddler and said, "Hmmm, I wonder whose gift I should open first?"

Aina quickly blurted out in the unabashed manner typical of toddlers, "Mine!" As she thrust the small package into Hale's hands.

Hale looked down at the small box that Aina had just given him. It was wrapped in festive red and silver wrapping paper that had clearly been used and reused many times. Hale made a great show of raising the package to his ear and shaking it gently while saying, "I wonder what's in it?"

"Open it and find out!" Aina urged him.

Hale carefully removed the wrapping paper, so as not to damage it, and pulled out a tiny wooden box. He recognized the box as one he kept under his bed. The previous summer he had collected several bugs out in the woods and kept it in this very box. After they all promptly escaped, he quickly forgot about the empty box as it collected dust under his bed. His sister had located it and repurposed it for this occasion. He smiled down at her and said, "What a wonderful gift! Thank you."

Hale leaned down and gave Aina a hug and a kiss on the top of her head. As he stood back up his Grandfather handed him a larger box and said, "This is for you."

Hale made eye contact with his grandfather and smiled. The older man was deep into his fifties with iron gray hair starting to give way to white. His features were well weathered from many decades of exposure to Finland's harsh winters. His smile revealed yellowing teeth. Hale took the box excitedly. It was wrapped in festive green paper. This time he tore into the paper with relish. Within was another wooden box about twelve inches long. Inwardly he sighed and thought, *Another box? At least this one doesn't already belong to me.*

Before his thought could continue his Grandfather said, "Open it."

Hale did as he was instructed and gently removed the lid of the wooden box. A sharp intake of breath was quickly followed by a smile that spread across his face. Within the box was a pukko blade. His eyes slowly panned up and down the length of the knife. The pukko was ten inches in length from the tip to the end of the pommel. The end of the blade had a slight curve to it which as Hale knew made it easier to gut an animal with. The pommel was a work of art. Hale marveled at the ornately carved moose bone handle with creatures of the forest meticulously carved into it.

"Try it." His grandfather said.

Hale held his breath and took the blade into his hand. The pommel was a bit large for his grasp and he awkwardly held it aloft, "You'll grow into it." His father said.

Hale noticed a second item at the bottom of the box, it was a sheathe for the knife. The supple well-oiled brown leather glistened up at him. He took the sheathe out of the box with his left hand and gently slipped the pukko into it. The blade was a perfect fit. Hale smiled up at his grandfather and said, "Thank you!" Before taking a step forward and embracing the old man.

Hale's grandfather returned the hug and said, "You're welcome. A man needs a good blade to make his living."

Hale took a step back, stood up straight, and said, "A man?"

"Yes, now that you are thirteen you are a man of this family." Hale's father said.

Hale smiled so widely he thought his face would crack. *I'm a man now!* Hale thought excitedly.

His father's next sentence dampened his enthusiasm somewhat, "Being a man comes with a lot of responsibility. You must provide for your family."

As Hale's father spoke, his mother slipped into the kitchen and came out with a long wooden box. The box was about nine inches wide, six inches tall, and nearly as long as Hale was tall. Hale's father took the box from his mother and thrust it into Hale's outstretched hands, "A man needs the right tools to put food on the table."

Hale looked down at the long and slender wooden box, *This must be a rifle!* He thought. The wide-eyed expression on his face unabashedly displayed his excitement, "Go on open it." His father urged.

Taking a deep breath and then letting it out slowly Hale lifted one brass catch and then another. He paused for a moment as his father placed a hand on his shoulder. He looked back at him nervously. His father gave him an encouraging smile in return. Hale slowly lifted the top of the box. Within, was a brand-new rifle.

Hale's eyes widened as he slowly took in the weapon. The metal parts of the rifle were covered in gun oil to prevent it from rusting, "Go on, pick it up." Hale's father urged.

Trying to calm his nerves, Hale took another deep breath and let it out slowly before reaching out and placing his hands on the wood of the rifle. As he ran his fingers along the grain of the wood, it felt smooth and cool to the touch. Finally, he wrapped his fingers around the stock and the wooden piece that nearly surrounded the barrel toward the tip and lifted the weapon out of the box.

Hale's mind snapped back into reality as he spotted the corpse of the Russian he had slain. Walking up to the slain soldier, he noticed that the cap was missing. He looked about and spotted the furry green hat a few feet away from the man's head. *It must have flown off when I shot him in the back.* He thought.

Hale quickly scooped up the hat and made his way back to the camp. He spotted Corporal Pekka leaning back on the bench seat behind the wheel of the truck as the engine idled. The Corporal was smoking a cigarette and blowing smoke rings into the air of the cab. Hale walked around the dark green truck and opened the passenger side door. A cloud of smoke billowed out of the truck as he pulled himself up into the empty seat.

The smoke tickled the back of his throat and Hale coughed. Taking a quick sip from his canteen to wash the tickle away he asked, "So what's the plan?"

Pekka turned his gaze to Hale, and blew a cloud of cigarette smoke over him, "I figured we would drive until we catch up with the next column. Dressed like this, we should have no problem falling in with them. When they make camp, we can figure out what to do from there."

"You honestly think that we will be able to make camp with the Russians and pass ourselves off as them until they all conveniently fall asleep for us?" Hale asked exasperated.

"Why not? We'll just keep to ourselves. If anyone asks us, we'll use the Russian we learned in class." Pekka replied.

"Why not?" Hale rolled his eyes and snorted, "Unless your Russian language skills are a lot better than I think they are, it won't work." Hale snapped back.

"Do you have a better plan?" Pekka paused for a moment before adding, "Private."

"As snipers, what was the mission given to us?" Hale asked.

Pekka's eyes narrowed as he replied, "To delay the enemy as much as possible and demoralize them."

"Parts of your plan has some merit. If we could somehow make our way into a Russian camp during the darkness of night and slit a lot of throats. They would be utterly demoralized and easy work for our boys on the Mannerheim line. Another way we could use this truck to our advantage is to drive back towards the Soviet Union and leap out of it the moment before it smashed into the lead vehicle in the next column." Hale replied.

Pekka rolled his eyes and laughed, "Because that worked so well for you the last time you did it. If I hadn't come along to rescue your dumb ass, you'd be a frozen corpse right now."

Hale joined in the laughter, "Perhaps you're right. I have another idea. Maybe instead of trying to use the truck as a weapon, or as a means to sneak into a Russian camp, we use it as bait." Hale said.

"Go on, I'm listening." Pekka replied.

"What if we drove towards Russia for a bit and just parked it. We could then set up good firing positions a few dozen meters further north from the truck and use it as bait." Hale said.

Pekka pondered Hale's words for several moments before replying, "I like it."

"I think if we picked a spot where we had enough

room to turn the truck around so that it was pointed into Finland, and then parked it in a way that blocks the road it would maximize the time, we had to get some kills." Hale said.

Pekka nodded, "In fact it will probably seem pretty normal to them since Russian equipment is crap. Those idiot peasants they draft and use as cannon fodder don't know how to maintain the vehicles and equipment they are issued. To capitalize on this, we should also put the hood up, so they are less suspicious about a truck that is detached from one of their columns."

Pekka put the truck in gear and started driving down the road to the south. He drove perhaps half a kilometer, until the abandoned Soviet camp was out of sight. He slowed the vehicle and looked about for a good spot to turn the truck around. After a few hundred meters he spotted a piece of the road where the trees thinned, and he was able to turn the wheel to the left and pull the front wheels of the Gaz-MM into the snow.

Pressing on the clutch, he threw the truck into reverse. He backed up until the rear end of the vehicle bumped a tree. Shifting into first he then drove forward and maneuvered the truck until the front end was pointing roughly northwest, so that it blocked the entire road.

The two men hopped out of the truck and looked around, "This looks good. What do you think?" Pekka asked.

Hale met the older man's gaze and said, "I agree, this should block the road while looking convincingly broken down."

"I'll kill the engine. You get the hood up." Pekka ordered.

Hale did as he was told. As the Corporal turned off the truck. The engine sputtered to a stop as Hale found the catch that held the hood closed. Tasks completed, the two men met each other by the left front bumper of the truck, "What about these uniforms?" Hale asked. "We definitely need to get out of them, this green is very visible against the white terrain."

Pekka let out a deep breath. The steam from his warm discharge created a large cloud of which slowly dissipated into the air around the two men, "Let's set up our firing positions. Then if we have time, perhaps we can build some snowmen and clothe them with these uniforms to use as decoys." He replied.

Hale grinned widely, "Clever."

Pekka paused and slowly looked out into the forest, "We will likely be come upon by a large column. I think one of us should set up so that we can target whoever gets out to investigate and the first few vehicles of the column. I think the other needs to set up a few hundred feet to the south, so that we can fire at them from two different positions."

Hale nodded in agreement, "Smart. That should maximize the chaos."

Pekka pointed at a large oak that was situated a few dozen meters alongside the road to the north of their decoy and said, "I'll use that large oak. It will provide me a great view of the column at a slight angle so I can shoot down the road."

"Are you sure you want to make yourself such a visible target for the column? The last time I was in a tree I got blown out of it by a Soviet T-28." Hale replied.

"I'll take the risk. It's too good of a position to pass

up." Pekka replied.

"You're funeral." Hale said.

"You have your orders private. I suggest you see to them." Pekka snapped back.

Hale stiffened to attention and saluted, "Yes sir!"

Uneasy silence hung over the two men before both broke down into laughter. Once they were able to bring their mirth under control, they stripped out of their Russian overcoats and hats. Pekka opened the driver side door of the truck and held it as Hale tossed his in. Pekka quickly followed suit and then closed the door.

Splitting up, they went about setting up their firing positions. Pekka reached his chosen spot first. He looked up at the imposing tree and smiled, *I think the kid is wrong about using trees as firing positions.*

Pekka started climbing up the venerable oak as Hale walked down the road looking about for a good firing position of his own. He spotted it off to his right, a large gray rock that jutted out of the snowscape. The rock had a large log wedged up against it that formed a natural point between the two objects. Hale left the road to investigate more closely.

As the young sniper examined the spot closely, he saw broken remains of a tree scattered in front of the rock. *This tree must have fallen, struck this boulder, and the top part of the tree broke into smaller pieces as it struck the earth.* He thought. He walked around the south side of the boulder trying not to disturb the snow that had piled up on the gray stone, and the log.

Getting down on his knees, he pulled out his rifle and sighted it up and down the road as it stretched out in front of him in either direction, *This is a great field of fire and I have plenty of cover.* He thought, excited.

Hale set about piling up snow underneath the log, so that the gap between the ground and the log was blocked. He then counted off the steps to the road from his spot so he could gauge the distance. He did this several times at different angles and wrote down the distances in his notepad with a pencil. After half an hour or so, he was satisfied that he had the distance of the road from his firing position calculated for every part of the road that was visible to him.

Task complete, he pulled a small hatchet out of his pack, and cut down one of the small evergreen trees that grew near the road. He began to walk back to his firing position with the tree dragging behind him, in each of the spots where he had left tracks. After another half an hour of this, he had successfully covered up all of the tracks that led back to his spot.

Satisfied that all was ready, he walked from his spot back to the truck. He was careful to walk north in the forest for a time, so that his tracks would not be visible from the road. He walked past the truck about a hundred feet and then made his way toward the road. He tread carefully through a depression that made its way toward the road. He was confident in the knowledge that he was well beyond the point that an approaching column would see his footprints before they reached the truck. Finally making his way onto the road, he walked down one of the tire tracks in the road southward. Reaching the truck, he looked around for Pekka. The older man was not visible.

Hale moved his eyes up the road to the oak tree several hundred feet to the north that Pekka had proposed using as his firing position. He slowly looked up and down the tree but didn't see Pekka. He was surprised by a sudden shout coming from the direction of the tree, "Bang, you're dead."

"Where are you?" Hale asked.

Pekka waved an arm at Hale from behind the trunk of the oak, "I'm here."

"How are you hiding behind the trunk of the oak, and ten meters in the air?" Hale asked.

"I'm standing on a thick branch pointed toward the north. Turn away and I'll get into my firing position." Pekka replied.

Hale did as he was told, "Now look." Pekka said.

Hale turned around and looked back at the oak tree, "Is your gun pointed at me?" Hale asked.

"Yes." Pekka said.

Hale looked at the spot where he had seen Pekka's arm a minute earlier. All his eyes could make out was a small black shadow that filled the light gap between two of the branches on the tree, "Are you in your spot?" Hale asked.

"I've got my gun pointed in your direction." Pekka replied.

"Perhaps you're right then. Maybe that is a great spot. I personally would not get back up into a tree though. It's too easy to get blown out of it by a tank." Hale said.

Pekka ignored Hale's statement and said, "Let's get to work on building some decoy snowmen, so we can put those uniforms to work for us."

Hale waited, as Pekka climbed down the tree, and then walked toward him on the road. Like Hale, Pekka was careful to stay in the tire tracks that had been cut by the wheels of the previous Soviet column to rumble through this part of Karelia's vast forest.

As Pekka reached Hale, who was leaning against the truck, the older man asked, "Any thoughts on how we should set up our two decoys?"

"To make the scene believable I think we should set them up at the front of the truck." Hale said.

Pekka nodded in agreement, "Yes, that's good, perhaps we can even make it so that only their backsides are sticking out from under the hood to keep their heads out of sight."

"I like it." Hale said.

The two men set about building the two decoys with Finland's most common resource on a cold December day, snow. As the two men toiled, they made a game of it by occasionally lobbing snowballs at each other.

Hale ducked under one such surprise assault and said, "You missed!"

As the younger man scooped up a handful of snow to return fire, a second round struck him right in the head and exploded. Peals of laughter immediately followed, as Hale's hood was knocked off his head, "Got you!" Pekka said.

Hale quickly prepared his own frozen missile and threw it at the laughing corporal. Pekka deftly sidestepped Hale's snowball, rolled to his right, grabbed another handful of snow, and came back to a standing position. He immediately threw another snowball at Hale. This time the nimble young sniper was able to dodge out of the way and yelled, "You missed!"

As Hale scooped up another handful of snow, his ears registered a faint rumble. He held up his hand to Pekka and said, "Shhh. I think I heard something."

Snowball fight forgotten, the two men stood and listened, "I think I hear it too." Pekka said.

Hale nodded in response before saying, "It's getting louder."

The two men quickly checked their decoy snowmen one last time. Satisfied that the pair resembled two men working on the truck wrapped in their greatcoats, they turned to each other. Pekka spoke first, "May God be with you."

Hale smiled to break up the somber mood, "And with you my friend."

The two brothers in arms clasped arms in the old way and shook. Hale glanced in the direction of the growing noise and said, "I've got to get to my position."

Without another word the two men broke company and headed to their prepared firing positions. As the rumble grew louder Hale ducked into the trees and made his way through the frozen forest to his spot. He got down on his knees and sighted his rifle along the road, *I hope this works.*

As the noise of the approaching column grew louder, the snow on several of the tree branches closest to the approaching Soviets began to shake loose from the branches and slowly fall to the earth. Hale marveled at the beautiful sight of snowflakes slowly drifting downward. The beauty of the scene and the constant thrum of the approaching engine's caused his mind to drift.

Wanting to stay focused, Hale pushed away his drifting thoughts and brought his mind back into sharp focus. He pulled out a magazine from his right coat pocket and nervously fingered the five bullets in the clip. With the sound of groaning metal and clanking tracks, the first vehicle in the Soviet column rolled into view, it was a T-26 tank.

Why must they always have tanks? Hale inwardly cursed. He sighted his rifle on the tank commander who jutted out of an opening in the top of the turret. The tank, painted dark green, stood in stark contrast to the background of snow and trees as it slowly lumbered up the road. As the clanking monstrosity's tracks tore up the surface of the road, it belched acrid black smoke from its hindquarters.

Hale observed the tank for several moments as it made its way from his right towards his left on the road in front of him. He noted that the T-26 was smaller than the tank that had blown him out of the tree yesterday. *I think this one would be easier to kill. Assuming I had the proper equipment.* Hale thought. As the tank disappeared from view to his left, he sighted his rifle on one of the many Gaz-MMs in front of him.

Knowing that the tank must be in Pekka's sight, and that it must stop soon because of their decoy, he reached down to the ground and scooped up a small handful of snow and pushed it into his mouth, *The cold of the snow in my mouth will keep my breath from giving me away.* Hale thought.

Task complete, he brought his rifle up and sighted it on one of the many truck drivers in front of him. Hale could make out the outline of the man as he stood in contrast to the light coming from the passenger side window of the truck. He kept his shot lined up as he waited for Pekka to engage first.

The T-26 rumbled to a stop as it drew close to the decoy truck. The commander turned toward the driver of the Gaz-MM immediately behind him and gestured at the stalled truck. The driver nodded in acknowledgement and banged on the window that separated the cab from the cargo area of the truck.

Several moments later, a squad of soldiers emerged and formed up on either side of the road. The leader, probably a sergeant, called out, "Privet?"

The man paused for several moments waiting for a response from one of the uniformed snowmen. The Soviet Sergeant called out again, "Privet? Neispravnost' avtomobilya?"

Frustration growing, the Sergeant took several large steps toward the decoys. As he raised his hand to grasp the shoulder of the decoy closest to him, his forehead exploded in a fountain of blood as Pekka's first shot smashed through bone and brain before exiting out the back of the unfortunate's head. Before the tank commander could react, Pekka operated the bolt on his rifle and put a bullet in his head as well. Given the haste of his aim, his second shot was not as perfect as the first.

The squad of soldiers behind the sergeant, four on either side of the decoy truck, dove to the ground upon hearing the first shot. Simultaneously, Hale fired his weapon at a truck driver in the middle of the column. His shot broke the glass of the Gaz-MM and struck his target in the side of the head.

Chaos erupted across the column, as men began to pour from the cargo areas of the canopy covered trucks. Pekka and Hale, slew several more Soviets with their rifles, as more and more of them emerged from the covered rear cargo areas of the trucks. Hale, being careful not to expose himself, worked the bolt on his rifle quickly and slew five men in ten seconds.

When he heard the click signaling his gun was empty, he ducked back down, and pulled the bolt of his rifle open. Next, he reached into his right coat pocket for his next clip and with a well-practiced movement, slammed it home into the slot. When he heard the click that told him the bullets were in place, he pulled the thin metal clip, now devoid of bullets, out of the rifle. He then slid the bolt of his rifle forward.

Sitting back up into his firing position, he took a moment to marvel at the scene of chaos before him that two snipers have caused. Most of the men that were in the backs of the trucks had emerged and quickly dropped to the frozen earth. As Hale took in the scene, he targeted one of the last men to emerge from the trucks and put a bullet in him. The quickly aimed shot was far from perfect as it slammed into the unfortunate's abdomen. Hale had been aiming for the center of his chest.

Before the men, now laying in the frigid snow, could draw a bead on Hale's location, Pekka shot one of the soldiers from the first squad crawling up the road in his direction. One of the seven survivors thought he saw movement up ahead, so he jumped to his feet and let out a loud whoop as he began charging up the road in Pekka's direction.

The Russian made it about five meters before Pekka's well-aimed shot put an end to his career in the Red Army permanently. Unfortunately, this gave away his position to the now dead soldier's squad mates. They leapt to their feet and began charging up the road in Pekka's direction. As they closed the distance to the solitary sniper, they bellowed a fearsome war cry.

Pekka, ignored the screaming meant to intimidate him, quickly dropped another Russian with a well-placed shot. Unfortunately, the six survivors closed the distance to his oak tree all too quickly. Cursing in frustration, he pulled out his German grenade, yanked the pull cord to activate it, and tossed it at the charging Soviets. The grenade spun end over end as it sailed through the air toward the Russians.

With a dull smack, the device struck the frozen mud at the feet of the lead Soviet and exploded a moment later. This had the result of tearing this unfortunate into about a dozen different pieces which were flung in random directions as the column of flame billowed upward. The two men immediately behind him were also killed instantly, as they were flung backwards by the expanding explosive cloud.

The other three members of the squad were peppered with shrapnel from the case of the grenade as the deadly bits of metal sailed through the air in a twenty-foot circle around the initial point of explosion. These men dropped to the ground and began groaning from their severe injuries. Pekka immediately raised his rifle and looked to see if any other Russians had spotted his firing position. None were looking in his direction.

In the middle of the column, Hale quickly used up his second clip of ammunition. As the Soviets ran around indiscriminately trying to determine where the gun fire was coming from, young man after young man panicked and sprang to their feet. As these panicked targets presented themselves, Hale took a deep breath, held it, took aim, and fired.

Back at the front of the column, Pekka noticed that the driver of the T-26 had poked his head up out of the metal monstrosity and was looking up the road in his direction. The Finnish Corporal took a deep breath and held it as he took aim at the man's leather skull cap covered head. The driver caught a glint of metal coming from the large oak tree down the road. Seeing the sniper that had been tormenting the column, the driver's eyes widened, and he dropped back down into the tank.

The moment before the driver spotted him, Pekka squeezed the trigger and immediately cursed as the driver disappeared. The bullet sailed through the spot where the driver's head had been just a moment before and impacted harmlessly on the armor of the tank with a loud ping.

A moment later, the barrel of the tank began traversing upwards in Pekka's direction, *Oh shit.* The veteran thought.

Pekka slid his rifle onto his shoulder and pulled himself behind the oak. He turned away from the tank and began climbing down the tree as his world exploded into flame and wooden splinters. The impact of the high explosive shot, and subsequent explosion flung Pekka to the ground before metal and wooden shrapnel had a chance to tear into his body.

He landed in the snow a second later with a loud thump and passed out. Hale heard the explosion, looked in Pekka's direction and cursed, *I warned him not to get in the tree.*

The young sniper ducked behind his log and reached into his pocket, *Only one magazine left.*

He crawled the short distance to the rock and peered around it. The Soviets had organized into several squads of men and were fanning out in all directions to search for him. *It's time to go.* He thought. He slung his rifle onto his shoulder and began crawling from his firing position in a westward direction away from the road and the Soviet column.

As the voices of Soviet sergeants barking their commands filled his ears, he reached a small gully that ran to the north. He slid into the gully and began scrambling on all fours as quickly as he could manage northward without exposing himself to the approaching Russians. The Soviets, seeing enemies in every shadow, began indiscriminately firing as they advanced.

Bullets whizzed by overhead as Hale continued his progress northward. Finally, the gully deepened into a depression and he was able to stand up, while leaning far forward, and managing a run of sorts. This odd posture kept him just below the top of the gully. He continued in this manner, tripping and falling a few times, until he felt that he had drawn parallel with Pekka's oak tree.

Stopping, Hale brought his rifle out, and opened the breech, it was empty. He reached into his right pocket, grabbed his last clip of bullets, and slammed the bullets home before deftly removing the now empty metal clip. He then peeked up over the edge of the depression he sat in. Ahead, the tree that Pekka had occupied was missing its top half. The rest of what remained of the tree was engulfed in flames. He inwardly cursed at the sight.

Thank God they don't have him yet. Hale thought.

He looked down the road to his right towards the column and cursed again. Several squads of Russian soldiers were advancing towards Pekka's last known position. Not knowing the fate of his comrade, Hale stood up so that he could see the ground at the base of the flaming oak tree. He instantly spotted Pekka's prone form. *Is he alive?*

Pekka rolled over onto his back and groaned. *Thank God!* Hale thought.

Satisfied that his companion still lived, he ducked back down behind the edge of the depression. He quickly pulled out his two empty clips, opened his white coat so he would have access to his bandoliers, and quickly plucked five bullets off the leather straps. Working quickly, he slid the bullets into the empty clip and dropped the now full magazine into his right pocket.

Hale hastily repeated this sequence to load the second empty clip. He checked over all his equipment to ensure it was in readiness. Nervous, he took a deep breath and let it out slowly before raising his head above the edge of the gully. He immediately spotted the advancing Russians. Raising his rifle, he took aim at one of the soldiers in the middle of the three squads that approached his injured comrade, held his breath, and squeezed the trigger. A moment later, the unfortunate Russian grabbed at the left side of his neck as the impact of the bullet simultaneously knocked him off his feet.

In reaction to Hale's shot, the three squads of Red Army soldiers immediately plunged to the ground. Hale quickly operated the bolt on his rifle and chambered another round. He then scooped up a handful of snow and placed it in his mouth to hide his breath in the frigid air. Satisfied that his breath would not give him away, he waited.

He began to hear the voices of the Soviets on the ground. *It won't be long before an NCO orders one of the poor beggars to stand up.* Hale thought.

He wasn't disappointed. Thirty seconds later one of the twenty-five or so men lying prone on the road, slowly stood up, and began moving toward Pekka. Hale ignored the man for several moments as he patiently waited for another to stand up. The Russians disappointed him.

Pekka let out an audible groan as he brought his left hand up to his head and rubbed his forehead. The sound caused the approaching Russian to pause, spotting Pekka, the man raised his rifle to take aim. Before the butt of the rifle touched the young soldiers' shoulders, Hale ended his war permanently.

Not wanting to give away his position, Hale ducked back down into the gully and waited several moments. The nervous enemy soldiers fired off several shots in random directions. *Well, the buggers know I'm here now*, but *they haven't figured out where I am.* Hale thought in relief.

He crawled a few dozen feet to the south, scooped up another handful of snow, and placed it in his mouth. He then raised himself into position to observe the Soviets. Through the tangled snow-covered underbrush, he could see a bit of green contrasting with the surrounding white. Smiling, he took aim at the patch of dark green and pulled the trigger. He was awarded with a scream as his bullet slammed into the prone form of a Soviet private.

This caused his nearby comrade to lose his nerve and stand up. Before the man had a chance to take a step, Hale put a bullet in him. This soldier joined his squad mate in death, as his body toppled over and landed on his injured companion. The snow around the two men quickly turned red as their life blood leaked out onto the frozen earth.

Before he was spotted, Hale quickly ducked back down into the gully and made his way fifty meters to the north. He briefly peeked over the edge of the gully to keep tabs on his enemy. His face broke into a smile as his eyes took in the scene. Nearly two dozen Soviets were hugging the frozen earth, paralyzed by their fear.

As he ducked back down into the gully, he ejected his nearly empty clip, opened his coat, and calmly reloaded the magazine as his thoughts slipped back to his training.

A middle-aged man stood at the front of the class. He was resplendent in his grey uniform. Multiple metals caught the light from the classroom's electric light which faintly buzzed overhead. Wrinkle free and neatly pressed, the man obviously took pride in the uniform he wore. Using a wooden pointer, he indicated a spot on the map, "What does this deployment and subsequent reaction by the opposing force to two snipers tell you?"

A squad member of Hale's raised his hand to reply. The officer, standing at the front of the room, raised his pointer and gestured at the young Finnish soldier. You there, with your hand raised, speak, "Sir-"

The man's face instantly turned red as a vein bulged in his forehead. Cutting the hapless private off he roared, "The name is Sergeant Virtanen not sir!"

Sitting in the back of the room Sergeant Kivi smiled as the private nervously sputtered out, "Sergeant Virtanen, the change in deployment doesn't make any sense. Why would so many react to two men in such a manner?"

Sergeant Virtanen's eyes panned over the men of Hale's training squad. Most looked away, but Hale dared to make direct eye contact. Sergeant Riku raised his pointer and said, "You there. Why do you think the larger group is reacting to the two snipers in this manner?"

Hale leapt to his feet, snapped to attention, and said, "Fear."

Sergeant Virtanen ignored the fact that Hale failed to properly address him, smiled and said, "Precisely. The sniper's best weapon against a foe, especially one that will outnumber us like the Red Army, is fear."

Hale's mind snapped back into reality as he finished preparing. Satisfied all was ready, he slid the clip back into place on the rifle. As soon as he heard the click of the magazine as it locked into place, he operated the bolt of his Mosin-Nagant to put a round in the chamber.

Hale leaned up against the wall of the gully and took a deep breath. He raised his right, gloved hand, and looked at it for a moment, it trembled slightly. *Stay calm, Pekka needs you.* He took another deep breath, let it out slowly, and then scooped up a handful of snow and shoveled it into his mouth.

Moving very slowly he peeked over the ridgeline. None of the Soviets had stood up and advanced during the few minutes he had reloaded and collected himself. Smiling slightly, he cast a glance in Pekka's direction. The injured Corporal had not moved, *Come on, you've got to wake up and get out of there!* Hale thought. *These bastards are going to figure out that there is only one of me out here very soon, and then the fear will be gone.*

Suddenly, a whistle blew, and all the enemy soldiers stood up simultaneously. With a loud roar, they charged up the road toward Pekka and the smoldering tree. Desperate, Hale began firing, hit, work the bolt, hit, work the bolt, and hit. The fourth time he took aim, a bullet kicked up the snow about a foot to his right, spoiling his aim as he pulled the trigger. *They've spotted me!*

Hale ducked back down into cover, rolled to his side, and came to his feet. As he ran away from the approaching horde, he worked the bolt on his rifle. As the final bullet in the Mosin's internal magazine slid into the chamber, he turned back toward the enemy. Having his choice of targets, he quickly took aim, and reduced the long odds against him by one.

The young sniper turned away from the enemy and ran. As he zigged and zagged trying to make himself a difficult target, he pulled the bolt back on his rifle. Seeing a gully just in front of him, he jumped into it, pulled a clip of bullets from his right pocket, and slammed it home into the opening in his rifle. With practiced ease, he pulled the thin metal clip that had held the five bullets together free, and slid the bolt forward on his rifle, closing the breach. He then peeked up over the edge of the gully. An entire squad of eight men were bearing down on him, *Shit!*

He quickly took aim at the lead soldier and squeezed the trigger. With an audible grunt, the bullet struck the man in the chest and he went down. This brought the other seven to a stop and they raised their rifles and took aim at Hale. Hale's eyes widened as he met the angry gaze of the Communists glaring back at him. As he ducked back down into the gully the roar of seven rifles discharging simultaneously pierced the forest.

The volley was followed by a loud series of screams as the squad bellowed and charged. Hale, heedless of being spotted, stood up, took aim, and killed another one. In the time it took him to operate his bolt, they closed to fifty meters. He nervously took aim at another, as his arms trembled slightly. Fortunately, hitting center mass when they were charging right at him was easy.

His shot dropped another of the advancing soldiers to the ground. This one clutched his gut and started screaming in agony. Hale stood his ground and calmly fired until his clip was exhausted. Despite his failing nerves he was able to put a bullet into each of the targets he aimed at.

As the two survivors drew within twenty feet of Hale, they stopped and took aim with their rifles. Hale ducked back down into the gully just as the two men pulled their triggers. Dropping his rifle, he pulled out his pistol and stood back up. The two surviving Soviets were working the bolt on their rifles to eject their spent round and pull another into the firing chamber.

Hale, now fully visible, raised the pistol and took aim at the Russian on his right. The man's fur lined green cap fell to the earth as he violently wrestled with the bolt on his rifle, it had frozen. Hale squeezed the trigger on his pistol. A moment later the frustrated enemy soldier clutched his shoulder and fell to the earth.

The other Russian raised his rifle and took aim at Hale. The young Finn dove for cover as the invader pulled the trigger. Hale could feel the wind of the bullet as it flew through the space, he had occupied only a moment before. With a grunt, he hit the hard-frozen earth.

Hale maintained his grip on the pistol and rolled over onto his back as the Russian appeared at the edge of the gully standing over him. The man smiled, his yellowing teeth catching the sunlight. He then dove at Hale, leading with the bayonet on his rifle. Hale raised his pistol and shot the man in the mouth.

Yellow teeth crumpled and flew in all directions as the bullet shattered them. Still alive and now very angry, he tried to stab Hale with his bayonet. Hale attempted to roll to the left to avoid the blow. He failed. Searing pain erupted in his right shoulder as the bayonet bit into his flesh.

Shocked, he dropped his pistol as his instincts for survival kicked in. He grabbed his pukko with his left hand and drove it into the back of the Soviet's head as the man struck the ground beside him. The man let out a deep breath as Hale drove the blade through his skull into his brain.

Hale sat up and looked over at his shoulder. His white

coat was stained red with blood and his shoulder throbbed. He quickly unzipped his coat and pulled it off. His injured shoulder screamed in protest as he pulled the coat off his right arm. Keeping the coat partially on, as it was ten degrees below zero. He looked down at the wound.

The bayonet had not gone into the shoulder, instead, the edge had scraped across the top until it was deflected by the bone. Hale rummaged around in his pack until he found a bandage. Holding it with his right hand, he tore it open with his left and slapped over the wound. He quickly secured it in place with a wrap and pulled his coat back on. Ignoring the pain, he thought, *Pekka needs me.*

Fighting back tears, he holstered his pistol, picked up his rifle, and pulled himself up to the edge of the gully. His stomach sank at the sight that greeted him. The survivors of the other two squads had reached Pekka. Inwardly cursing, Hale slipped back down into the gully and pulled his last clip of ammunition out of his pocket. *This isn't going to be enough.*

He opened his white overcoat and patted his bandoliers to check for more ammo. There were no more bullets, *Dammit!*

Taking a moment to calm his nerves, Hale peeked up over the edge of the gully. The Russians had pulled Pekka to his feet. The gathered crowd of Red Army soldiers had made a lane for a new figure that approached. Hale looked at this man, his dark green overcoat was of a better cut than the rest of the group. On his overcoat, affixed to the collar were three red squares. Squinting, to see the man's features, Hale's heart sank, *The Commissar!*

Hale watched as the man who had captured him the day before reached Pekka. He could hear his voice but couldn't make out the words. Suddenly the Commissar punched Pekka in the gut. Pekka crumpled at the blow, but the two soldiers' firm grip on his arms kept him on his feet. The Commissar shook his black gloved hand.

Enraged, Hale raised his rifle and took aim at one of the men surrounding Pekka and the Commissar. Calming his rage, he held his breath and pulled the trigger. A moment later the impact of the bullet knocked the unfortunate off his feet, and he tumbled to the ground face first.

The rest of the squad, knowing that Hale was alone, turned, raised their rifles, and fired in his direction. Hale ducked back down into the gully and worked the metal bolt on his Mosin-Nagant. He calmly stood back up and ended the life of another young Red Army soldier just as the rest of the group were raising their rifles. Seeing him reappear they quickly took aim.

With a loud roar, the Soviets let loose a barrage of fire in unison. This time the bullets flew and buzzed around Hale. *They know precisely where I'm at.* Hale thought.

The Russians bellowed in unison and charged. Hale, down to his last three bullets, was forced to turn and flee from the advancing Red Army soldiers. *I will return for you as you did for me my friend.* Hale thought as he fled from the advancing tide of Red Army soldiers.

Chapter 5

Afternoon Karelia Finland, December 1st, 1939

Hale stumbled through the woods in a headlong rush. Branches and thorns grabbed at his white coat as he hurtled through the underbrush. Fear drove him forward as his lungs heaved in protest from the effort of running in the frigid air through the snow. After half an hour of running, Hale collapsed in exhaustion and laid on the ground. He rolled over and looked back toward the direction he had just come.

Expecting to see dark green clad soldiers emblazoned with red stars break over the horizon at any moment, he raised his rifle and took aim. As he waited, his breathing began to slow and his thoughts raged, *How can I get Pekka back from that traitorous jackal? That coward is always surrounded by too many soldiers.*

After several minutes, his breath finally stilled itself and he was able to listen. The sounds of the forest filled his ears. Absent were the sounds of boots upon snow. *They didn't follow me.*

Hale stood and looked around. The sun was low on the horizon. Off to the north was a line of clouds that had advanced across the sky all afternoon, and now were nearly upon him. He pulled his pack off his back and rummaged around in it for several moments. Pulling out a compass, he held it up with his right palm to get his bearings.

Satisfied he knew where he was, more or less at least. Hale set off toward the south west. Without his skis, the journey through the snow-covered woods was a difficult one. Even for one such as Hale who had spent his entire young life wandering through woodlands such as this in search of meat for his family's table. The effort of pushing one's self through the endless piles of snow would quickly wear down the strongest of men.

As he trudged through the thick blanket of frozen snow, his mind was cluttered with thoughts of Pekka and the recent fight with the Red Army, *What could I have done to save him? Why did you run? You yellow coward, if you would have just stayed and fought a little longer, you could have saved him. Instead you filled your boots with piss and fled.*

Hale's mind raced as his brain filled with these disjointed thoughts again and again. He was becoming overwhelmed by a growing sense of guilt. His thoughts tried to coalesce around a moment that if he went left instead of right, the engagement would have turned out differently. *You had no choice but to run. You were hopelessly outnumbered, and they were charging right at you!*

In response, another piece of Hale's mind still raged at him. *You could have stayed and fought!* Heedless of the cold, he reached into his mostly white overcoat and felt his bandoliers, there were no bullets left. *That doesn't matter, you could have taken bullets from the dead man at your feet!*

Hale paused and leaned up against a tree. He looked

up at the sky, with tears in his eyes. As he started to weep and said, "I had no choice. There was no time!"

His sudden outburst caused the woods around him to grow silent. Sighing deeply, he adjusted the rifle slung over his uninjured shoulder and continued slogging toward his destination. As he walked, the weak light of the arctic sun disappeared behind the western horizon. Soon, the bank of clouds he had observed earlier, while it was still daylight, covered the sky overhead.

A snowflake lazily drifted down from the sky and tickled Hale's nose as it found its way to the earth. A moment later another one brushed his chin as it fell to the ground below. Then the snowflakes came a few at a time. Finally, they began falling in earnest, obscuring Hale's visibility through the dark and frosty forest.

The sound of millions of snowflakes striking the ground filled Hale's ears as he plodded ever onward toward his destination. To protect his face from the cold and endless barrage, he donned his white mask that shielded his face from the weather. He walked for a few hours through the growing maelstrom of falling snow that swirled around him as the wind picked up. He shivered as he thought, *Am I lost?*

He paused and rummaged around in his right coat pocket for his compass. Pulling the little metal device out, he strained to see the position of the dial in the darkness. Frustrated, he slipped his pack off, and let it fall to the ground. Bending over at the waist, he rummaged around in it until he found what he was looking for. He struck a match and it flared to life. Careful to keep it sheltered from the wind, he held it up so that it cast its feeble light on the face of his compass.

Hale was relieved when he saw that he had been

maintaining his course through the darkness and the storm, *Southwest.*

He dropped the match to the ground. The wind whisked away the small puff of smoke as it sizzled for a moment in the snow and winked out. Hale slipped his compass back into his coat pocket and pulled the heavy pack back onto his back. He grimaced as shooting pain erupted from his right shoulder. Biting his lower lip, he picked his rifle up off the ground and slipped the strap over his left shoulder.

He resumed his journey through the icy conditions. As he walked, the storm intensified until he could barely see ten feet in front of him. Despite the physically arduous trek through the snow, he began to shiver as the temperature dropped.

Approaching a rise, his teeth began to openly chatter from the cold as he started to struggle putting one foot in front of the other. His thoughts receded as his world shrank to the pain in his shoulder, and the cold. Always the cold.

As he reached the small hill, his strength began to ebb as the frightfully cold conditions drew the strength from his tired muscles. He paused for a moment at the bottom of a small knoll and looked up. All he could see were a few trees in front of him and snow falling from the sky. The snow fell with such intensity, it was as if a giant was standing over him dumping buckets of the stuff onto his head.

As he climbed, he fought against the weather, the cold, and his own fatigue. As the last of his energy fled him, his steps up the rise became a struggle. With each step, his feet sank deeper and deeper into the ever-growing volume of snow on the ground.

Reaching the top of the hill, he paused and looked down into a small valley below. His eyes caught the faintest hint of dull yellow light through the murk. His dry and cracked lips turned faintly upward as a new emotion warmed his frozen body, hope. Ignoring his pain, and the ever present cold, he hastened towards the inviting glow. As he approached, he smiled in relief, *I made it!*

The glow came from a tent that had been set up at the base of a large fir tree. The snow-covered branches seemingly reached around the tent as if the tree were embracing it. Smoke wafted lazily from a pipe that jutted out the top of the dark gray hued shelter. The branches of the tree broke up the tell-tale cloud of smoke up as it drifted upward. The positioning of the tent ensured that the smoke emerging from the pipe would not give the location of the tent away to the invading Soviets.

Hale slipped through a flap and stepped inside. He was immediately greeted by a blast of warm air. Sighing in relief, he collapsed to the floor of the tent, exhausted. Within a moment, a man with penetrating blue eyes loomed over him, "Hale?"

Hale let out a groan as the warmth of the tent began to thaw his frozen extremities. He took a deep breath and smiled as the warm air flowed into his lungs helping the feeling to return to his numb body. Lieutenant Maki looked down at the red stain on Hale's shoulder and said, "You've been injured."

The blond-haired man squatted and pushed Hale over onto his side, "I need to get this pack off, so I can see what's going on with you."

Hale held up a hand as he said, "It's fine, just a flesh wound."

The Lieutenant's lips pursed as he said, "A flesh wound? That's an awful lot of blood for just a flesh wound. Let's have a look."

Hale nodded. He carefully slipped his right arm out of the straps of his pack. As he did so, his face twisted into a frightful visage betraying the pain he was feeling. With a dull thump, the pack dropped to the wooden floor of the tent. He then slid his rifle off his left shoulder and gently placed it on top of his pack.

The exhausted sniper then unfastened the buttons of his white overcoat and pulled it off. As he did so Lieutenant Maki gasped, "It's still bleeding."

Hale swooned as his thoughts dulled. His superior officer knelt down and helped pull Hale's sweater off. Several more layers of clothing later, Maki had reached the bandage. He gently pulled it off as Hale grimaced, "I was right. It's still bleeding." Maki said.

The Lieutenant stood up, walked to the back of the tent, and opened a large grey chest. Pulling a box with a red cross on it out of the chest, he returned to Hale. He opened the first aid kit and pulled a small packet out. Quickly ripping the top off the packet, he poured the contents of it over Hale's wound as he said, "This will help to stop the bleeding."

Hale nodded dully. He looked over at his shoulder. His mind tried to process what he was seeing, but it was clouded by fatigue. A moment later awareness fled as his exhaustion and blood loss overtook him.

Hale opened his eyes. The pleasant smell of brewing coffee filled his nose. His head was laying on something soft. *A pillow?* He thought. He looked down at his injured shoulder. It had been expertly wrapped in a clean bandage. Unlike the bandage Hale had applied earlier, this one was not soaked in blood.

Noticing that Hale was awake, Lieutenant Maki stood and walked over to Hale, "How are you feeling?"

"Better." Hale replied.

"Good. You want some coffee?" Maki asked.

Hale nodded, "Yes sir."

"You don't have to keep calling me sir. It's just you and me in here right now, and I'm not that much older than you." The Lieutenant replied.

"What should I call you then sir?" Hale asked.

"Maki is fine."

Maki returned with a tin cup full of steaming black liquid, "Sorry, I don't have any sugar or milk."

Hale looked up at him and reached for the cup, "Thank you."

Hale took a small sip from the cup. The warm liquid slid down his throat. After nearly forty-eight hours in the cold, Hale relished the feeling of warmth in his core.

"Are you hungry?" Maki asked.

Hale met Maki's gaze and smiled, "Famished."

"I've got some venison and hardtack. I'll get a stew going on the stove." Maki said.

The Lieutenant walked across the tent and began rummaging around the stove. Hale took another sip of the coffee and sat up. He looked around. The tent had a small black stove situated in the middle of it. A small pipe, made from some black metal as the stove, connected to the top of the stove. The stovepipe continued upward to the ceiling of the tent where it jutted upward through a small hole.

Lieutenant Maki stood over the stove. He wore dark grey uniform pants, but like most of the soldiers of Finland who lacked a full proper uniform, he sported a non-regulation wool sweater. The sweater looked like it had been lovingly knitted by hand. Maki looked back and saw Hale's eyes on him, "My wife made this for me."

"It looks really warm." Hale said.

Maki smiled, "It is. The wool came from our heard of black faced sheep. She spun the wool herself into thread and then knitted it."

"You are a lucky man to have a woman who loves you enough to take that kind of time making you a shirt." Hale replied.

"Indeed. Is there someone special you are fighting to protect?" Maki asked.

"Other than my sister, and parents?" Hale asked.

"Yes." Maki said.

Hale's thoughts drifted inward for a moment as the memory of that last afternoon with Nea filled his mind. He jerked himself back into the present before the growing warmth in his loins gave his thoughts away, "Her name is Nea."

"What's she like? How did you meet her?" Maki asked.

"Someone I grew up with. The daughter of the couple

that owned the farm down the road from ours. When we were younger, we used to play dirty tricks on each other all the time. Then our relationship evolved." Hale said.

Maki chuckled, "Oh I bet it started evolving the moment you both began growing hair in new places."

Hale flashed him a look of anger, "It wasn't like that. She became my friend and confidant. We talked for hours about our innermost thoughts and desires for the future. Over the years it became unimaginable that such a future wouldn't include the other."

The Lieutenant left the stove and walked up to Hale, squatting, he met Hale's gaze and put a hand on his uninjured shoulder, "Peace my friend. I did not realize the depths of your feelings for Nea. It's tradition for soldiers to talk lewdly of what we left behind at home."

"I just can't talk about Nea like that. Even though we. . ." Hale's voice drifted off as his thoughts returned to that afternoon in the woods.

"I can see she means everything to you." Maki stood and ran his right hand over his chest almost caressing the sweater, "My Sade evokes such feelings within me as well. It is good to have such thoughts of a woman. It fills our Finnish hearts with fire."

Hale nodded in understanding, "We will need that fire if we are to keep the invader from our homes."

"Exactly," The Lieutenant stood and brought a second tin cup over to Hale, "Drink up, I'm not a great cook, but this will help your strength to return."

"Thank you." Hale replied.

He took a small sip of the broth, *Not bad.* He thought.

Hale held the cup with both hands relishing the warmth his fingers felt. Looking down at it, he saw pieces of meat floating within a brown looking broth. Steam came from the liquid and filled his nose with the smell of boiled venison. There were small bits of bread within the cup. As the bread dissolved, it helped to thicken the broth.

Hale took another sip of the stew and looked at the left side of the tent. There was a campaign table with a map sitting on it. Helping to hold the map down on the table were two objects, a large stone, and a radio microphone. Hale's eyes followed the cord attached to the bottom of the round black microphone. His eyes came to rest on a large gray box sitting on the floor next to the table.

Maki followed the course of Hale's gaze and said, "One of our few radios. It helps me to stay abreast of what is going on."

"What have you heard so far? How bad is it?" Hale asked.

"It's pretty bad. We're facing the Soviet 7th Army's 19th Rifle Corps, specifically the 24th Rifle Division." Maki replied.

Without warning Hale suddenly stiffened. He turned to face the Lieutenant and said, "I've got to get back out there. They've captured Pekka."

Maki shook his head, "No, you need to rest, you're exhausted. The snipers we have put in place have nearly ground the bastards to a halt. At the pace they are moving it will be a week before they even reach the Mannerheim line."

"But Pekka-"

Maki held up a hand, "Knew the risks the same as the

rest of us. He would want us to focus on the invader and not some half-cocked attempt to sneak past half a million Soviets to rescue him."

Hale's nostrils flared as his cheeks began to turn red. As the fire of anger burned through his blood, Hale's eyes narrowed. With clenched fists he turned to face Maki and squared his shoulders. The action caused him to grimace in pain. The Lieutenant placed a hand on Hale's good shoulder and said, "I understand. The thought of those bastards having one of my snipers makes me sick inside. Especially Pekka. During his many years of service, he's given much to Finland."

"He has a family. A wife, and two daughters." Hale replied.

Maki sighed, "I know." He repeated himself, this time in a low whisper before saying in a louder voice, "He would want us to keep fighting to protect them."

Hale nodded and turned to look down at the map. It was a detailed map of the local area. The chart had a transparent sheet of plastic over top of it. Two grease pencils laid on the table at the edge of the map, one black, the other red. Hale's eyes were drawn to a red arrow that hugged the only northward running road in this area. The red line was labeled with a 24.

Hale traced the red line back to the border of the Soviet Union. There were several more numbers written on the Soviet side of the border 43, 70, 123. Each number had a question mark written behind it.

Maki saw what Hale was looking at and said, "Those are the other three divisions in the 19th Corps. We haven't detected them yet."

"So many." Hale's voice drifted off into a whisper.

"Aye. To many." Maki said in a low voice.

The radio crackled to life interrupting the two men, "Loki do you have a copy? Over."

Maki picked up the radio microphone and said, "This is Loki go."

The radio speaker replied, "Loki, this is Asgard. Uncle Lenin is going for a walk. Over."

Maki pressed the button on the side of the microphone and replied, "He'd better bundle up it's cold this time of year. Over."

The voice coming from the radio speaker on the floor replied, "Indeed, he wouldn't want to catch a cold. Over."

Maki pressed the microphone button again as he said, "Go Asgard actual. Over."

"The Titans are rampaging toward the north. They will reach the brook soon. Over." The voice on the other end of the radio said.

Maki replied, "Understood, what does the all father wish me to do? Over."

"He's dispatching a group of Valkyries to make a stand. He feels that delaying the Titans at the brook would be worth the blood price. Over." Asgard actual replied.

"Then we shall ride forthwith and partake in our mischief in support of the Valkyries. Over." Maki replied.

"Excellent. Do what you can to punish the Titans from your side. Over" Asgard actual replied.

"There are few of us here. I shall go forth myself. Antti will be here soon to mind the store. Over" Maki replied.

"Understood and good luck. Over." Asgard actual replied.

Hale looked at Maki, his face etched with confusion, "What did all that nonsense you just spewed mean?"

Maki chuckled, "It was code. The Soviets have radios too. We wouldn't want them listening in and understanding what we just said."

Maki pulled a book out of his right uniformed pants pocket and began thumbing through it, "Ahh here it is. The brook is the codeword for the crossroads at the village of Kivennapa."

Maki turned to the map and quickly located the village. He placed a finger on it and said, "Here."

"What are we to do?" Hale asked.

"Command wants me to dispatch as many snipers as I have available to the village to harry the invader. They're sending up a battalion to delay the bastards." Maki replied.

"Why? Many villages along that road have already fallen. What makes this one different?" Hale asked.

"Because it sits on a crossroads. If the Russians take the village, they'll have access to this road that runs east and west. Right now, they are limited to the north and south running road they are currently on. Since they have confined themselves to the road. If they reach that crossroads, they'll be able to spread themselves out."

Hale's eyes focused on the map, "Oh, I see what you are saying. Right now, we have them in a bottle neck. If they are able to gain the crossroads, they'll be able to work their way loose. So, you're sending me there?"

Maki nodded, "And I'm going with you."

Hale looked incredulous, "No offense, but you grew up in Viipuri. What do you know about sneaking through a forest and using a rifle?"

"Not much," Maki admitted.

"Then why?" Before Hale could finish his sentence, Maki held up a hand.

He crossed the room, picked a gun out of a pile of them lying on the floor in a corner and said, "I can help you with this."

Hale's eyes widened as they took in the weapon Maki was holding up, "A machine gun?"

Maki nodded, "A PPD 34. It's a submachine gun to be precise."

"Where did you get it?" Hale asked.

"Onni brought it in. He collected two of them from the corpses of a squad of Soviets he slew." Maki replied.

"If I had something like that when they took Pekka, I could have saved him." Hale replied.

"Perhaps." Maki paused, then added, "Perhaps not. You are only one man and you were engaged with an entire battalion."

Hale sighed loudly, "I know. I just can't help but to think that if I made different decisions, that somehow he'd be here with me right now."

"You did everything you could for him, and then you

did what was best for Finland. You preserved yourself to fight another day." Maki replied.

"I know but-"

"Peace Hale. I need you focused on what's ahead, not what happened yesterday. Put it behind you. I need you in the here and now. Your family needs you."

Hale nodded slowly. His features revealing the turmoil within him, "I know you're right."

"Of course, I'm right! I'm your commanding officer."

Hale laughed, "You're barely older than I am!"

Maki joined in the laughter, "Aye, and I would have gotten lost in the woods getting here if not for the rest of you holding my hand." Maki stopped laughing and patted the PPD 34, "But I can contribute. I can cover you so you can use your skills on those swine."

"You know, they are young men just like we are. They've been told to fight just like we have." Hale replied.

"Fuck them. We are fighting for our homes and our way of life. They are fighting, because if they don't, the party will riddle their families with bullets." Maki replied.

"Dark the world has become. A place where the candlelight of freedom sputters and blinks in the growing winds of tyranny." Hale replied.

"I thought I was the university graduate. Who taught you philosophy?" Maki asked.

"My dad. Though we have a hard life living off the land, he always challenged me to exercise my mind as hard as I exercised my body." Hale replied.

"He sounds like a wise man." Maki replied.

"He is." Hale replied softly.

"You'll get to see him again when this is all over." Maki reassured.

Hale nodded slowly. As Maki added, "Eat up. We've got to get moving."

As Hale sipped on his stew and coffee, Maki wrote a note. When he finished, he nailed it to the tent post that was prominently visible upon entry."

"What's that?" Hale asked.

"It's a letter to the rest of the squad to join us. We'll need all the help we can muster." Maki replied.

Maki then worked to load his pack. He placed within enough rations for several days, and six drum magazines of ammunition that appeared to fit the Russian submachine gun. He then walked over to grey chest and opened it. Pulling out the first aid kit, he took several fresh bandages and wraps from it for Hale's shoulder. He placed the kit back into the larger chest and dropped the bandages and wraps into his pack.

Turning to Hale the Lieutenant asked, "How are you doing on bullets?"

"I'm completely out." Hale replied.

Maki's eyes narrowed, "You were out of ammo, yet you've been lamenting about not saving Pekka this whole time?"

Hale nodded sheepishly, "Yes." Before Maki could fire off a retort Hale held up his hand and continued, "I know it doesn't make any sense."

"No, it doesn't. This is why you need to clear your head of this nonsense. The mental energy you are wasting on what you couldn't have hoped to prevent is best saved for our mission."

"I'll try." Hale replied softly.

"No, you'll do. That's an order." The Lieutenant barked sternly, "There are several boxes of 7.62mm ammo for your rifle next to the grey footlocker. Fill up your bandolier, and your clips. Hell, fill up your pockets too. We are probably going to need every last bit of it."

"Yes sir." Hale replied.

Hale quickly finished up his meal and strode over to the spot Maki had indicated. Looking down he immediately spotted several wooden boxes. The unpainted boxes smelled faintly of freshly cut wood. The ammunition containers were about four inches wide and a foot deep. The two ends of the boxes sported handles made from a black colored rope.

Hale knelt and wrestled the top off the box closest to him. His eyes took in the gleam of the box full of 7.62mm rifle rounds. The bullets, about four inches in length, started with a sharp point on the business end, and ended with a flat circular base. In the middle of the flat circular base, surrounded by numbers, and contrasting with the brass coloration of the rest of the bullet's casing, was a silver circle. *The percussion cap.* Hale thought.

Hale worked quickly to fill his bandolier with the new rounds of ammunition. Task complete, he began filling up his empty magazines with the new bullets. Finally, he located his rifle, still on the floor by the entrance of the tent and ejected the bullets. Only two remained inside the rifle's internal magazine. He quickly filled the clip back up and slammed it home into his rifle. Then pulled it free, before refilling it.

Finishing up, he helped himself to some ration tins, and then turned to see what Maki was up to. The Lieutenant had gone through a transformation. Gone was the relaxed looking officer in his white sweater, and gray uniform pants. He was now suited up in white pants, and an overcoat just like Hale had worn outside.

Like Hale's, the white coat had a large hood that would help to protect the wearer of the jacket from the sub-zero temperatures of a Finnish December. Maki had donned his pack which hung on his back. On his right shoulder he wore the PPD 34. He also sported a gray colored utility belt with a pistol holster, and several grenades attached to it. The grenades were the German style wooden handled variety with the metal top that the Wehrmacht called the Stielhandgranate or stick grenade, "Ready?" Maki asked.

Hale nodded, "Yes."

"On the side of the tent I have several sets of skis. We'll use them to quickly make our way over the snow to the village." Maki said.

Hale smiled, "Good. After slogging through kilometers of this knee-deep snow, I've learned my lesson about losing track of my skis."

"The skis are a huge advantage for us. Without them we wouldn't be able to move around the Russians like we have been able to. Those idiots have been hugging the roads and ignoring the woodlands. We've made them pay dearly for their ignorance thus far. By hitting the bastards by surprise, then disappearing into the forest using our skis, we drive fear into their hearts. The same group of

Finns, using their skis, can easily hit them again elsewhere in a short amount of time. This gives those Marxist pigs the impression there are a great many more of us than is actually the case." Maki said.

The two men quickly attached the skis to their boots and began the journey northward toward the village of Kivennapa. As they traveled away from the tent, the two men set a steady pace. It wasn't long before Hale's injured shoulder began to ache with the effort of using his ski poles to push himself forward over the snow.

As Hale's discomfort grew, he began to give it away with heavy breathing and a slowing pace. Worried, Maki turned and asked, "Are you well?"

"It's my shoulder, the effort of pulling myself forward with the ski pole is causing it to hurt." Hale replied.

"Let's take a break for a few minutes. I may have something to help." Maki replied.

Hale gently lowered himself to the frigid snowpack, careful not to cause any additional discomfort. As he did so, Maki took off his pack and began to rummage through it. He pulled out an object, wrapped in brown paper. Tearing the paper open, he dropped the contents of the pack into his open palm. It was a syringe.

Turning to Hale, he said, "Take off your coat."

Hale leaned back so that the bottom of his pack rested on the ground. He then gently slipped his arms out of it. Once the pack was laying on the ground, he stood up and removed his coat. The freezing air immediately made him regret his choice as the force of the icy air slammed into him like a brick wall. He unconsciously grabbed himself with his arms trying to retain his warmth.

"Lower your right arm and let it relax." Maki asked.

Hale did as he was told. Looking over at Maki he said, "What's that?"

"It's a syringe of morphine. This will help you forget about the pain in your shoulder." Maki said.

"I thought we were supposed to save that for serious injuries." Hale replied.

"I need you to get to the village in fighting condition. This will help." Maki said. Then added, "Stand still." As he plunged the needle into Hale's arm.

Hale winced at the sharp pain in his arm. A few moments later he smiled as the pain in his shoulder began to disappear. He met Maki's gaze and said, "Wow."

"That is going to have to do you for a while. I brought most of our base camp's supply, but I need you to be able to shoot straight when we get there." Maki said.

Hale nodded as a numbing haze began to descend over his awareness, "Let's get moving." Maki added.

Hale reached down and picked up his pack. He slid it onto his back, left arm first, and then very slowly slipped his right arm in. There was almost no pain. Smiling he picked up his rifle, slung it over his left shoulder, and picked up his ski poles.

With Hale's pain greatly diminished, the two men were able to set a steady pace. The kilometers quickly fell away as they headed in a northerly direction. Occasionally, Maki would bring them to a halt for a few minutes so they could catch their breath. As the sun touched the south western horizon, they changed direction. They were now heading northeast with the sun almost behind them.

The golden rays of the setting sun glistened off the white blanket draped across the countryside. The snow-covered countryside, sparkled in the light, making it seem as if there were tiny diamonds embedded everywhere. Hale, basking in the natural beauty of the Finnish countryside, was startled when Maki raised his right arm and made a fist, the signal to stop.

Hale dutifully came to a stop. His ears, uncluttered by the sound of their skiing, he heard the noise of engines ahead. In a whisper Maki said, "Let's take a break and eat. Once it's fully dark, we can continue toward them quietly."

"How close are we to the Russians?" Hale asked.

"About half a kilometer or so to the east is the road. The sound echoes and carries through this frigid night air." Maki replied.

The two men opened their packs and pulled out some ration tins, "What are you going to try sir?" Hale asked.

"Hmmm." Maki responded, "I wonder which one of these would taste the best frozen?"

Hale looked at the two tins that Maki was holding up, "Probably the chicken. If we dig a hole in the snow behind one of the thicker trees, we could build a fire. The enemy probably won't see it."

"I'd rather not risk it." Maki replied.

Hale sighed, "As you wish." Trying to take his mind off the numbing cold he asked, "Tell me about Sade. How did you meet her?"

"We met in the fall of '34, I was attending the University in Helsinki." Maki replied.

"Was she in one of your classes?" Hale asked.

"No, we met by chance. She was sitting in the park one day, and I was out for a walk. It was a warm day for late September, and I was enjoying the feel of the sun on my face. When I rounded a bend in the path, there she was." Maki said.

"Did she see you?" Hale asked.

"No. She was leaning up against a tree next to a small lake. The sun was setting behind her, and I could see the rays shining through her golden tresses." Maki said.

"What did you do?" Hale inquired.

"She seemed really focused on a book she was reading. The book was sitting in her lap, so she did not notice me standing there. I found a spot nearby and pretended to watch the water." Maki said.

Hale laughed, "How did that go."

"Not very well. She noticed me almost immediately." Maki replied.

"I bet. What did she do?" Hale questioned.

"I feel like I am being interrogated by the Soviets. You're asking more questions than a commissar." Maki chuckled.

Hale, in his best imitation of a Russian accent said, "You will tell me what I want to know, or it will go badly for you Finn."

Maki laughed and relaxed a bit, "Very well. If you must know."

"It's helping. We've got a lot of time, and this story is

helping to keep my mind off the cold and my shoulder." Hale replied.

Maki closed his eyes and smiled, "She looked up and saw me gazing at her. She hesitated for a moment and then returned my smile."

Hale leaned in, "Caught! What did you do?"

"There was only one thing I could do, to salvage the situation. I walked over to her and introduced myself." Maki replied.

Hale whistled softly in appreciation, "Bold. How did that go?

"Better than I thought it would. My heart was pounding, my bladder was weak, and I prayed that she did not see that my hands were shaking." Maki paused for a moment and then continued, "She didn't, so I asked if she would like to get some coffee at a nearby café."

"I don't think I would have been brave enough to do that." Hale said.

"I couldn't believe that I was either, but what did I have to lose at that point?" Maki said.

Hale chortled, "True. So, what happened?"

"She said that she would be happy to have coffee with me, but first she wanted to watch the sunset." Maki said.

Hale swallowed a bite of his dinner, "Then you got coffee?"

"Well it was a bit late to have some coffee at that point, so I asked her to dinner." Maki said.

Hale whistled softly in appreciation, "A courageous

move! Do they teach you such things at the university?"

"No, it just felt right." Maki replied.

"What happened next?" Hale wondered.

"This isn't very fair." Maki said.

"How so?" Hale asked.

"You're finding out all about Sade, without telling me anything about Nea." Maki replied.

"There isn't much to tell. It was a lot different than how you met Sade." Hale said.

"Let me be the judge of that. Before I continue about Sade, you are going to tell me about Nea." Maki said.

"Yes sir." Hale said.

"I didn't mean it like that. I'm just curious too." Maki said with a soothing voice.

"Oh." Hale paused for a moment to collect his thoughts, "Me and Nea were different than you and Sade. Nea belonged to the family that owned the farm next to ours."

"Here in Karelia?" Maki prompted.

Hale nodded, "About forty kilometers north of here."

"Viipuri is not much beyond that. We both have a lot to lose if we can't stop these bastards. Tell me more about Nea." Maki said.

"As I was saying."

"Before you were rudely interrupted." Maki added.

Hale started again, "Nea was part of the family that worked the farm next to my parent's."

"How did you meet?" Maki asked.

"I don't remember." Hale replied.

Maki's eyes widened, "What do you mean you don't remember? How can you forget the moment you met the woman you fell in love with?"

"Because I was like two when it happened." Hale shot back. A hint of frustration tinged his voice as he added, "Are you going to let me tell the story or not?"

Maki nodded, "Continue. I'll keep my mouth shut."

Hale smirked, "See that you do." The young sniper let his mind drift back to a happier time, "We were the best of friends for many years. We'd play together in the forest. Often by a little creek that ran between our family's two properties."

"Sounds romantic." Maki said.

"Oh, it was. We did what children often do. We dropped insects down each other's shirts, made mud pies together, tried to help injured frogs, and generally made a mess of ourselves." Hale closed his eyes and smiled as his mind drifted back to the past, "This went on for many years. We sought each other out daily. When it was too cold for our parents to let us wander about unsupervised, they made sure we were brought together frequently to sip hot cocoa in front of a warm fire."

Maki smiled, "A warm fire and hot cocoa, that sounds amazing right now."

Hale exhaled a large cloud of mist, "Yes it would.

Around the time we turned eleven, we began to see each other differently. She slowly went from being my friend to something more. We continued to share our innermost feelings with each other, but things changed."

"Oh, something changed all right. It's called puberty." Maki teased.

"We used to snuggle and touch each other all the time and think nothing of it. Then, slowly over time, whenever we would touch, I would feel this electric shock through my whole body." Hale said.

Maki poked fun at Hale, "I'm sure you were feeling warmth in places you didn't realize were there up to that point in your life."

Hale's pale cheeks turned a deep shade of crimson, "Yes. I began to see her differently. She was still my friend, but something more too. These feelings were fleeting at first and we continued much as we had the previous several years. Every once in a while, when looking upon Nea, I would feel this unexplained warmth in my loins."

"When did the dreams come?" Maki asked.

Hale lowered his eyes, embarrassed, "About the time I turned thirteen."

"What did you think about it when you first awoke? Maki asked.

Hale drew in a deep breath, "I was a cornucopia of emotions, horror, embarrassment, shame. I thought I had pissed myself that first time."

"How did things evolve with Nea after that?" Maki asked.

"I think we were both feeling much the same thing. Every so often, I would catch her looking at me intently." Hale paused and looked up at the stars, "Then I noticed that she would brush my hand with hers more and more often."

Maki grinned, "She was trying to make it easier for you to hold her hand."

Hale returned the Maki's smile and nodded slowly, "Yeah, and I was too stupid to realize what was going on."

Maki placed a reassuring hand on Hale's good shoulder, "Not stupid, just inexperienced and full of nerves. So, what happened to change the stalemate?"

Hale shivered at the growing cold, "We were sitting on the bank of the creek just gazing at the water as it flowed by. The sun was high in the sky and reflecting the light on both of us. I looked over at Nea and she looked up from the stream and smiled at me. I could see the waters of the stream and the sunlight reflecting off of her green eyes. A cascade of feelings erupted inside me and I couldn't control myself. I got this overwhelming urge to kiss her."

"Did you?" Maki asked.

"I did." Hale replied.

"How did that go?"

Hale's face crinkled as it took on a happier countenance, "Better than I thought. It was very fast and over before we both knew it."

"So just a peck then?" Maki inquired.

Hale nodded, "I was totally shocked by what happened next." Hale paused for a moment to rub his gloved hands over his numbing face, "She kissed me back!"

Maki leaned back and laughed heartily. Quickly realizing how much noise he was making, he lowered his volume and said, "Sorry I got so much into the story, that I forgot the Soviets were nearby."

Hale nodded and held up a hand to silence the conversation. The low thrum from idling engines off in the distance filled his ears, "I doubt they heard you with all the racket their metal monstrosities are making."

"They are making less noise than earlier. It seems like they've stopped moving." Maki said.

Hale nodded, "They probably are keeping the engines running to stay warm."

The Lieutenant said, "Let's get some sleep. We'll wake early so we can cause some mayhem while they still slumber."

"I'm too cold to sleep sir." Hale replied.

Maki sighed, "I am too. Let's dig ourselves a chamber in this snow and squeeze together in it. Our body warmth should help." The Lieutenant said.

"Yes sir." Hale said.

The two men pulled their pukkos out and started chipping away at the top layer of the snow. Before long they had created a dug-out chamber that was just large enough for both of them to squeeze into. The close proximity to Maki in the small chamber began to warm Hale back up. Thanks to the increased warmth, the two men's breathing became even as they drifted off to sleep.

Chapter 6

Early Morning Karelia Isthmus Finland, December 3rd,

Hale was jostled awake by a hand. He groaned, tried to roll away from it, and said, "Dad just a few more minutes. It's too early to go hunting."

"Hale." Came the voice of Lieutenant Maki.

Hale opened his eyes and saw nothing but darkness. Startled, he tried to sit up and his head struck the top of the dugout. Awareness of where he was filled him as he groaned and rubbed the spot on his head that had struck the ceiling.

"Are you with me now?" The Lieutenant asked.

Hale nodded and replied, "Yes."

Maki smiled, "You're not much of a morning person, are you?"

Hale's eyes narrowed as they glared at Maki's back, "No."

"Let's get out there, stow our bags, and go hunting." The Lieutenant said.

They emerged into the bitterly cold darkness. Looking for a place to store their packs, the two men looked about for possibilities. The moonlight revealed a promising looking birch tree with thick branches nearby.

Maki approached the tree. The Lieutenant brushed the snow off a thick lower branch of the tree and then hoisted himself upward. Once he was standing on the thick branch, he located a smaller counterpart jutting from the trunk and hung his pack from it. Spotting another, similar in size to the one that he hung his own back from attached to the trunk nearby, he gestured for Hale to pass his pack upward.

Maki hung Hale's pack and then lowered himself to the ground. Turning to Hale he asked, "How should we approach?"

"Straight at them at first. Stay low and try to keep as quiet as possible. We need to get close enough to figure out how they are laid out." Hale replied.

Maki gestured in the direction of the Russians, "Lead the way."

Without replying Hale turned toward the east and slowly began creeping toward the road. Based on the thrum and rumble of the idling engines, he figured they were about a half kilometer distant. About every fifty feet or so he would pause and listen. Maki was careful to follow in his exact footsteps as quietly as he could manage.

Hale paused, turned toward Maki and whispered tersely, "You sound like a fat moose in a glass factory."

Maki's face turned crimson from his embarrassment, "Sorry. What am I doing wrong?"

"You're leading with your heel when you take a step. Try leading with your toes instead." Hale suggested.

Maki frowned, "How am I supposed to manage that in these thick boots?"

"Just do it! It's not the most comfortable way to walk, but it helps with the noise."

Hale turned and continued toward the road. The noise Maki was creating diminished considerably. They took about half an hour to cover a quarter of a kilometer. Hale, like he had done so many times before, paused and listened. This time he heard movement up ahead.

Turning to the Lieutenant he whispered, "Do you hear that?"

Maki listened intently and nodded, "I hear noise, but I'm not sure what I'm hearing. It's very faint."

"That's the sound of someone trying to stay warm while standing guard. I think he keeps shifting his feet in place causing those faint crunching noises in the snow." Hale said.

"What can we do?" Maki asked.

"You stay here. I don't think you're ready to sneak up on someone without being detected. Those city legs of yours need more practice out here first. Get your gun ready and come running if I get into trouble." Hale said.

Maki nodded as he quietly pulled his PPD 34 from his shoulder, "I'll be ready."

Without replying, Hale turned and began moving toward the sound. As he made his way slowly forward the sound increased as the man standing guard grew colder and therefore increased his movement.

About fifty feet out Hale paused. He looked through the trees trying to see the man he knew lay ahead. As he sat in silence, he heard the tell-tale crunching noise of someone approaching. Somewhere near the guard a voice called out, "Kak delishki."

The guard turned toward the voice and said, "Kholodno."

Hale heard a chuckle, "Da, bodrstvovat."

The guard replied, "Da ser."

Satisfied, the second man, probably a sergeant, moved away. Hale used the opportunity to take advantage of the noise the man was making. Under the cover of the loud crunching noise the man's boots made, he moved forward toward the shivering guard. Incredibly the man pulled out a cigarette and lit it using a match.

The glow of that cigarette is silhouetting his face! Hale thought gleefully. *What luck! I picked an idiot to sneak up on.*

The cigarette brightened as the guard took a long pull on it. He exhaled in satisfaction. The combination of warm air and nicotine rushing through his blood stream, combined to give him a warming sensation. As Hale crept forward, the guard stamped his legs on the ground several times to prevent them from going numb.

The Soviet paused for a moment and slowly looked around. Satisfied that nothing was amiss, he took another long pull on the cigarette. He relished the warm smoke that filled his lungs. It was the second to last feeling he ever had. As he exhaled the smoke into the frigid night air, creating a giant cloud, Hale's hand covered his mouth. A second later, the sharp edge of the Finnish Sniper's pukko blade bit deeply into the flesh of the guard's neck.

Hale held the struggling figure until he stopped moving. Feeling the life leave the body of the young soldier, he slowly lowered the corpse to the ground. As he did so, the pain in his right shoulder intensified causing him to grimace. He bit his lower lip to stifle the urge to cry out.

As Hale started to search the body of his victim, he heard the familiar crunching of Maki's approach. Ignoring it, he checked the man's pockets. He found a flare gun in a holster attached to the man's belt. There was no vodka, grenades, or alcohol of any kind. Turning to Maki, he said, "Odd, usually these bastards have vodka on them."

"If you were in charge of the guards, in enemy territory, would you want them to have access to alcohol why they stood guard?" The Lieutenant asked.

"No, I wouldn't. I guess they are starting to wise up." Hale replied.

"Or they are getting a little less overconfident. Perhaps the efforts of our little group of snipers are beginning to have an effect on their morale." Maki said.

Hale held up a hand to silence Maki. In the silence, Hale could hear the sound of crunching boots nearby. He held up his index finger to his lips and made eye contact with Maki. *Be quiet.* He thought at Maki hoping the Lieutenant could understand his meaning.

The sound of crunching snow under booted feet intensified as whoever it was, seemed to be walking right towards them. Maki laid on the ground next to the body of the guard, afraid to make the slightest move. The Russian paused about fifteen feet away and said, "Gregory?"

Maki's mind raced, *Should I respond?*

The Lieutenant turned to whisper in Hale's ear. The younger man had vanished. *What the?*

Maki's thoughts were interrupted when he saw a figure suddenly appear behind the Soviet. The Sergeant, seeing the shadows moving behind him, whirled around while he grabbed at a whistle hanging around his neck with his left hand and raised it toward his lips.

It was the last thing he ever did, as Hale's blade slammed into the side of his neck severing his jugular vein. Before Hale could cover his mouth up, the man took a step back and grabbed his neck. He opened his mouth to scream, but all that came out was a wet gurgle as blood erupted from his mouth like a fountain. The man again tried to cry out, but his mouth filled with blood as he sank to his knees. A few moments later he fell forward as he drowned in his own blood.

The young Finn grabbed the dying man's shoulders and gently lowered the cooling corpse to the ground. "That was close." The familiar voice of Maki whispered.

Hale nodded in acknowledgment and began rifling through his second victim's pockets. This time he found what he was looking for. Smiling he pulled a metal flask from the dead Sergeant's inner coat pocket, "For later." He whispered.

The Lieutenant grinned, and replied in a whisper, "As long as you're sharing."

Hale raised a finger and placed it on Maki's lips. *It's*

time to be quiet again sir. Maki got the message and nodded.

Hale stood still and listened for several minutes. He heard no further sound beyond the constant thrum of the Russian's engines. Turning back to Maki he whispered, "We're inside their outer picket perimeter. I don't know if there is another line of guards or not. I'm going to move forward and find out. Stay about fifty feet behind me and watch for my signal. If I hold up a clenched fist, stop moving. If I hold up an open palm, get ready to help me. Got it?"

Maki smiled and said, "Yes sir."

Hale returned the smile, "Good. With luck these bastards are being sloppy and there are no more guards between us and the vehicles."

Hale pulled the dark green overcoat off the dead Sergeant and put it on. He grimaced at the shooting pain in his right shoulder as he put his arm through the right coat sleeve. He then stood and silently crept toward the sound of the engines. Maki continued laying on the ground next to the corpse of the unlucky man, and covered Hale's advance with his PPD 34.

Hale paused to listen. He could see the faint outline of vehicles, perhaps two hundred feet ahead in the flickering light from a cluster of campfires next to the road. The sound of the engines was making it difficult to hear anything else.

Hale continued to cautiously advance toward the Soviet column on the road. As he drew within a hundred feet, he could see the faint outline of men sleeping inside the warm cabs of the trucks. As he drew closer, the sounds that men made while sleeping filled his ears, *The squads of soldiers that rode in the back of the trucks set up camp beside them. They must have built campfires to stay warm enough to sleep.* Hale thought.

He laid down on his chest and observed the scene for several minutes. Satisfied that no one was moving about, he resumed his slow and silent advance towards his slumbering enemies. He was about twenty feet from a truck sitting on the road when he came upon the edge of a campsite. He turned and looked in the direction of Maki and held up an open palm.

Turning back to his objective, Hale crept forward until he was standing over a group of Russian soldiers. Attempting to stay warm they were practically sleeping in the fire. The uneven flickering light of the campfires illuminated many of their faces and cast shadows around them. Like all of the Russians Hale had encountered, they wore dark green uniforms, and greatcoats. Each had a matching dark green hat with a red star pulled down over their head.

Hale turned and looked to see if anyone or anything was moving nearby. The only movement his eyes detected were the dancing shadows on the nearby tree line. The Finnish sniper looked down and saw the face of a young man. *He looks so innocent in slumber.* He took a deep breath and sighed. *It's a lot easier to kill them at a distance. You can't really see them as people.*

Inner turmoil raged within Hale as he fought the feeling in his heart that he couldn't bring itself to murder a defenseless and innocent young man. Then he thought about his family and all the other Finns whose farms the Soviets were here to steal. Images of families fleeing their homes with a few hastily gathered possessions filled his mind.

His mind drifted into darkness as it was filled with visions of Russians raping the women of Finland. and casting their babies into flames. Images of Nea's legs being pushed apart, and tears running down her face. Then came the inevitable screams. Hale shuddered at the scenes that swirled through his mind. Clenching his teeth, he pushed the imaginings away and filled the void with a single feeling, rage.

The anger steeled him for what he was about to do. It was as if a piece of his own innocence departed from his soul and floated up to heaven. That bit of him that was lost joined the smoke from the nearby fire and disappeared into the sky. Forever lost.

As he hardened his heart for what he was about to do, the boiling rage erupted from within. The anger coursed through his veins and despite the frigid temperature warmed him. He quietly pulled his pukko blade from its sheath secured to his left hip. Next, he placed his hand on the Russian's mouth, and dragged the blade across his throat.

The young soldier woke up and his eyes widened at the sight of Hale. Those seemingly innocent eyes bulged from his face as he struggled for a moment against the man that had slain him. He fought desperately against the young Finn with every ounce of his fading strength until he lay still.

Satisfied that the man was dead, Hale moved on to the slumbering form that lay on the ground beside him. He repeated this process over and over, until the entire squad of soldiers lay dead around the fire. Each time Hale drew a blade across a throat and committed murder against a defenseless man, a small piece of his innocence left him, *How many more will I have to kill to get them to leave us in peace? How many will it take to keep Nea safe?*

His grisly task complete, the troubled Finn quickly searched the bodies. He found several bottles of vodka amongst them, but most importantly six Russian RGD 33 grenades. He smiled at the thoughts of mayhem he could create with six of them. Hale slipped the handles of each one into his belt.

Turning in Maki's direction, he saw the Lieutenant's outline against the moonlight about fifty meters away. *He's still covering me.* Hale looked up at the nearby truck. Within the truck's cab, lay two men fast asleep.

The truck gave a steady low tone rumble as it idled. Like the dozens of other Gaz-MM trucks Hale had seen in the last few days, this one had a large red star painted on the driver's door. Glancing at the rear of the truck his eyes settled on the rusty tailpipe. He saw a steady stream of exhaust fumes floating upward into the icy night air. *With the driver sitting right on the horn it would be too risky to open the door and try to kill the two men inside the cab. I'll accomplish more, by finding another camp site.*

Hale looked down the road toward the south. About twenty feet away, lay another truck. Beside the truck, next to the road, another campfire blazed. This campfire also had eight bodies huddling for warmth clustered around it.

Hale slowly crept toward the group of men huddled around the campfire. As he drew near, one of the men coughed violently and sat up. Several of the other men groaned at the noise. Hale, fearing discovery, crouched low and ducked in-between the two trucks. As he waited for the man, who again let out a long string of violent coughs, to settle back down, he basked in the warmth the engine was producing.

As the young sniper waited, his heart pounded in his chest as his confidence waned, *Did someone see me? Are they even now surrounding me?* Calming his panicked thoughts, his mind shifted to his perceived ill fortune. *Just my luck, this squad has a man with consumption keeping them awake. I'll need to kill him first.*

Hale crouched behind the engine for what felt like an eternity. In actuality it was perhaps ten minutes before the tell-tale sound of steady breathing took hold of the group, but to him it felt like an eternity of uncertainty and fear. *They have fallen back asleep.*

Satisfied that everyone was slumbering, Hale began his slow creep toward the man with tuberculosis. He was extremely careful to not make a sound as he cautiously placed each step in the snow. This time, instead of killing the nearest slumbering Soviet, he circled around the group asleep next to this campfire. As he reached his chosen victim, one of the men on the other side of the fire awoke, saw Hale looming over his comrade, and yelled, "Narushitel!"

Without hesitation Hale plunged his blade into his target and took a step back. As he did so, he pulled his pistol from its holster and put a bullet into the yelling man's face to silence him. He then jerked a grenade lose from his belt, twisted the top half until he felt the click, and dropped it into the middle of the camp site. The desperate sniper then turned to run in the direction of the tree line.

The sound of automatic weapons fire erupted as Maki laid down some fire to cover Hale's retreat. Hale could hear the buzz of Maki's bullets as they flew past him. As his mental count reached ten, he threw himself to the ground as the grenade he left in the camp site exploded. Several of the Russians had stood and started fumbling with their rifles to take a shot at Hale. These men were instantly cut down by the expanding cloud of shrapnel from the exploding grenade.

Hale jumped back to his feet and ran as fast as his legs would carry him through the snow. Looking over his shoulder he saw the men from the next campsite down the line stirring and looking about in confusion. He stopped and pulled his rifle from his shoulder. As he took aim, Maki's gun barked out a series of shots. Several of the men were cut down, the rest threw themselves to the ground.

Deciding he didn't have enough time to use the rifle, Hale jerked another of the grenades free from his belt, pulled the pin, and threw it. His throw was a little short. He slung the rifle back onto his shoulder and resumed his awkward run through the deep snow. As he reached the relative safety of the tree line, the grenade exploded sending shrapnel into the enemies that hadn't been hit by Maki's fire.

Covered by the trees, Hale turned to observe another group of Russians up the road to the north as they emerged from their slumber and looked about in confusion. Hale took aim with his rifle and put a bullet into one of the men. The enemy soldier clutched his chest and fell backwards from the force of the bullet. The other men of the squad paused and looked at their comrade as his body fell back into their campfire. Their wide eyes full of shock and surprise.

The flames quickly took hold on the fabric of his greatcoat. As he turned into a writhing fireball, his screams filled the night air. Maki's gun erupted and cut down the men gawking at their burning squad mate. Hale threw his rifle onto his shoulder and began pushing through the snow as quickly as possible. His breath began to come in ragged gasps as his Lieutenant fell in beside him.

Looking back to check behind them, Maki looked at Hale and said, "Great work, I think we must have killed around thirty of the bastards."

Hale smiled at the compliment, "What now?"

"Let's get to our skis and packs. After that we'll travel further north towards the village and engage them again. This column stretches for kilometers, so we can rinse and repeat this tactic several times before dawn." Maki replied.

"Won't they all be roused now?" Hale questioned.

"Perhaps, but we have to try. If we can't get close enough to take out a few more squads, then at least we are keeping the bastards up all night." Maki replied.

"True, that will make them less effective tomorrow morning when they attack the village." Hale said.

Maki smiled, "Exactly."

The two men found the path that they had created earlier to reach the road and began to make better time. A few minutes later they were back at the tree that held their packs. Leaning up against it was their two sets of skis.

The two men, exhausted from their recent ordeal, rested. Over the course of several minutes, their breathing went from ragged gulps, to deep breaths, and then finally slowed back to normal.

Satisfied that they had adequately recovered, the Lieutenant said, "Let's get our skis on and move about half a kilometer north."

"Then we hit them again?" Hale asked.

Maki nodded, "Yes." He gestured toward Hale's belt, "I see that you came away with several prizes. Perhaps this time, instead of sneaking into individual camps, you can just toss two or three of those at the camp sites."

"Won't we need these later for the defense of the village?" Hale wondered.

"They would certainly help, but I need you alive more

than anything." Maki replied.

Hale didn't reply. The two men skied in silence for about twenty minutes until the Lieutenant broke the silence, "This is far enough. Let's head toward the road. This time let's keep our skis on so we can make a faster getaway."

Hale nodded, "Yes sir."

The pair turned toward the east and continued skiing. After about a quarter of a kilometer, Hale held up his right fist and the two men stopped. The pair spent several minutes listening. Like before, the sounds of the idling engines filled their ears. Conspicuously absent, despite their proximity to the road, was the noise of boots crunching on the snow made.

Turning to his commanding officer Hale said, "If we get much closer with the skis, we may be heard over the noise of the engine."

"Very well. We can leave them here. I just don't relish the idea of having to push through the snow to get away again." Maki replied.

"I relish even less, getting shot by an alert guard." Hale fired back.

The two men quickly unclipped their boots. They leaned their two pairs of skis up against a tree, "Perhaps we should hang our packs again so we can find them quickly?" The Lieutenant said.

"Agreed. I don't like the idea of trying to make a get away with this weight on my back." Hale said.

The two men quickly hung their packs from the tree that they had leaned their skis up against. Maki asked, "Same as before?"

"Yeah, except this time, once we are inside the perimeter, I'll do as you suggested. Tossing a few grenades at the camp sites should get them all stirred up.

"And missing out on sleep." Maki added.

"Exactly, then I'll make a break for it." Hale replied.

"Sounds good. Let's get moving. I want to be able to do this one more time before dawn." Maki said.

Hale nodded and turned toward the sound of idling engines. He slowly crept forward, careful not to make any noise. After a few hundred meters, he raised up his right hand and clenched it into a fist again.

About twenty meters ahead was a figured outlined by the moonlight. Hale pointed at Maki and then down at the ground to indicate for him to stay there. Maki nodded in understanding and carefully pulled his PPD 34 from his shoulder.

Hale moved off to the north, he slowly angled his way toward the road. He was careful to keep the trees between him and the guard. Wanting to ensure all was well, he would pause every few dozen feet and just listen for several minutes. Each time he paused the only sound he could hear was that of the engines droning in the distance.

Finally, he drew parallel to the Soviet standing guard. Satisfied that he hadn't been spotted, Hale slowly crept from tree to tree, as he drew closer to his intended victim. This one, was a lot quieter than the smoker Hale had snuck up on and slain earlier. Catching wind of something amiss, the guard turned in the direction of Hale and said, "Privet?"

Hale stopped moving. His heart thundered in his ears as he waited for the enemy soldier to make the next move.

"Ya slyshal, ty perestal igrat' v igry." The man said as he pulled his rifle off his shoulder.

Hale inwardly cursed as his mind raced, *I think that last word was games. He thinks I am a friend trying to play tricks on him. What should I do? Anything I try is going to make noise.*

The young Finn quickly ran through his options in his head, *I could shoot him, but that would make too much noise. Using a grenade would definitely make noise. Pukkos make terrible throwing knives, besides in this darkness I'd probably miss anyways.* His mind went back to the class on basic Russian. *There was one phrase that might work.*

Staying hidden, Hale said in his best imitation of a Russian accent, "Pomogi mne."

The Russian wasn't buying it, he squared his shoulder, raised his rifle, and said, "Pokazhi sebya."

Summer of cunts! Hale raged. He stepped out from behind the tree with his pistol raised and put a bullet in the man's face.

Before the Soviet's corpse hit the ground, Hale was running toward the road. He could hear several whistles being blown to rouse the men from their sleep. Reaching the edge of the tree line, he saw several different squads standing around their campfires. The light from the fires revealed looks of confusion on many of their faces as they hastily prepared their rifles for combat.

Hale pulled a grenade from his belt, twisted the cap, and threw it at the nearest campfire. He repeated this motion two more times, hurling the grenades at the campsites on either side of the first. Without waiting to see the results, he turned and ran toward Maki. Frantic screaming erupted from the first campsite as the Russians quickly realized what had flown out of the darkness and landed amongst them.

Before Hale could get five meters through the deep snow, the first grenade erupted cutting down several of the soldiers. A few moments later, the second and third grenades exploded, adding to the chaos and the body count.

A few moments later, he reached Lieutenant Maki, "Well that was sloppy."

"The damn sentry was too alert. I had to shoot the bastard." Hale replied testily.

"Did you get any more besides the sentry?" The Lieutenant asked.

"Yeah, I should have gotten several with the grenades." Hale replied.

Gunfire erupted from the direction of the Soviet column. Maki threw a glance in that direction and said, "We'd best get going, before they start heading in this direction."

Hale gestured toward the west, "Lead on."

The two Finns made their way back to the spot where they had left their skis and packs. They hastily buckled their boots to the skis, placed their packs on their backs and set off to the west. Back on the road, the Russian officers had finally managed to organize the chaos into a semblance of order and sent several squads toward the location they suspected Hale to be.

By the time this was accomplished Hale and Maki were a kilometer away and turning toward the north. The two men skied in silence across the countryside. As the chaos they caused faded away behind them, the only two sounds Hale could hear was his own breathing and the noise his skis made. After nearly an hour, Hale turned toward Maki and broke the silence, "How much further is the village?"

"About three or four kilometers by my reckoning." Maki replied.

"Then shouldn't we be hitting them here? Before we get much closer." Hale asked.

Maki stopped and pulled a map from inside his coat. He frowned as he struggled to read the map in the fading moonlight, "The moon is setting, I can't see the map."

Hale pulled out a box of matches, turned his back toward the road to conceal what he was about to do, and struck one. Careful to keep it lit, he protected the flame by cupping his hand around it and held it over the map, "Thanks." The Lieutenant said.

"Well?" Hale impatiently snapped.

Maki flashed Hale a glare and stabbed an index finger at a spot on the map, "I believe we are here."

Hale stared at the map for a moment, "That puts us about three kilometers south west of Kivennapa."

Maki nodded, "Exactly, so as you say, we need to go ahead and hit them here."

Hale cast a glance in the direction of the moon, "The moon is setting. That means dawn isn't far off. How much time do we have?"

Maki pulled up the left sleeve of his coat, and then several more layers of clothing underneath until he found his wristwatch. It showed six o'clock, "About two hours until dawn."

"How shall I attack this time? I've got three grenades left." Hale said.

"I would say to try and conserve at least one for our attack on the group assaulting the village." The Lieutenant replied.

"Very well that sounds prudent. I think that I should try sneaking up on them all the way again. Perhaps I can find more grenades." Hale said.

Maki made eye contact and placed a hand on Hale's shoulder, "Just be careful. As a result of our previous two attacks, the guards are probably very alert. Not to mention the fact that dawn is near."

Hale gave Maki a reassuring smile, "Piece of cake, let's get going."

The two men turned their skis toward the Soviet column that resided on the road and began moving. They skied in silence for about ten minutes before Hale raised his right fist into the air. He turned to Maki and whispered, "I think this is close enough. Let's lose the skis."

Maki nodded and the two men removed their skis. They leaned them up against a stout looking birch tree and carefully hung their packs from two of the mighty tree's lower branches. Maki pulled his PPD 34 from his shoulder and checked the weapon to ensure all was in readiness.

Hale slowly crept forward toward the sound of the idling engines. The moon had set, so there wasn't as much light to see by. He grew more and more nervous as he made his way further and further eastward without spotting a guard, *The two previous times, I would have been past the guard by now. Where is he?*

Hale's thought was answered by a shadow up ahead blocking the flickering light from the campfires off in the distance. *There he is. Why is he so close to the camp?*

Hale concealed himself behind a tree and observed the

guard for several minutes. *He doesn't appear to be moving. I guess I can try sneaking up on him, but if he alerts and I'm that close to the road, I'm screwed.*

Gritting his teeth, Hale made his way slowly toward the guard. Just like he did the last time he approached a guard, the young Finn angled to go around the man, instead of heading right toward him. As Hale drew closer, he saw that the guard's back was turned toward him, *If he stays where he is at, this is going to be easy.*

Hale slowly crept up behind the man. A moment before he reached the guard, the man started to whirl around, and grab for the whistle hanging around his neck, *Too late.* Hale thought. He stuck a hand over the man's mouth and used his other to drag the sharp edge of his pukko blade across the Soviet's neck.

The Russian struggled for several moments as his lifeblood flowed out and dripped onto the snow below him. Satisfied that life had left him, Hale slowly lowered the corpse to the ground. He quickly rifled through his victim's pockets. As before on a perimeter guard, he didn't find any vodka. Instead of the alcohol he coveted, he managed to find a pocketful of 7.62mm bullets and a pack of Russian cigarettes.

He pocketed the cigarettes, wiped his blade on the man's green pants, and carefully removed his overcoat. He pulled the coat on to conceal his own white one that gave him away as a Finn and set off toward the nearby road.

Like before, he spied several figures huddled around the flickering light of the campfires. The campfires were near the road close to the idling dark green Gaz-MM transport trucks. Each group of sleeping Soviets was arrayed in a tight circle around the small source of heat. They used the warmth being cast by the crackling flames and each other, in an attempt to stay warm in the sub-zero temperatures.

Hale quietly tiptoed up to the closest group of slumbering soldiers, careful not to make any sound as he approached. Luckily this group didn't have a cougher, and all seemed to be in a deep slumber. He reached the closest man, put his hand over the man's mouth, and with a quick jerk of his arm, ended the nameless Russian's war forever.

Hale would never know that he ended the life, not of a Russian but of a Siberian. This man, a father of two, had been swept up into the Red Army against his will, and made to fight in Stalin's wars. Now, on a frozen field far from home, his family would never know his fate. Never again would he feel the tender embrace of his wife's arms, the adoring smiles of his children, or the satisfaction he got from watching his children play.

For Hale, the man represented an invader who must be destroyed to save his home. With each instance such as this, an innocent man killing an innocent man, the horrors of the conflict grew. This horror had been perpetrated by the greed and hunger for power of a single man. While men fought and died, he lay in his warm comfortable bed in Moscow hundreds of kilometers away.

This evil man, through lies and deceit, had perpetrated this tragedy that was unfolding in the frozen forests of Karelia. A tragedy that put fathers, brothers, and sons against each other for no other purpose than his greed. Comrade Stalin slept on as men continued to die for his greed.

Hale methodically repeated this process over and over, until all seven of the men sleeping by the fire's lifeblood leaked into the hungry Finnish soil. With each new victim a piece of the young Finn's innocence left him forever. His grisly task complete, he took the time to methodically search each body.

Besides the usual large quantity of vodka and cigarettes, the young sniper came up with two grenades, and a PPD 34 for himself, *What luck! With two of these wonder weapons, we are sure to be able to make a difference during the stand at Kivennapa.*

Hale quietly slipped the sub-machine gun onto his shoulder and checked his surroundings. None of the men belonging to the squads of the nearest fires had stirred as Hale went about his grisly task. *I should move down the road away from the village.*

Hale started his slow silence and movements southward to the next group. As he focused on his steps and making the least amount of sound, he failed to notice the driver of the truck closest to him wake up and watch him. The man, noticing the white coat underneath Hale's stolen dark great coat, pretended to be asleep as Hale drew abreast of the Gaz-MM's door.

Without warning, the Russian flung the door open. The door, emblazoned with the Red Star of the Soviet Union, narrowly missed the startled Finn. The man lunged at Hale tackling him to the ground. Hale was completely surprised as the weight of the driver hit him on his left side. Grunting Hale fell toward the right and struck the frozen earth.

As the truck driver wrapped his arms around Hale, he started yelling for help. Hale, desperate to escape, managed to get a hand on his holstered pistol. As the men from the nearby campsite began to stir, Hale elbowed the driver in the abdomen. This won him a few inches of precious separation.

The Soviet grunted in surprise and loosened his grip for the barest moment. Hale, taking advantage of his efforts, shoved his pistol against the driver's chest and pulled the trigger three times. The man's body shuddered as each bullet pierced his skin. By the third shot, the enemy soldier offered no further resistance and collapsed to the ground in a heap.

Hale, reacting quickly, saw the Sergeant stirring in the cab of the truck. He pulled a grenade from his belt, twisted the cap, and threw it onto the empty drivers' side seat. He then turned toward the nearby campsite, where all of the bleary-eyed Russians were coming to their feet in alarm. Without emotion, he pulled the newly won PPD 34 off his shoulder and sprayed the entire clip of bullets into them.

The bullets leapt from his gun in a rapid series of muzzle flashes. The projectiles Hale was spraying at the unfortunate group of Russians penetrated flesh, and smashed bone. In the few seconds it took Hale to unload the entire clip of his new dealer of death, all eight of the Soviet's had been cut down as if a giant scythe had swept through them.

Hale, ignoring the cries of pain and agony from his dying victims, turned to his right, took three steps, and flung himself to the ground just as the grenade in the truck went off. The exploding force from the grenade slammed into the Sergeant who was struggling to get out of the cab. A moment later, the expanding cloud of flame found the vehicle's fuel tank causing a larger, much brighter explosion to pierce the night sky.

As debris from the nearby truck landed in the snow around him, Hale stuck his head up to assess the situation. He quickly saw that the men from the next campsite had reached their feet and were looking for the source of the mayhem. Hale, pulled another grenade from his belt, twisted the cap, and flung it toward the group.

Hale's throw came up a meter short, and the grenade struck the snow just shy of the circle of light shed by the fire. An alert man instantly noticed the explosive and yelled, "Granata!"

All eight of the Russians, trained to instantly react to such a proclamation, collapsed to the ground. The grenade exploded spraying shrapnel and flame over the space they had just been occupying. Hale, taking advantage of the confusion, jumped to his feet, and started running in the direction of Maki.

The Russians, seeing Hale's retreating form, stood, and attempted to raise their rifles to attack. Before the first one could line up a shot, the sound of automatic weapon fire erupted from the tree line. Maki's bullets quickly found flesh, as Hale flung himself to the ground in reaction to the sound of the gunfire.

Hale looked back over his shoulder and saw Maki's bullets cut down the Soviets. Before the last one fell, he was able to get off a single shot in Maki's direction. Hale's worry over his commander quickly dissipated when he heard Maki's voice cry out, "Hale, move your ass. It's time to go!"

Hale leapt to his feet and ran toward the voice. The Russians, roused by the noise, began firing at every shadow they saw in the forest. Before long, the entire column, stretching out for kilometers, had been roused from the growing racket of gunfire. The impenetrable forest of Karelia greedily digested the lead projectiles the frightened Russians wasted.

As the two Finns retreated from the road, they heard the growing crescendo of gunfire coming from the Soviet column. Laughing, Maki said, "I think you succeeded beyond my wildest expectations. It sounds like the entire division has been roused from slumber!"

Hale nodded in acknowledgement at his superior

officer's words. Maki quickly noticed Hale's lack of enthusiasm over the success of his efforts, "What's wrong?"

They reached their skis and put them on in silence. As they started to make their way to safety Hale replied, "I feel like every time I have to kill, a piece of me dies inside."

Maki stopped skiing. Startled, Hale shot past him, noticed the Lieutenant had stopped, and turned himself around, "What's wrong sir?"

"In my jubilation, I had forgotten that we sent at least thirty men to the grave." Maki replied solemnly.

Hale nodded slowly, "As this night has unfolded, I have thought more and more about the lives I have been taking. It's senseless really, but as soldiers of Finland, what choice do we have? These men have been fooled into thinking that our country attacked their mighty nation."

"And now, filled with lies of our tiny nation's aggression, they are here in a perverted sense of patriotism." Maki replied.

"You talk as if they had a choice sir. The system they live under, while it has put food in their once empty bellies, has taken away their right to think, and the freedom to choose their own path." Hale replied.

Maki gave Hale a faint smile, "Hearing you philosophize, if one didn't know any better, one would think you are the university graduate and I the back woods peasant."

Hale snorted with laughter, "No, just a small-town boy who listened to his pastor in church with a thirst for reading. There isn't much to do during our long winter nights other than read."

"Oh, there are other things you can be doing. You'll find that out when you marry Nea." Maki said.

Hale's eyes fell, "I'm not even sure I want to. Do I deserve her now? All of this killing. Every time I do it, I feel like I'm surrendering a piece of my soul to the devil that the fat preacher used to extort us to ignore. Is there going to be anything left of my soul for her when this is all done?"

Maki halted and turned to face Hale, "Man slaying man is indeed a tragedy. Whether from the word of God or a philosopher like Marcus Aurelius, who spent too much of his life killing to defend his home, men try to rationalize the feelings we get from killing."

"The bible says that murder is one of the ten biggest sins you can commit. That committing sin is evil. Here in this desolate forest, I have done much evil, and for what?" Hale said.

"To stop the greater evil of what would happen if many of these men reach our homes." Maki replied.

"Not all of those men are evil. Many of them are here because they were forced into the army against their will. Thanks to Stalin's propaganda machine, they think they are here in the righteous cause against Finnish aggression." Hale said.

Maki's eyes narrowed, "The world knows that the attack was a lie."

"But these men clearly don't." Hale snapped back.

Maki put a comforting hand on Hale's shoulder, "True. Their Commissars work day and night to fill their heads with bullshit."

The word Commissar reminded Hale of Pekka, "I don't

want to think about what those self-righteous bastards are doing to Pekka right now. Those damned evil men, Marxist to the core, have taken on an almost religious holy quality to themselves. They act like they are the prophets of a new religion."

"That's a good analogy, the Commissars are indeed preachers of Lenin and Stalin's unholy new religion. They extort us to adhere to the tenants of the new faith. These evil men rail against the old faith and demand that we abandon God and Jesus Christ. Instead, we must turn to the holy way, Socialism, and the holiest of holies, Communism." Maki drew in a breath and placed a comforting hand on Hale's shoulder, "I don't want to imagine what Pekka must be going through. Though there is nothing you can do about it to bring him back. use the anger from his capture. Let it fill your heart." Maki said.

"Why should I fill my heart with anger?" Hale wondered.

"Because it's better to give up a piece of righteous anger every time you have to kill an enemy instead of a piece of your innocence." Maki replied.

Relief flowed out of Hale, "Could it be that easy?"

"It has to be. Otherwise, the men forced to fight throughout the ages would lose their souls to the God of War. Be angry with Stalin, and his preaching crusaders of socialism, the Commissars." Maki urged.

"Then I will be angry today, so that the love in my heart and what's left of my soul can be spared for Nea." Hale said.

Maki glanced over Hale's head and saw the first tinge of gray on the horizon, "Come my friend, we must get into position to support the defense of Kivenappa."

Chapter 7

Dawn Karelia Isthmus Finland, Near the Village of Kivennapa, December 4th, 1939

Hale and Maki sat in silence as the sun slowly pushed the darkness away and cast its light on the endless kilometers of snow-covered forest. During the last hour, they had made their way to a position just to the south west of the village of Kivenappa. Through the trees they spied a small cluster of buildings at the center of a crossroads.

Hale couldn't quite put his finger on it, but the village was missing something, "The village seems odd to me somehow. I know the people that lived there were evacuated two days ago."

"It looks odd because you are used to seeing signs of life from such a place." Maki said.

"How so?" Hale asked.

"For instance, there isn't any smoke." Maki replied.

Hale nodded, "I couldn't put my finger on it, but that's what must be weird about it then. You think the Russians are going to notice?"

Maki smiled, "I doubt it. Those poor bastards have been brainwashed to the extreme. They are incapable of independent thought. The party exacts a terrible price for the food that fills their bellies. There is no greater price a person can endure than the loss of independent thought. The very thing that makes you who you are is demanded by the party in tribute for the pittance that you are granted."

"Well that would explain why it's been so easy to kill them." Hale replied.

"If the party allowed them to have thoughts, they would be dangerous. A man that can think, is a man that will see through all the nonsense the party feeds them, to keep them in line. Thanks to that fact any one of us is worth ten of them on the battlefield. That is why so few of us will be able to beat so many of them." Maki said.

"From what I have seen, I would agree with you. One of us is certainly worth ten of them, but what if there are eleven?" Hale asked.

Maki laughed, "That's what I love about you Hale. You would think that someone with your background would be an unintelligent country bumpkin, but your mind has a sharp edge to it."

"Thanks. I think." Hale replied.

"It was meant as a compliment. The circumstances of your birth, and the life you led growing up, would dictate that your body is strong, but your mind is weak. You aren't like that. You've worked to foster strength in both." Maki said.

The two men fell silent and turned their attention to Kivenappa. The thatched roofs of the small cluster of buildings gathered around the crossroads were visible through the trees. As they talked, the eastern horizon slowly morphed from a gray, to a purple, then deep red, and finally a brighter and brighter orange. A moment later the sun broke the horizon. Hale could see the dull red orb through the countless sea of trees.

Suddenly, the silence of the woods was pierced by the droning of engines. Faint at first, but ever louder as hundreds of vehicles rumbled their way toward the village. Hale closed his eyes and listened to the sounds. His ears could pick out the difference between the dull rumble of trucks, and the higher pitched squeal of tank tracks.

The sound slowly grew over time until Hale's eyes caught movement on the road. The lead vehicle came into view. Hale shuddered as he recognized it, an unstoppable behemoth, a T-28 medium tank.

The T-28s long body was covered in a dull dark green paint. In addition to the deadly looking main gun that sprouted from the front of the tank's turret, were several smaller machine guns. Two of the machine guns flanked the large main gun in the middle. Two more surrounded the opening from which the driver peered onto the road. The side of the turret had a red star emblazoned upon it.

Hale saw the torso of a man sticking out of the top of the turret. This man who leaned up against the metal door of the open hatch was the tank commander. Of the six men that occupied the metal beast, the only other vulnerable crewmember was the driver. This man likely sat just behind the opening in the front middle section of the behemoth.

Hale raised his rifle and took aim at the driver. A hand

touched his shoulder, "Not yet. We have a battalion deployed in the village. Let them deliver the first surprise blow. We mustn't show ourselves too early. We are here, to keep the Soviets off balance when they start pressing home their attack. By distracting them we increase the chance that our men in the village can hold." Maki said.

Hale lowered his rifle, turned, and made eye contact with Maki. The young sniper threw him a faint smile and a slight nod, "We wait then."

"It won't be long." Maki promised, "Patience."

The two men sat in silence behind their protective log. Earlier that morning, they had found a downed tree. Deciding the position offered a great view of the road while affording them some protection, Hale and Maki worked to turn it into a firing position. Using snow, loose branches, and other logs, to build up a protective barrier between them and the road. Now they watched the column from their concealed position.

The T-28 kept slowly rumbling northward toward the village. As the tank moved past them, they could see the acrid black smoke that belched from its back panel. Following closely behind the tank, was a dozen Gaz-MMs. Each truck carried a squad of enemy soldiers, eight men in all.

As the tank closed to within two hundred meters of Kivenappa a very loud bang sounded from the direction of the village. A moment later something struck the front of the T-28. The projectile, whatever it had been, Hale was unsure as he couldn't see it and was unfamiliar with the sound it made, struck the front of the tank. The dark green juggernaut abruptly stopped as the men inside screamed.

"What was that?" Hale asked.

"An anti-tank rifle." Maki said.

The tank commander leapt from the top of the turret, as smoke began billowing out of the opening. Before he could lower himself to the ground, weapons fire rang out from the village and peppered his body. The commander staggered back a step, then two, and finally his corpse toppled off the tank and onto the ground.

This caused the Soviet infantry in the twelve trucks behind the T-28 to vomit forth from the bowels of the vehicles. Several seconds elapsed as these men gathered themselves behind the trucks. As soon as the Sergeants were satisfied that all was ready to deploy, they simultaneously erupted from behind the trucks and fanned out as they began charging the village.

The Finnish defenders in the village allowed these men to advance about one hundred meters before a lone voice from somewhere in the village barked the command to, "Fire!"

The instant the order was given, it seemed as if a giant wave swept out of the sky and broke across the charging Soviets. The lead men jerked to a stop as if they had run into an invisible wall. They fell to their knees clutching the fresh holes that had erupted on their torsos a moment before. A cacophony of sound roared over Hale and Maki as the noise of both automatic weapons fire, and single shot bolt action rifles created a deafening roar.

The Soviet charge broke and they fell to the earth trying to save themselves from the lead onslaught that blazed forth from the village. When the last enemy soldier still standing was slain, the roar of weapons fire abruptly stopped. Eerie silence reigned where moments before the loud crescendo of weapons fire had filled the forest.

Smiling, Maki turned to Hale and said, "They've completely stopped the first attack cold."

"What happens next?" Hale asked.

"According to the training I received from the war college. Whoever is in charge of the Soviet's will now take their time to deploy the regiment. They won't move forward again until they form a large front. When all are ready, they will advance again." Maki replied.

The two men sat in silence and watched as the men that survived the first assault on the village slowly crawled south back down the road. The engines of the advancing regiment dropped in volume as they came to a stop and began to idle. As the two men sat in their position and listened, the voices of angry Sergeants began to pierce the forest. It took nearly an hour for the Russians to form themselves up into a brigade sized formation.

"Does it normally take this long to form men up for an attack?" Hale asked.

Maki shook his head, "No, it should have taken maybe ten minutes at most to debark this amount of men from the trucks, ensure all was at the ready, and then form them up into a line. The amount of time this is taking is beyond pathetic. It really shows just how poorly trained these communist swine are."

"With such a large well-equipped army, why send the untrained against us?" Hale wondered.

"It doesn't make any sense does it?" Maki replied.

"No. Why waste the resources when you don't have to?" Hale said.

The pair of men fell silent as they watched the Soviet brigade sized formation cautiously advance toward the village. To Hale's trained eye, they looked fearful and uncertain about the forest. They stepped in all the wrong places, made too much noise, and failed to use the trees as cover, as they slowly crept toward their goal.

Whoever was in charge of the battalion of Finns in the village was a smart tactician. The Finns held their fire until the Soviets had advanced well beyond the position they had been engaged at earlier. The closer they drew to the village, the sloppier and more incautious the invaders became thinking the Finnish defenders had fled. Finally, when Hale's heart seemed as if it would burst from the anticipation of the coming attack, the weapons in the village burst to life.

Simultaneously a series of explosions ripped through the advancing line of Soviet soldiers. The kinetic energy from the detonations flung the hapless Russians and pieces of Russians in all directions. Those that still stood, were quickly cut down by the wall of steel that slammed into the brigade. Hale watched as nearly a thousand men perished in the course of a minute.

Those that survived broke and fled back the direction they had come. Sergeants and Commissars roared with displeasure at the fleeing men, but their calls to turn around went unheeded. Ignoring their leaders, the broken men fled away from the Finnish battalion as fast as their legs would carry them.

Maki laughed openly at the scene. Curious Hale turned to his Lieutenant and asked, "What is so amusing about this?"

"There are maybe three hundred Finns in Kivenappa. The Russians have the entire 24th Motorized Rifle Division bearing down on them. Thus far three hundred men have held up ten thousand for the better part of an hour while slaying around a thousand of them."

"When you put it that way it is pretty amusing. Maybe they can hold, and we won't even have to engage?" Hale said.

Maki made eye contact with Hale, "No, sadly our time will come. They'll be more careful this time. They'll probably take the time to bring up some tanks and have another brigade advance behind those metal monsters."

"Will our men be able to stop more than one tank?" Hale asked.

"I don't know. Maybe, if in addition to the explosives they set, the men had time to lay some mines. Then with some luck, perhaps they can hold a third time." Maki replied.

The Lieutenant took a breath to keep speaking, but Hale raised an index finger to his lips to shush his superior officer. Maki nodded and gave Hale a little shrug as if to ask what is going on? Hale picked up on the non-verbal cue and pointed south east.

Maki stared in the direction for nearly a minute before his eyes were able to pick out what Hale had been pointing at. A lone Soviet soldier was very slowly climbing up a tree. Like the Finns, the man wore a white colored overcoat that helped him to blend into the terrain around him. On his back, was a rifle with a long scope mounted to the top.

Maki whispered, "A Russian sniper."

Hale nodded in response before saying, "Let's keep an eye on him."

"Good plan. We can't kill him now. There may be others that we can't see, and we would only draw attention to ourselves." Maki said.

"When the Russians attack the village again, I'll use the noise to take him out. For now, we should duck down into our cover. We don't want to become targets ourselves." Hale replied.

The two men lowered themselves to the frozen earth. For the next hour they sat safely behind the firing position they had built, invisible to curious eyes. Finally, as the Sun neared its zenith, the ground began to vibrate beneath them. The two men shared a look as if to say this is it.

A few minutes later the vibration manifested itself into the loud rumble of a dozen tank engines. In between the noise of the engines, the sounds of the squeaking tank tracks permeated the air as the metal monsters slowly advanced toward Kivenappa.

The two men, one at a time, careful not to make too many sudden moves that would attract the eyes of a sniper, peered out from their protected enclosure. Their eyes took in the scene. As Maki had feared, at least a dozen Soviet tanks advanced toward the village. The metal monsters were a mixture of T-28 medium and T-26 light tanks.

Behind the tanks, careful to use them and the trees as cover, advanced a line of Russian Infantry. They stayed low and advanced cautiously as the metal beasts slowly lumbered forward through the trees. Hale noticed that there were no exposed men jutting from the tanks this time. All the hatches were buttoned up neatly to afford the crew inside maximum protection.

Maki stole a quick glance, and then sat back down on

the frozen earth. He leaned toward Hale and whispered into his ear, "Get ready to take out the sniper. I don't know how many anti-tank rifles they have in the village, but I suspect its only one or two. If that is the case, they will have to engage momentarily. Otherwise, they won't have a chance of stopping the tanks before they reach the village."

Hale nodded in response and peeked out over their barricade. He quickly spotted the Russian sniper. The man hadn't moved since he took up his position in a large oak tree some four hundred feet south east of their position.

"Go ahead and take aim at him." Maki said,

Hale scooped up some snow with his hand and placed it in his mouth. He then slowly raised his head. He spotted the sniper in the distant oak, still sitting still. *The man hasn't moved for at least an hour. He must be freezing.* Hale thought. He slowly brought his rifle up and rested it on the log the two men had been using for cover.

Looking down the long barrel of his Mosin-Nagant, he took careful aim at the distant figure of the Soviet through his iron sites. Hale slowed his breathing as he waited for the sound of the anti-tank rifle. A few seconds past, then a few dozen, and finally a few minutes. Hale began to wonder if the battalion of his countrymen had abandoned the village when a sudden very loud, low-pitched rifle report rumbled through the forest.

The lead tank in the Soviet advance, a T-26, suddenly erupted into flames as the anti-tank rifle round struck its front armor and penetrated. The thin armor of the light tank did little to stop the anti-tank rifle round. As the round passed through the crew cabin, it cut the loader in half, and tore the legs off the gunner below the knees.

Now covered in blood, it kept moving through the tank until it slammed into the ammunition bin in the back of the crew compartment.

The ammunition was ignited and detonated with a spectacular explosion shooting the turret into the air and lifting the body of the tank off the ground. Simultaneously, Hale held his breath and gently squeezed the trigger. His rifle kicked against his shoulder, sending forth 7.62mm of brass jacketed death and a shot of pain to his injured shoulder.

The young Finnish sniper's aim was perfect, as it struck the Soviet in the left side of the torso. The bullet shattered two of the man's ribs as it passed into his chest and cleaved a path through the man's lungs. The Soviet sniper toppled forward and struck the ground with a thud that was drowned out by the sound of weapons fire.

Hale smiled as he watched his adversary fall from the tree. His jubilation was short lived as a bullet slammed into the log just a few inches from his head, "What the?" He said as Maki pulled him down.

As Hale looked up at his Lieutenant looming over him with wide eyes, Maki said, "Stay down, there must be another sniper out there!"

Tank guns, anti-tank rifles, rifles, and automatic weapons fire continued to create a horrible racket. Coming out of his shock Hale said, "Do you have any idea where the shot came from?"

Maki pointed up at the top of the log they hid behind and said, "The shot hit there. It struck slightly below the top of the log and deflected splinters toward you."

"Which means it did not come from behind us." Hale replied.

"If the sniper was set up to our west, one of us would be dead by now. Thankfully these Russian swine don't stray too far from the safety of the road." Maki added.

"Since the splinters flew toward us, the shot really couldn't have come from the north or south." Hale said.

"Which leaves one direction, east." Maki said.

"East makes sense as that is the direction of the Soviet force. Could it have been a stray bullet that almost got lucky?" Hale asked.

Maki shrugged, "There is one way we can find out."

Maki took off his white, fur covered hat, and drew his pukko blade from its sheath. He placed the hat on the curved blade and slowly raised it above the top of the log. A moment after the top of the hat passed above the threshold of the log, and became visible, a shot rang out and struck the log narrowly missing Maki's hat.

Maki dropped his arm and plucked his hat from the end of the blade. He glanced in the direction of the village in time to see a large explosion engulf one of the buildings as a high explosive tank round struck it, "It's a good thing the bastards haven't brought up their artillery yet."

"Why." Hale asked.

"They could use it to level the village. Our men wouldn't stand a chance." Maki paused and sighted in frustration, "Never mind that for now. We've got to figure out where that second sniper is so we can get into this fight. Judging by that last explosion the Soviets are finally pressing home their attack. I wish we could see what was going on."

"I have an idea." Hale said.

Maki met Hale's eyes and waited a few moments before impatiently blurting, "Well spit it out already."

"I'll shift positions. When I'm set, you can play that trick with your hat again. Hopefully the sniper will expose themselves to take the shot." Hale proposed.

Maki pondered the idea for a few moments and then slowly nodded in understanding of Hale's plan, "That seems logical."

Hale flashed the Lieutenant a smile and then slowly began crawling to the north. When he reached the end of the log they were using for cover, he shifted his direction and began crawling to the west, directly away from the log. By staying low, he was able to use the log as cover. He quickly reached the nearest tree and paused for a moment. The sound of his heartbeat thundered in his ears. *The sniper didn't see me. That means he is a bit to the south east of our position instead of straight east.*

Here comes the hard part. He looked back and made eye contact with Maki who waved his PPD 34 above the log. Another shot rang out and struck the earth behind the Lieutenant. Maki quickly jerked his arm back behind the cover the log afforded.

Hale used the distraction to dash forward twenty feet and dove for cover behind another fallen tree. He took his rifle off his shoulder and made ready to shoot. *I'm pretty sure the shot came from a position two hundred or so meters further north from the first sniper's tree.*

"I need one more distraction and I think I'll have him." Hale said loudly over the din of battle.

"You had better figure it out this time. These distractions are going to get me shot." Maki fired back flippantly.

"I'll get him this time. I swear." Hale promised.

Maki took his fur lined white cap off again, drew his pukko blade, and proceeded to slowly lift his hat above the top of the log so that it was visible to the sniper. Nothing happened. He moved the hat from side to side a bit, creating movement to attract the enemy sniper.

"Well, go ahead and shoot it already. Try something else." Hale said.

"I am trying, the bastard isn't cooperating." Maki fired back.

"Try harder!" Hale demanded.

"Fuck you too Private!" Maki roared in response.

Suddenly a shot rang out. Hale moved out from his hiding place and took aim at the position he thought the sniper occupied. There was no one there, "The bastard moved!" Hale yelled.

"Great! Any idea where he moved to?" Maki asked.

Another shot rang out. This one smacked into the tree trunk right next to Hale's head with a dull thud. The young Finn jerked back under cover and yelled, "He's on me now, can you see him?"

Maki raised his head and peered out from behind the log he was using as a hiding place. As he drew in the breath to yell no, a bullet slammed into the log sending small splintery bits into his face. Maki dropped to the earth a moment before a second shot buzzed by overhead. This one missed the log and impacted into the ground behind him with a dull thud.

A moment after the sound of the second shot

registered in Maki's ears. A third shot rang out. After a brief pause Hale said, "Got him."

"Are you sure this time? Are there any more out there?" Maki asked and then added, "I don't really feel like eating a bullet for lunch today."

Hale removed his white, fur-lined cap, placed it on the end of his pukko, and stuck it out from behind the tree he was using as a hiding spot. He waved it back and forth trying to attract attention from the enemy. Nothing happened.

"I think that was all of them." Hale said. Before he could continue, a pair of the Soviet T-28 tanks fired simultaneously into the village. Two wooden structures erupted into gouts of flame, as high explosive rounds tore into them, flinging bits of wood in all directions. A moment later the dull rumble of the anti-tank rifle responded to the salvo taking out another T-26.

With a roar, the brigade of Soviet infantry abandoned their positions behind the tanks, and trees and charged toward the village. The Finns responded with intense automatic weapons fire. A heavy machine gun fired continuously at the oncoming Russian horde. The bullets from this gun quickly zeroed in on the advancing wall of flesh. In the space of a few moments, the Finnish gun crew sent nearly a hundred Red Army soldiers to their party dictated afterlife.

Maki stood up and watched the advancing Soviets as they bore down on the village, "It's too late, once they reach the village, our men won't be able to hold."

Before he could continue his lamentation, a series of explosions erupted, as the enemy drew within fifty feet of the village. The explosions sent shrapnel flying through the air. The metal fragments shredded the bodies of hundreds of advancing Russians. In reaction Maki started laughing.

"What is happening? Where are those explosions coming from?" Hale asked.

As the two men watched, the momentum of the attack broke, and the men of the Red Army turned away from the village and fled. The pressure on the Finns relieved, the heavy machine gun was soon joined by automatic weapons fire, and single shot rifles. Many of the bullets found their way into the backs of the retreating Soviets before the tanks fired another salvo with their main guns at the Finnish line. The tanks quickly followed this up by laying down a suppressing fire into the village with their machine guns. This fire helped to protect the backs of their retreating comrades as they fled from the Finnish wall of lead.

"Here's our chance to get into this fight. Grab your PPD 34, we're going to put the bastards in a crossfire and cut them down so their yellow asses will keep running until they reach Leningrad." Maki ordered.

Hale nodded, slung his Mosin-Nagant onto his right shoulder and drew the PPD 34 submachine gun from his left. He slipped the safety off the submachine gun with his gloved hand. He felt awkward running with the gun he had taken from the Russians earlier that morning. The two men rushed forward about three hundred feet to get in position for their attack. Breathing hard from their exertions, they stopped and sought the cover of two trees.

From behind the safety of his chosen tree, Maki made eye contact with Hale and said, "Wait until they are abreast of us, and then let them have it."

"Yes sir." Hale responded.

Each second seemed to take a small eternity as they slowly ticked by. Finally, the ragged line of retreating Soviets drew near. Maki moved from behind the tree he was using as cover and opened fire on a dozen Russians as they ran by. The fleeing Soviets were quickly cut down by his attack.

This caused another nearby group, who were beginning to rally and slow their headlong rush away from Kivenappa, to resume their flight. Hale opened fire on this group, sending many of them to their graves. The rest dove to the ground seeking any shred of cover that would protect them from this unexpected assault.

The two men quickly spent their bullets and ducked back behind the trees they were using as cover. Maki ejected the magazine from his gun and slammed a new one home. Hale looked over at him and said, "I don't have another magazine for this gun."

"See what you can do with your rifle, I'll cover you." Maki ordered.

Hale slipped the PPD 34 onto his left shoulder and pulled his rifle off his right. Now armed with a loaded weapon, he peered around the tree. The young Finnish sniper immediately spotted at least a dozen different Soviets in full flight from the village. He raised his rifle and began taking shots at the fleeing men. One by one, with the occasional miss, he cut down the retreating invaders. Panic intensified as the fleeing soldiers quickly realized that they were now taking fire from the west as well as from the village to the north.

When his rifle clicked, informing him that his bullets had been spent, Hale slipped behind the tree to provide cover. Protected from the enemies' return fire, he grimaced at the intense pain his wounded shoulder was emitting. He glanced down at his shoulder, a small blood stain had become visible on his white great coat, *That can't be good, but I must continue fighting.*

Nearby, several Russian officers realized the shift in behavior of their fleeing men and noticed the new direction that they were taking fire from. Having held an entire battalion in reserve, the Soviet brigade commander, Colonel Ivkin, decided to put his three hundred men to good use. Especially since they would not be required for the attack on Kivenappa. Turning to his aide he ordered, "Prikazat' lyudyam atakovat na zapad k finskoy linil tam!"

The aide nodded at the order, turned around, and made eye contact with the reserve battalion's commanding officer, a major, pointed in the direction of Maki and Hale, and blew his whistle.

The Major drew his pistol, turned to his men, and pointed in the direction of Hale and Maki with the weapon as he screamed, "Ataka!"

The men let out a fierce roar and charged toward the two Finns. Maki, a brand-new magazine in his PPD 34, emerged from behind the tree he had been using as cover and emptied the clip into the densely packed Russians as they charged.

As the Lieutenant cut down at least two dozen of the enemy, Hale emerged from his own hiding place. He selectively used his rifle to take out several Russians that had stopped rushing forward and were taking aim at Maki with their rifles. As soon as Maki expended his clip, he slipped back behind the tree into cover. As Maki ejected his second clip, and slammed the third and last one home, Hale continued to rapidly kill the enemy with his Mosin-

Nagant.

With Maki out of sight, the advancing battalion forgot that he existed and turned their ire toward Hale. As bullets began buzzing through the air and striking the trees all around Hale, the young sniper was forced to take cover behind a tree. As Hale disappeared from sight, Maki emerged from his hiding place and laid down fire. The Soviet advance stalled momentarily under Maki's withering fire.

Unfortunately for the Finns, the Russians were better prepared for Maki's sudden appearance. They instantly reacted to the fresh attack by diving for the ground and seeking whatever cover the frozen forest could provide. As a result, the Finnish officer was only able to wound about a dozen of the enemy soldiers.

The moment Maki's clip was expended the Russians roared and charged toward him, firing as they came. Once again, the Finnish Lieutenant was forced to seek cover as dozens of bullets slammed into the tree he was using for cover. The Russians, intent on taking down the man who had killed so many of their comrades, ignored Hale's efforts with his rifle to stem the tide rushing toward his commanding officer.

Hale's mind raced, *They're going to reach Maki!* As the advancing line drew within fifty meters of Maki's position, Hale began to throw his grenades at the charging Soviets. One after another the grenades detonated sending shrapnel and death buzzing through the frigid forest.

The Russians that weren't immediately killed by the explosions or were cut down by the shrapnel, dove to the ground seeking cover from this new attack. Several of them noticed Hale ducking back behind a tree and screamed in outrage. Overwhelmed by the urge to avenge their fallen comrades, they leapt to their feet and charged toward the young Finn.

Desperate to stop the onslaught, Hale started shooting at the advancing horde with his rifle. He worked the bolt of his rifle as quickly as humanly possible; it was not nearly quick enough. Maki, now free to act thanks to Hale, and desperate to help his subordinate, drew his pistol. He rapidly emptied the clip into the backs of the advancing Russians. He was rewarded with a red-hot fiery pain that slammed into him, knocking him over.

Out of the corner of his eye, Hale saw Maki go down. Expending the magazine on his rifle, he dropped the weapon to the ground and drew his own pistol to make a final stand against the oncoming horde, *There's just too many!*

Hale pulled the slide back on his luger, took a deep breath, and peered around the tree. A dozen Russians, their faces red with rage, charged toward him less than ten feet away. *I'm going to die. God please keep my family and Nea safe.*

As he made his mental prayer, Hale stepped out from behind the tree, raised his pistol at the approaching Russians, and fired in rapid succession. Luckily for him, the squad of enemy soldiers was so close to him, that those further back, couldn't get a clean shot at him. He emptied his pistol into the advancing squad of enemy soldiers. The luger just wasn't fast enough to stem the tide.

The first Russian to reach him, was a six-foot-tall brute with broad shoulders. The brute flung himself through the air at Hale. The Finnish sniper tried to swing his pistol toward the left to shoot the large Russian, but it was too late. Hale was knocked flat and dropped his pistol as the big man crashed into him. As Hale's back struck the hard-frozen earth, the air in his lungs was squeezed out of him, leaving him breathless.

Gasping for air Hale gazed up into the eyes of the enraged enemy soldier, who now lay on top of him brandishing a knife. The Russian, who was missing several teeth, smiled down at him for a long moment before he raised the blade above his head with both hands. The Russian was clearly moving to plunge the ten-inch blade into Hale as hard as he could. Hale, powerless to stop the large Russian, closed his eyes waiting for the blow that would end his life. *Nea, I'm sorry I won't be coming back to you like I promised.*

Hale's thoughts drifted back to the final moment they were together. He had just hugged his family goodbye. Following Finnish custom, they turned away from Hale to give him a private moment with Nea but remained on the train station platform a few feet away. Turning to Nea, Hale pulled her into an embrace, they were both crying. Stepping back, she looked up at him with her emerald orbs and said, "Promise me you will come back to me. I can't imagine a life without you."

Guilt flooded Hale's heart. He tried to fight the emotion that was overwhelming his mind. *Stop it! You have no choice. Only cowards avoid their duty.* Outwardly he smiled down at the girl he grew up with, and the woman he had fallen in love with, "I will my love. The entire Red Army cannot keep me from you. Even if I must kill a hundred of them with my bare hands, I will come home to you."

The sound of automatic weapons fire registered in Hale's ears jerking him out of his memory. He kept his eyes firmly shut waiting for the pain that would signal the end of his life and the breaking of his promise. It never came.

Confused he opened his eyes. The large Russian

soldier still lay atop him, his immense bulk continuing to pin Hale to the ground. The green clad soldier had dropped the knife and was now clutching his chest as blood poured through his fingers.

Hale pushed the dying Russian off and snatched up the man's knife. He drew the blade across the dying brute's throat to finish him off. He then picked up the dead man's loaded rifle and looked about. The entire squad of enemy soldiers that had overrun his position was down on the ground bleeding. Their moans of pain filled his ears.

In shock from the sudden turn of events, Hale just stood there numbly for several moments. A voice startled the stunned Finn and brought him back to the horrible reality around him, "Stop lollygagging around and get moving. This will only hold them for a moment."

Obeying the command, Hale, picked up his own rifle and slung it on his back. Keeping the loaded Russian rifle in his hands, he turned and ran toward the voice as best he could. Between his injured shoulder, the two weapons on his back, and a third in his arms, he was weighed down and made slow progress toward the voice.

The exhausted and injured sniper moved as quickly as he could manage through the snow toward the sound of the voice he had heard. As he ran, his ears registered the click of a magazine being slammed into place. Then a man, dressed as Hale was in a white overcoat, and white trousers, emerged from behind the cover of a tree.

Recognizing the man, Hale exclaimed, "Onni!"

The older man smiled, "It's good to see you too. Where's Maki?"

Hale stopped and pointed toward the spot where he had seen his commanding officer go down, "Over there. I think he's been hit."

Suddenly a chorus of war cries erupted from the village and a platoon of Finns emerged from the fire and smoke screaming and firing as they came. This caused the nearby Russians, who were busy regrouping for another attack against Hale, to lose their nerve, break, and run to the south toward home.

A short time later, a pair of men, dressed as Hale and Onni, suddenly appeared. The one on the left, barked, "Hands up!"

Hale and Onni obeyed the command, dropped their weapons, and raised their hands. Onni smiled and said, "We're on your side."

"Who are you?" The man on the left, he had the three stripes of a sergeant on the gray shoulder epaulettes of his white overcoat demanded.

"We're snipers with Lieutenant Maki's squad." Onni replied.

The corners of the Sergeant's mouth started to turn upward, before he caught himself and demanded, "How do I know you aren't Russian spies dressed as Finns?"

"The phrase of the day is, "Stalin's silk panties."

The Finnish soldier standing on the Sergeant's right, a private, burst into laughter at the phrase. The older man cast him a glare which caused the young soldier to abruptly cut his laughter off. He then turned to the two snipers and said, "It is indeed. Do you require assistance?"

"Yes, our Lieutenant is about fifty meters that way," Hale pointed. "He's been hurt."

The Sergeant craned his neck toward Kivenappa and bellowed, "Medic!" He turned back toward the two snipers and said, "Go to your Lieutenant, I've got to continue leading my squad forward, we're trying to break these bastards up with a counter attack and send them scurrying back to Comrade Stalin with full pants and piss filled boots."

"God go with you." Onni replied.

The two soldiers dug their ski poles into the snow and began moving toward the fleeing Russians. Onni turned to Hale and said, "Reload all of your weapons in case they are unsuccessful in driving those red swine off."

Hale, exhausted, collapsed to the earth. He pulled his thick gloves off, exposing his fingers to the cold. The young Finn started the process by ejecting the clip on his pistol, the Luger, and refilled the empty magazine. His fingers quickly grew numb in the sub-zero conditions as he painfully pushed bullet after bullet into the magazine. Finished, he slammed the cold metal home into the stock of the gun. Next, he turned to his empty rifle magazines. As he worked Onni changed the magazine on his PPD 34 and made his way over to Maki.

As soon as Hale had completed reloading all his weapons, he joined the Corporal at his Lieutenant's side. Onni was down on his knees holding Maki's hand. Maki, seeing movement out of the corner of his eyes, turned to Hale and said, "There you are. I'm glad you made it. You've got to keep your promise to Nea after all."

Hale's eyes widened, "How did you know about that?"

Maki began to chuckle, but his laugh was interrupted by a cough. Spitting up blood he looked up at Hale and said, "We all make that promise." He closed his eyes for a long moment before they fluttered open, "I'm so cold."

Onni gripped the young officer's hand, "You'll be warm soon lad, a medic is coming."

Hale took Maki's other hand and said, "Sir don't leave us. We need you." He paused to fight back tears, "I need you. You saved my life." As he said the last sentence his voice trailed off into tears.

Maki smiled up at Hale. Blood stained his teeth. He squeezed his subordinates' hand with his fading strength, "We saved each other. It's what comrades in arms are supposed to do." He was interrupted by another long cough and then added, "Did we save the village?"

"Yes, Kivenappa is still in our hands. Though there isn't that much of the actual village left. A platoon has counter attacked and driven the invader off." Hale replied.

Maki smiled up at Hale and said, "Good, then it was worth it.

Maki's body shuddered, and he let out a final gasp of pain, and then forever lay still. Hale looked into the unblinking eyes of his dead commander. Unmoving, they stared up into the blue gray sky shrouded in the golden light of the setting sun. With tears running down his cheeks, that quickly turned to ice in the frigid air, Hale gently shut his friend's eyes for the last time.

A voice from behind Hale and Onni said, "I'm sorry."

Hale looked in the direction of the voice. A man wearing the gray of a regular army soldier of Finland looked down at the pair. Instead of a rifle, he had a leather satchel with a large red cross slung over his shoulder that rested on his left hip, and no rifle. He also wore a white arm band around his right bicep with a red cross emblazoned upon it.

"Where can we take him so that he gets sent home?" Onni asked.

"North of the village. There is an aid station there." The medic replied.

Onni nodded dully in response. Turning to Hale he said, "Help me with him."

Together the two men lifted Maki's cooling corpse up. As they did so Hale winced in pain, "What's wrong?" Onni asked.

"My shoulder was injured a few days ago." Hale replied.

"Let me get a look at it." The medic said.

Onni looked over at Hale, "You're bleeding! I can take care of Maki, you let him check that shoulder. I'll see you at the aid station as soon as you can manage." Onni said.

"I can help." Hale said.

"Nonsense, you're hurt. Let the medic patch you up." Onni said.

Onni hefted Maki's corpse over his left shoulder and began walking slowly toward the smoldering remains of the village.

"Unbutton your coat and let me have a look at that shoulder private." The medic, a Corporal as indicated by the two stripes on his epaulettes of his coat, ordered.

"Yes sir." Hale replied.

He unbuttoned the top four buttons of his overcoat and winced as he pulled his right arm out of the sleeve.

"Take your shirt off too, I need to see the wound." The medic said.

Hale nodded dully and did as he was told. The moment his bare skin was exposed to the air, the hairs on the skin stood up on end and goosebumps formed. The medic poked and prodded the wound causing Hale to cry out in pain.

"Sorry, I had to check it. The wound isn't infected. You need to take at least a few days to let it heal though. It looks like you have reopened it several times. Luckily for you, you've kept it clean." The medic said.

Hale let out a bitter laugh, "There's a war on, I haven't exactly had time to take a holiday."

The medic placed a hand on Hale's uninjured shoulder and squeezed it, "I know, you have done what you must to save our country." His eyes briefly alighted on the corpse of Maki being carried away by Onni. "But if you don't get some rest, you won't be any good to us much longer. If you don't give yourself some time to heal, this wound will become infected. Then no matter how strong you are, you'll die in a pool of your own sweat."

Hale nodded in acknowledgement and said, "All right. Where do I go?"

"Follow your friend to the aid station north of the village. The doctor there will diagnose you. With luck, if you're from Karelia, you'll get to go home for a few days."

Hale's shoulders slumped, *Home!* "I'll do as you say Corporal."

The medic smiled, "I thought you might. I've got to keep moving with the counterattack to treat our casualties. I'm officially ordering you to the aid station. There the doctor will make sure that you are sent north so you can recuperate. You've earned the rest soldier."

Hale smiled faintly at the Corporal and turned toward the village. No longer caring about the battle, he dropped his newly captured Russian rifle on the ground and began walking in the direction of Kivenappa. Through the fuzz of his exhaustion and pain, his mind started to race as he walked.

What would it be like to see his family again? To see Nea? His thoughts were interrupted by shooting pain in his shoulder. *The killing, it's changed me so much. Will they accept me, or will they despise me for all of the butchery I've committed?*

Hale's thoughts were interrupted as his eyes registered the smoldering hulk of a T-28. The smell of cooked flesh filled his nostrils as tendrils of flame snapped and danced from the open hatches of the green metal beast. As he reached the front of the vehicle, his eyes took in a grisly sight. The charred remains of one of the crew members lay half out of a hatch in the top of the tank. Black smoke billowed out from the opening and circled lazily into the sky.

As he moved past the tank a voice said, "Don't come any further."

Hale looked toward the sound of the voice that came from the direction of the village. His eyes teared up as he tried to see through the clouds of smoke, "Why?" He replied, "I've been ordered to the aid station."

"Mines. Stay where you are at. Private Rinehart, escort this young man through the minefield."

A younger less confident sounding voice responded with a, "Yes sir."

Hale stood there for about a minute. His shoulder hurt, his stomach churned from the stench of burnt flesh, and his body trembled slightly with exhaustion. The adrenaline from the recent battle was leaving him and being replaced with an overwhelming wave of exhaustion.

A strong hand grasped his right arm and he winced in pain, "Sorry." Private Reinhart said.

Hale gave the man, who was about the same age as himself, a dull smile, "It's my shoulder, I was stabbed."

The Private swallowed nervously and said, "I see. Let me get you to the aid station."

The Private released Hale's right arm and moved around to his other side. He looked nervously up at the befuddled sniper before he grasped his left arm. This time there were no cries of protest. Reinhart pulled gently on Hale's arm and said, "This way. The safe path is over here."

Hale let the Private lead him through the safe path. He couldn't see any difference between this snow-covered spot, and the rest of the land in front of the village. As they walked, Hale became aware of dozens of Russian corpses strewn about. The corpses were in various states of dismemberment. Some looked as if they had just laid down on the frozen soil to take a nap. Others had horrible wounds that had frozen in the sub-zero temperatures.

Many more had been blown into smaller pieces and strewn about in front of the village. As the two men walked slowly through the safe path, a young Russian's eyes snapped open, surprising the two Finns, "Vody."

Startled, the two men stopped and looked down at the man. The injured Russian's dark green overcoat was torn to pieces. His front torso was riddled with bullet holes, at least a dozen in all. The air had quickly frozen the wounds preventing the injured man from bleeding out. Miraculously, thanks to the sub-zero temperatures, he still lived.

Hale dispassionately looked into the eyes of his enemy. Expecting to see nothing but hate, all he saw was hopelessness and fear. Private Reinhart gasped at the state of the wounded Russian as Hale said dully, "He's asking for water."

Reinhart nodded, unbuttoned his gray overcoat, and pulled out his canteen. As he knelt beside the dying man. The mortally wounded Soviet made a feeble attempt at lifting his arms to grasp the canteen. Unmoved by the plight of the young Russian, Hale placed a hand on Reinhart's shoulder and said, "No. Don't give it to him. Let him suffer. Let them all suffer for what they've done. To our land." He paused for a moment to fight back tears thinking of Pekka and Maki, "To our people."

Reinhart's eyes widened as they looked up at Hale, indecision etched on his face. Hale, losing patience, slapped the canteen from the Private's hands, "No!"

The liquid, all the more precious in its unfrozen state, poured out of the canteen where it had struck the ground and mixed with the blood of the Russians. Reinhart threw Hale a look of horror, and then picked his canteen up. He wiped the blood off of it with a dead Russian's sleeve, pulled out a pistol, and shot the injured Russian in the head. Turning, he met Hale's angry gaze and said, "He's suffered enough."

Hale stared at Reinhart for a long moment before slowly nodding and turning toward the village. Ignoring the Private, he turned and stalked into the village. *What have they done to me? My mind is filled with such rage. I've become a monster!*

The defenders of Kivenappa eyes followed Hale as he slowly trudged past their lines. Tortured by his own thoughts Hale ignored them.

Chapter 8

Dusk Karelia Isthmus Finland, Village of Kivennapa, December 4th, 1939

Hale reached the aid station. The gray tent, bathed in the golden light of the setting sun, had a large white square on it's top, with a red cross in the middle. Several men lay outside the tent groaning from their wounds. A nurse knelt by one of the men and helped him take sips from a steaming cup of tea. Noticing Hale, she stood up and turned to face him, "Are you injured?"

Hale nodded and said, "Yes. I've been stabbed in the shoulder."

The nurse wore a mink coat that would have been the height of fashion in London or New York. Here, amidst the forest that was home to the animals harvested for the pelts to make the coat, it was a common sensible garment for anyone to wear in the cold. She looked him up and down. Quickly noticing the tear and flecks of red on his coat, "Pull your coat off that shoulder so I can see." She asked.

Hale was taken aback by the business-like attitude of the woman. She was the first female he had seen since Oda, who had tried to teach him some Russian a few months back. Irritated by her cold brusqueness, the young woman, pushed a blond lock of hair from her face with her left hand and said, "Don't stand there with a stupid look on your face. You're taking me away from these dying men."

Hale mumbled an apology and exposed his injured shoulder to the poking and prodding that was sure to come. He wasn't disappointed, "Ouch!" He exclaimed.

The nurse flashed him a look of apology, "It's not infected. You're lucky."

"How does being stabbed, poked and prodded make me lucky?" Hale asked.

"Because it looks like this wound has been reopened several times. Why didn't you seek help sooner?" The nurse admonished.

"I'm sorry, I was a bit busy killing the monsters that have invaded our country." Hale replied gruffly.

The nurse flashed Hale a smile, "Sorry, I feel like we got off on the wrong foot. My name is Tora."

"Hale."

"Well Hale, head on into the tent and get warmed up. Try not to disturb the doctor, he is in the middle of an operation. When he finishes he'll take a look at you." Tora said.

Hale relaxed, "Thanks Tora."

The two shared a long gaze. Hale lost himself in her

ice blue eyes for a long moment before she looked away as her cheeks turned crimson, "I've got to get back to my patients."

"Of course." Hale replied politely.

Hale walked over to the entrance of the tent and pulled a flap back to enter. A wall of warm air hit him as he stepped into the surprisingly brightly lit interior of the aid tent. At least a dozen lanterns hung from the ceiling brightly lighting the room. It took a few seconds for the shift in temperature to register, then the stench hit him. The stink of the place overwhelmed him. Looking down he saw the floor was covered in blood and bits of other things he'd rather not think about. The thought abruptly cut off as he inwardly shuddered.

Hale looked up and saw two figures. In the middle of the tent was a man in a red stained lab coat. Next to him, a woman wore a blood-stained apron. Hale's eyes immediately went to her dress underneath the apron. It was form fitting and complimented her figure. The woman, a nurse presumably, stood beside the man and held the tray up where he could easily reach it.

The man in the white lab coat, was using a metal instrument that resembled a large pair of tweezers. Using the tweezers, he pulled a piece of shrapnel from a grisly wound in the gut that the poor unfortunate on the table had. The man in the white lab coat, presumably the doctor, didn't turn to look as he released the shrapnel into a small metal bowl on the tray.

The nurse had calmly shifted her tray, so that the metal bowl was underneath the Doctor's hand, when he released the shrapnel. The tiny piece of metal made a faint tinkling noise as it landed in the bowl.

"I think that's the last of it. Let's close him up." The doctor said.

The nurse set the tray she had been holding on a table behind her and picked up another tray. This one was covered by neatly arranged rows of instruments. The Doctor turned to look at the tray. For a moment his gaze met Hale's. Ignoring the young sniper, he selected two items. The first looked to be a needle and thread. The second item was a small packet. Satisfied he had what he needed, he turned back to the injured soldier on the operating table.

The Doctor worked quickly on the unconscious man as the nurse looked on. Hale, seeing an unoccupied chair by the wood burning stove that kept the tent warm, walked over to it. Wanting to sit, he removed the two weapons from his back, and sat down. He let out a small gasp of pleasure as his exhausted body was finally able to relax.

As the Doctor worked, Hale slowly warmed up. As he did so, he removed his white great coat, then his pants. Underneath was several layers of garments that had helped keep him warm in the subzero temperatures. He glanced at his shoulder. Through several layers of torn shirts, he could see the wound slowly oozed blood. The skin on the edge of the wound had a very angry looking red shade to it.

As the Doctor finished up, a truck pulled up outside. Two men entered, like the medic that had directed Hale to this tent, they were dressed in the gray uniform of Finland and sported white arm bands with a red cross. The Doctor turned to the two men and said, "Good timing, I just finished up with him. You can go ahead and load him into the truck. Don't leave before I've had a chance to look at the Private sitting by the stove. I think he'll be joining you."

The two men stiffened to attention and said, "Yes sir."

"You know I don't like that yes sir crap." The doctor admonished, "I'm a healer not a damned pretentious prick with a command stick shoved up his ass."

Hale, unable to stop himself, laughed loudly at the Doctor's words. Those sharp eyes immediately fell on him again. Noticing that Hale was not wearing a uniform underneath his clothing, the man said, "What seems to be the issue?" He paused for a long moment before adding questioningly, "Private?"

"Private would-be correct sir. I'm not in the regular army. Just a volunteer reservist trying to keep my home safe. There aren't enough uniforms to go around for everyone, since I usually work alone, I don't need one." Hale noticed the blank look on the Doctor's face as the exhausted man waited for Hale to get to the point, "It's my shoulder sir, I was stabbed a few days ago."

"I see. Out on a mission?" The Doctor inquired.

"Yes sir." Hale replied.

"Like I was telling these two." The doctor gestured toward the two orderlies who were busy removing the patient to their truck, I'm a healer not one of these damned pompous asses that need their boots licked every morning to feel good about themselves." He paused to take a deep breath and let it out slowly before adding, "Call me Gar."

Hale laughed at the Doctor's words and said, "Well met Gar. My name is Hale."

"Let me get a look at that shoulder. Take off all those shirts." Gar ordered.

Hale nodded in acknowledgement of the Doctor's request and took off his shirts. He started with the baggy woolen sweater his mom had knit him. She had spun the wool their flock of sheep had provided into thread and painstakingly knit the sweater over the course of many days. Seeing his mom's beautiful creation torn and bloody, made Hale's heart ache.

Next was another sweater, this one was tighter and more form fitting than the one his mom had knit. It has been purchased through a catalog from a department store in Helsinki. Hale couldn't remember which one. Next, was a button-down flannel shirt. Unlike the two sweaters, he was able to remove this one without wincing. Underneath this shirt, was a white undershirt. It had been stained with the sweat from his numerous exertions over the last several days and of course blood.

He stifled a cry as he removed the tight form fitting undershirt, and then looked up at Gar. The older man met his gaze, his eyes full of reassurance. The Doctor took a step forward and stared down into the wound. He poked and prodded the wound eliciting several gasps of pain from Hale.

"You're lucky, you've reopened this wound numerous times during the last several days. I think that is what has prevented it from becoming infected. You're going to have to take some time to heal. Let me put some sulfa in it and close it up. Then I'm sending you to the hospital to recover." Gar said.

"What's sulfa?" Hale asked.

"It's a powder that you put into wounds to prevent them from becoming infected. It was invented by the Germans a few years back. It is supposed to revolutionize the medical arts. For the first time ever, we can actually prevent and treat infections." Gar said. Noticing Hale's blank look the Doctor added, "Trust me, this is an exciting development."

"If you say so, Doctor." Hale replied.

"It's going to save millions of men who survive their injuries from infection." The doctor replied.

Gar looked around for the nurse and her tray, they had both disappeared. Frowning, he retreated to a gray metal cabinet set into the far corner of the tent and opened it up. He withdrew a small packet from one of the shelves. As he approached Hale, he tore the packet open. Next, he stood over Hale's injury and tipped the packet so that the powder slowly poured into the wound.

Hale winced as he felt the grains striking his open wound. The Doctor continued this process for about a minute as he spread the powder evenly over the knife injury, "There we go. Now I just have to close it up."

"Close it?" Hale asked nervously.

"Yes, I have to sew it shut or it will never heal." The Doctor replied. Seeing Hale suddenly turning pale he added, "Don't worry it won't hurt."

The Doctor was wrong. It did hurt, *A lot.* His shoulder now feeling like it had been kicked by an angry jackass, throbbed mightily, "Thank you." Hale winced as a shooting pain from his shoulder caused him to grimace, "I think. Am I free to get dressed and go?" Hale asked.

Gar smiled at Hale, "Don't worry. I know it hurts now, but you'll feel better later. Let me spread a bit more sulfa onto your stitches so they don't become infected."

Hale stood by patiently as Gar went back to the gray

metal cabinet. He pulled the latch to the right and tugged on the door opening it. The mechanism screeched in protest at being disturbed. Within seconds he had picked up another packet of the sulfa powder from the neatly arranged shelves and had torn the top off as he walked back across the small space to Hale. Gar then concentrated as he carefully spread the white powder into Hale's stitched wound.

"There you go, that should prevent infection. You need at least seven days of rest, and then you'll be good as new." Gar said.

"After seven days, will I be able to fire a rifle without pain? I'm a sniper, that's kind of important."

Gar eyes widened at Hale's words, "It will probably still hurt, but your shoulder should be able to take the kick at that point. What do you shoot with?"

"A Mosin-Nagant." Hale replied.

Gar pointed at Hale's weapon on the floor, "That hunting rifle?"

"Yes, my parents got it for me. The army used a conversion kit on it to upgrade it to military standards." Hale replied.

The doctor tilted his head back so that he was staring up at the ceiling of the tent and laughed mightily, "What's so funny?" Hale asked, irritated.

After Gar's mirth abated, he met Hale's gaze and said, "We are invaded by a large modern army with all of the latest equipment, countless technologies devised for the destruction of mankind and we send out the flower of our youth armed with hunting rifles to stop it."

Hale bristled, "I've killed many of the Soviet swine with my hunting rifle."

Gar held up a hand, "Peace Hale. It wasn't meant as an insult to you. On the contrary, it was meant as an insult to the Russians. Despite all the advantages they bring, young boys, like you, who were born free are able to make them pay dearly for every inch of our soil."

"One of us is worth ten of them." Hale added.

Gar smiled, "I don't doubt it. You, and many other good free-spirited Finnish boys are proving the value and ingenuity that growing up free instills in a man."

The horn on the truck outside honked. At the same moment Gar's nurse re-entered the tent. She reeked of tobacco smoke, "You had best get going. Enjoy your rest, you've earned it."

"Thank you, Gar."

Hale finished dressing. As he turned to leave, he shook hands with the doctor as the older man handed him a piece of paper.

"Your pass." Gar said.

Hale smiled at the older man in thanks, took the paper from the doctor's outstretched hand, and hastily walked out of the tent. As he emerged outside, a blast of cold air and darkness greeted him. A few feet in front of him, on the road, sat an ambulance. The vehicle had a cab much like the other trucks Hale had seen. On the back, instead of a canopy covered flatbed, it was fully enclosed. *How did I rate such comfort?*

Seeing Hale emerge from the tent, the passenger, one of the orderlies who had taken the man with the gut wound away, got out of the truck and said, "Let me help you into the back."

"Thanks. Where are we going?" Hale asked.

"We're taking you to the hospital outside of Perkjarvi" The man responded.

Hale smiled, *Perkjarvi is close to home!*

Seeing Hale smile the man asked, "What's so great about Perkjarvi? I grew up in Viipuri. Seems like a quaint little shithole by comparison."

"It's close to home." Hale responded.

The man's eyes widened as he realized the insult, he had just paid Hale. He quickly recovered from his blunder and said, "The hospital there is nearly full, and you don't seem to be that bad off. Perhaps they'll let you go home to recover."

Hale's heart leaped as he climbed into the back of the ambulance. Stepping into the dim interior, he saw that the right side of the space was occupied by the unconscious form of the man who had just gotten the operation. Opposite him was an empty stretcher, sitting securely in an apparatus designed to hold the stretcher in place.

The medic gestured at the empty stretcher, "Get some rest. It's a long trip to Perkjarvi."

Hale did as he was told. He set his weapons on the floor of the vehicle and laid down on the stretcher. The medic pulled a pillow out of a metal cabinet set into the forward wall of the ambulance. He handed Hale the pillow, along with a gray woolen blanket, and then retreated. The last sound Hale remembered was the sound of the door being latched shut and then nothingness.

Chapter 9

Early Morning Karelia Isthmus Finland, South of the Village of Perkjarvi, December 5th, 1939

Hale awoke in mid-air. Immediately realizing his lack of contact with any physical surface his stomach lurched. A moment later he landed back on the stretcher with a thump. As his heartbeat thundered in his ears from the adrenaline rushing into his bloodstream, he heard a groan from the darkness, *The man with the gut wound.* He thought as realization came back to him. *I must have been deeply asleep.*

The squeal of brakes filled the small chamber the two men occupied as Hale felt his body sliding forward. Not thinking, he stuck his right arm out to stop his forward motion. The sudden searing pain caused him to cry out. The moment the motion of the vehicle ceased; Hale heard the sound of a door opening up front. This was followed by the sound of boots on gravel as someone, presumably the orderly, made his way around to the back of the vehicle.

With a moan of protest, the latch on the door twisted and the door opened revealing a shadowy figure in the moonlight, "Is everyone all right?" The orderly asked.

"What happened?" Hale asked.

"There was a huge hole in the road. Maybe from a Russian bomb? I'm not sure. It wasn't there when we came through earlier today. The driver swerved to miss it, but he still caught the edge of it with the back tire on your side." The orderly responded.

"Russians here? Where are we? I thought we were going to Perkjarvi!" Hale's mind raced as he blurted out the words.

"Peace friend, we are. The hole didn't come from Soviet artillery. It likely came from an airplane. Bastards probably tried to bomb an ambulance or a supply truck yesterday afternoon." The man responded.

Hale calming asked, "I see, how far are we from Perkjarvi?"

"A kilometer? Five kilometers? It's hard to say. One stretch of frozen trees looks much like the next." The man responded.

Before Hale could ask another question, the other patient in the ambulance groaned and whispered in a cracked voice, "Water."

Hale pulled his canteen out. He kept a metal flask underneath his coat, so it wouldn't freeze solid. As he sat up, he was hit by a wave of nausea and lightheadedness for a moment before his head cleared. He rolled out of the stretcher and placed his knees on the floor of the ambulance. Next, he leaned over the other patient and twisted the cap off his canteen. Finally, he gently put his left hand underneath the man's neck and put the edge of the canteen to his lips.

The man drank greedily for a moment and then coughed, "More." He rasped, his voice a little stronger this time.

Hale obliged him. This time he was able to take in a lot more of the liquid without coughing it back up. When the man had drunk his fill, he pushed the canteen away with his left hand, "Thank you."

"What's your name?" Hale asked.

"Jani."

"Nice to meet you Jani. How did you end up here?"

"I got shot." Jani replied with an edge to his voice.

"Outside of Kivenappa?" Hale asked.

"That's right. Who are you? You're not a member of the battalion." Jani replied.

Hale gently placed a hand on Jani's right arm to reassure him, "No I'm not. I was a sniper with Maki's group."

"Never heard of it." Jani said.

"No, I don't suppose you would have. I've been

fighting the Russians with my hunting rifle since the first day they crossed into Finland. We were ordered north to do what we could to aide in the defense of Kivenappa." Hale replied.

As the truck started to slowly rumble forward Hale asked, "Are you good on water?"

"Yes, I've had enough, thank you." Jani replied.

"How did you get hit?" Hale asked.

"I was in the line with the rest of my brothers. We were trying to hold against a Russian charge. They had at least a dozen tanks, and over a thousand of the bastards charging right at us. I stood up to shoot from behind our barricade and felt a searing pain." Jani said.

"I saw that charge. I thought your unit was going to be overrun. Then the mines went off." Hale said.

"The mines?" Jani inquired.

"Yeah, the first wave of the invaders hit the mine field simultaneously. There was a string of explosions and then a hundred of the bastards were down on the ground screaming." Hale replied.

"The very last thing I remember before being hit was a bright flash." Jani said.

"What was the next thing you remember after that?" Hale asked.

"Waking up on a table. The room was blindingly bright. I couldn't see anything. My gut." Jani paused to take a breath, "My gut was on fire. I could feel something poking around inside my body!" Jani said.

"That was Doctor Gar. What did you do?" Hale asked.

"I tried to sit up, but my body wouldn't move! Then I screamed." Jani said.

"That doesn't sound like a pleasant way to wake. It's good you weren't able to move though. If you had, you would have injured yourself further." Hale said.

"No, it wasn't a pleasant way to wake up. Not at all. There was one bright spot, I heard a voice. The voice of an angel told me that I needed to lay still. That everything was going to be alright." Jani said.

Hale chuckled, "That was probably the nurse."

"Oh." Jani said, disappointed.

"Do you remember anything after that? When I walked into the tent you were unconscious and didn't wake up." Hale said.

"After I heard the nurse." Jani's features became downcast as he said, "I liked her being an angel better. I felt a prick on my right arm. Then I felt numb for a moment. The next thing I remember is waking up here." Jani said.

The sound of breaks filled the chamber once again as the ambulance came to a stop. The noise and vibrations created by the motor stopped as the engine was cut off. A moment later Hale heard the two doors of the cab opening nearly simultaneously. A few seconds later, the double doors were pulled open and two orderlies stared at the pair of injured men.

Looking at Hale the driver said, "We'll get Jani first and then we'll come back for you."

"No worries. I can walk." Hale said.

"Suit yourself. Just follow us into the hospital. A nurse will get you processed." The driver said.

Hale, noticing the two stripes on the driver's epaulets indicating the rank of Corporal said, "Yes sir."

"No need for that sir business. I'm enlisted the same as you, the name is Langston."

"Well met Langston, my name is Hale."

Langston flashed Hale a smile as the other orderly climbed into the back of the ambulance. Working together the two men lifted Jani's stretcher off the frame built to hold it and gently removed him from the vehicle. They walked slowly toward a set of double wooden doors set into the wall of a large two-story building made of concrete.

As the two orderlies carrying Jani neared, the double doors swung open. Two ladies, both in the form fitting white dresses that nurses wore smiled at the two men as they approached. The one holding the right door open, in her mid-twenties with raven black hair asked, "What have you got for us?"

"Gut wound. Gar pulled the metal out of him and sewed him up." Langston replied.

"Take him to room 210. We've got three in there already, but I think we can squeeze in one more." The raven-haired nurse replied.

"Yes ma'am." Langston replied.

As the two orderlies carried Jani into the building the nurse noticed Hale for the first time, "What do we have here?" The raven-haired nurse asked as her hazel eyes looked him up and down.

"The name is Hale ma'am. I was stabbed in the shoulder."

"You don't look that bad off. I'll get you seen by the Doctor, perhaps we can board you with one of the town's folk. There isn't much room here, and we must save what space we have for the seriously injured."

"Getting stabbed is pretty serious business." Hale retorted gruffly.

The nurse gave Hale a reassuring, if somewhat tired looking smile, "I wasn't trying to imply that your injury was less important Private. Just that you require less care to recover. Since you can walk, we can board you with one of the locals."

"My family owns a farm about five kilometers from here. Do you think I could stay with them?" Hale asked.

The nurse pursed her lips as she thought it over, "Perhaps. If the Doctor thinks you can make that walk every day. He's going to want to examine you regularly to make sure your wound is healing well." The nurse put a hand on Hale's uninjured shoulder, "Getting you better as quickly as possible is important. If we are to survive as a people through this crisis, we will need all of our fighting men."

Hale squared his shoulders and stood a little taller at the woman's words, "Thank you. When can I see the Doctor?"

"Come with me, he's asleep right now. Poor thing has been up basically since the war started." The nurse replied.

"Then we mustn't disturb him. What's your name nurse?" Hale asked.

"Astrid. What's yours?"

"Hale."

Astrid gestured down the hallway, "This way Hale. All I can spare for you is a chair while you wait for the Doctor to wake."

Hale met Astrid's gaze; he was captivated by her Hazel eyes. *So different from Nea's.* Forcing himself back into reality he said, "A chair will do quite nicely after a week freezing in the forest."

Astrid led Hale to a wooden door. As she opened the door, she turned back to Hale and placed an index finger over her lips to indicate for him to remain quiet. Once the door was open, Astrid stepped to the side so Hale could enter the room, he saw a middle-aged man in a white lab coat laying on the floor.

The bearded and clearly overweight man was laying on his back. As Hale took his first step into the room, he was startled by a loud blast that emitted from the Doctor. Hale narrowly prevented himself from crying out in surprise. *I've never heard someone snore so loudly.*

Astrid pointed to a chair set behind a large desk made of oak. Hale nodded to indicate he understood and tiptoed over to the chair. As quietly as he could, he removed the two weapons on his shoulders and set them on the floor. He winced as his right shoulder throbbed in protest from the movement.

Taking a deep breath, he bit down on his lower lip to avoid crying out. Successful in remaining quiet he then removed his coat, and his white snow pants, along with several layers of sweaters. Next, he picked the wooden office chair up and set it back a few feet from the desk. He ran his fingers over the wooden surface of the desk for a moment admiring its polished surface. He enjoyed the feel of the wood underneath his fingertips. As he moved them across the top of the desk, the sensitive nerve endings on his fingertips registered the feel of the grain and slight imperfections along the surface.

Finished admiring the desk, he lowered himself quietly into the chair. As Astrid gently shut the door, he put his feet up on the desk. Despite the racket the sleeping Doctor caused, Hale was asleep within minutes. As he slept, his mind was filled with dreams of conflict, killing, and hardship.

He awoke with a start. The bearded doctor was now standing over him, and sunshine streamed in through the room's window, "Good Morning." The man said.

Hale stifled a yawn and replied, "Good morning."

"I'm Doctor Nooa. Mind if I get a look at your wound?"

Hale, still a bit disoriented from his slumber nodded his head slowly but failed to take action. "Can you take that shirt off?" Dr. Nooa asked.

"Sure." Hale responded sheepishly.

He pulled his undershirt up carefully trying to avoid the shooting pain any kind of movement caused in his shoulder. Failing, he winced out loud. Dr. Nooa, ignoring Hale's discomfort, pushed the glasses up on his nose as he leaned over and examined the wound, "Whoever stitched you up did a good job. Do you remember his name?"

"Gar." Hale replied. Dr. Nooa frowned at his response

so he hastily added, "He never told me his last name."

"No matter, whoever this Gar was did good work. He sewed you up nicely. I'm going to put some sulfa on it, to keep the infection away, then we need to see about finding you someplace to stay." Dr. Nooa said.

Hale opened his mouth to speak when Dr. Nooa snapped his fingers and said, "I almost forgot. Astrid said that your family is on a farm nearby. How far are they from here?"

"About five kilometers." Hale replied.

"That's too far for you to walk everyday so I can check up on you. Do they have a car, or a wagon?" Dr. Nooa asked.

"With this much snow on the ground a wagon is impractical. We have a sleigh." Hale replied.

"Anything will do, as long as you don't have to make the walk. What's your family's name? I can send someone out in our car to tell them to come get you."

"Wouldn't it be simpler just to send me in the car?" Hale asked.

"No, I want them to come here so I can explain to them directly the care you will require."

"I see Doctor, Karhonen is my surname." Hale said.

"I just had another thought. Would anyone in the village know of you?" Dr Nooa asked.

Hale nodded, "We used to come into town a few times a month to shop at the store."

"Then I could get shopkeeper Olley to send one of his

boys with a message." Dr. Nooa replied.

"I thought you were going to send a car directly?" Hale asked.

"I changed my mind. If we can pay someone to do it, that will save me from having to send a nurse in the car. With the hospital beyond capacity, everyone is needed here." Dr. Nooa took a breath and pointed at the desk in front of Hale, "There's some pen and paper right there. Care to write a note to your family?"

Hale blurted out enthusiastically, "Sure!"

I'm going home! Hale wrote the note to his family and handed it to Dr. Nooa. The older man took the note from Hale and turned to leave. Simultaneously, Astrid entered the room with a tray of food. She stepped around the Doctor's impressive girth and placed the tray on the desk in front of Hale. Hale's mouth watered at the smell of sausage wafted up from a bowl of steaming hot soup.

"Care for some sausage soup?" Astrid asked, "You need to eat so you can heal."

"Absolutely!" Hale replied excitedly as his stomach rumbled, reminding him that he hadn't eaten in a day.

He quickly lost track of the world around him as he enjoyed the soup, and the rye bread. Simply not having to pay attention was a luxury after several days of being hyper vigilant. As he ate, the Doctor handed Hale's note to Astrid and said, "Can you take this to Olley and see if he can send one of his boys to the Karhonen farm?"
"Of course, Doctor." Astrid replied.

After Hale finished his meal, his eyes grew heavy. He pushed the tray to the side, propped his feet on the desk, and fell back asleep. He awoke several hours later. As he opened his eyes, he noticed a middle-aged man standing in the doorway with graying hair. Hale wasn't sure how long the man had stood there watching him. His eyes widened as he recognized the man and blurted out in surprise, "Dad!"

A middle-aged version of Hale stepped into the room. Behind him, his mother and Aina pushed his father to the side to get a look at him. The moment Aina caught sight of him, she squealed in delight and ran to him. As Hale stood up Aina wrapped her arms around his leg and his mother flung her arms around him and hugged him tightly, "Ouch!" Hale exclaimed.

Hale's mom took a step back, a look of horror spreading across her face, "I'm sorry! Where are you hurt?"

"In the shoulder. One of the bas-." Hale cut himself off as he looked down at Aina, "One of the Soviet's stabbed me."

"Did you get him?" His father asked.

"Yes father, he will not trouble Finland further." Hale said.

"I'd like to hear more about your experiences, but not in front of the women." Hale's father replied.

"Later then." Hale said. He kissed his mom on the cheek and then squatted down to look Aina in the eyes, "How have you been little pup?"

"Great! Mother has been teaching me how to bake cookies!" Aina exclaimed.

"Has she now?" Hale replied.

"Yes, and my kitchen has been a disaster." His mom added.

Hale's father interrupted, "You can both tell him all about it during the journey home. We must get going, the trip is a long one and it's nearly dark. Aina shouldn't be out after the sun goes down. It will be too cold for her."

"She'll be just fine underneath the blanket." Mom snapped.

Hale's father silently glared back at his wife without replying, "Fine. I guess we shouldn't keep Hale waiting. We'll get going, but first they should talk for a few minutes."

Dad sighed and then nodded slowly, "Agreed, but they should have the room to themselves."

Mom frowned. She met her husband's unrelenting glare and said sharply, "Fine."

Before Hale had a chance to ask what was going on, his family shuffled out of the room and closed the door behind him, *That was weird. What's with them?*

A few seconds later the door opened. Standing in the doorway was a young lady with red hair, green eyes, and a huge smile on her face, "Nea!"

Nea ran to him and they embraced, "It's so good to see you Hale. I'm so happy you're coming home!"

He looked down into her green orbs and lost himself. He leaned his head down toward hers and her lips eagerly found his. They kissed for nearly a minute fervently exploring each other's mouths with their tongues. Breathless Nea took a step back and said, "Let me get a look at you. Where are you hurt?"

"In the right shoulder." Hale replied.

His eyes slowly looked Nea up and down. His pulse quickened at the sight of the woman he loved. Everything was as he remembered, the long red tresses which touched her perky bosom, narrow waist, rounded hips, slightly bulging belly. *Bulging belly, oh my God!*

Nea saw Hale's eyes widened as they came to rest on her mid-section, "Surprise!"

Hale stood still for a moment stunned at this turn of events. As Nea's brow furrowed and her features began to contort into a look of worry Hale dropped to one knee, took her hands in his, looked up into her eyes and said, "Nea, will you marry me?"

Nea, with tears streaming down her freckled cheeks said, "Yes, Hale."

The door flung open and Aina ran into the room, embracing them both, "I'm going to be an Aunt!" She exclaimed.

Hale's parents stepped into the room smiling and said in unison, "Congratulations!"

Hale's mother, Jenna, turned to the couple and said, "We must plan the wedding quickly, so we can get it done before you have to go back. People will start to talk if Nea gets any larger. Luckily, it's wintertime. With her coat on you can't tell she's pregnant yet. Otherwise, we would have had to keep her hidden on the farm."

"Could we go to the church right now and do it?" Hale asked.

"No Hale, I want my parents to be there too when we are married. Perhaps tomorrow?" Nea replied.

"We should at least stop by the church and talk to the preacher about tomorrow." Jenna added.

Hale's Father, Raynar, looked down at Aina, "Are you sure she'll be ok under the blanket if we ride back in the dark?"

"It's plenty warm under the blanket, she'll be fine." Jenna replied.

"I suppose, if you think it is necessary to talk to the preacher today." Raynar replied testily.

"It is. We have to give him some warning that he will be expected to officiate a wedding tomorrow. Hopefully he'll agree." Jenna replied.

"He will. I'm sure of it. We don't know how long Hale's going to be with us." Nea said.

"The Doctor said I'll be fit for combat in about a week." Hale replied.

"Do you think the Army will be able to hold? We're south of the Mannerheim line here. The Government has been warning us to make ready to flee." Raynar asked.

"They've got us badly outnumbered. The first time I witnessed the regular army making a stand, they held." Hale paused for a moment before adding, "Barely."

"I'm sure our brave men will keep us safe." Nea said.

"We'll try our best, but the Red Army seems to have a bottomless pool of men to sacrifice. Plus, the Russians have modern weapons like tanks, artillery, and airplanes. We don't have those things." Hale replied.

Raynar frowned, "That's not entirely true. When I

fought in the Civil War against the Reds, we had some artillery. Plus, what about those tanks we bought from the French several years back?"

Hale quickly fell into a familiar pattern and disrespectfully rolled his eyes at what his father had to say, "Yes, I'm sure we have some artillery, but I'm hearing the Russians have thousands of guns. We have maybe a few hundred and not much ammunition."

"Still, that is something, is it not?" Raynar replied.

Hale held up his PPD 34, "Look at this. They have thousands of guns like it." Hale handed the weapon to his father and continued, "That gun can fire thirty rounds in thirty seconds. Now look at what I have to fight with." Hale picked up the rifle that Raynar had given him for his thirteenth birthday.

Raynar's cheeks began to turn crimson, "There's nothing wrong with the rifle I bought you."

"No there isn't. It's a fine weapon that has served me well for the last five years, for the purpose it was designed for, killing animals. On the modern battlefield it's simply too slow. It can only fire five rounds in thirty seconds." Hale replied.

"I see, but why does that matter? Aren't you a sniper? Surely a small gun like this, no matter how fast it fires, doesn't do you much good as a sniper." Raynar replied.

"That would be correct, if the Soviets were nice enough to stand off and trade rifle shots with me all day, but they aren't. I've had to use the PPD 34 several times, just to keep from getting overrun." Hale said.

The conversation continued as the family emerged from the hospital onto the street. Nearby, tied to a post was the family's horse. As Hale's father untied the horse he said, "We can talk about this later." He paused and threw the women a glance, "Alone."

"As you wish father." Hale replied.

The family, Hale, and Nea, climbed into the sled. After he finished untying the horse, Raynar took up the reins. He pulled on the right one and cracked the whip in the air above the family's horse, Liv, "Let's get going old girl."

Liv snorted in displeasure, but dutifully obeyed the command. Her hooves made clomping noises as she began pulling the sleigh, and the family along with it, down the road. Hale relaxed as Nea leaned into him. Everyone remained silent, lost in their thoughts, as the sleigh slid over the snow-covered main street of Perkjarvi. It took but a few minutes to reach the church. Raynar pulled back on the reins and brought the sleigh to a halt in front of the structure.

The family shuffled out of the sleigh as Raynar tied Liv up to the post in front of the church. The church was a simple wooden structure with a squat square shaped steeple also made of wood and painted white. Having weathered many harsh Finnish winters, the paint on the church, was cracking and chipping in many places. The only signs of life from the structure was a billowing cloud of smoke that emerged from a small chimney set in the back.

Hale opened the red front door and stepped into the sanctuary. Memories flooded his mind from the many Sundays he spent here, struggling to stay awake during the long service. His eyes scanned the sanctuary looking for the preacher, Oskar. The rotund old man was nowhere to be seen, "Hello?"

As Hale stepped forward to give everyone else room to enter, a plain wooden door opened in the back of the sanctuary and an older bald man entered the room. Oskar was as big around as a barrel. His eyes widened slightly at the sight of the Karhonen family standing by the front doors. Remembering himself, he asked, "How can I help thee?"

Hale put his arm around Nea and said, "We'd like to get married."

Oskar, his thoughts focused on his dinner that was now growing cold, frowned, "Hmm I see. Right now?"

"Tomorrow." Nea said, and then added, "I want my parents to be here too."

Oskar let out a sigh of relief. He didn't realize he had been holding it, "Very good, I have a funeral in the morning. The Heikkinen's lost their eldest son in the fighting. I'm giving a service tomorrow morning here in the sanctuary."

"What time is the burial? We can have the wedding after that." Jenna asked.

Oskar stuttered a bit as he said, "There wo- won't be a burial. According to the army, there." He paused a moment, steeling himself to say the words, "There wasn't anything left of him to send home."

Hale's mother and Nea simultaneously turned white as sheets before Raynar said, "I see. Then the afternoon would be good?"

Oskar nodded, "Yes, any time after two o'clock should be fine. Will there be many in attendance?"

Hale opened up his arms to indicate the people around

him, "Just my family and Nea's. We don't have much time to put together a large wedding. I'm due back to the front in a week."

"Very good then. I'll see you tomorrow, at two o'clock." Oskar replied.

"Two o'clock it is. Thank you, sir." Hale replied.

The family turned and left the little sanctuary. Outside, the wind had picked up and the biting cold made everyone pull their coats closer. The village was cast in a golden light as the Sun hung low on the western horizon creating long shadows.

Without warning a dull wale began to sound from the center of the village. The warbling alarm, faint at first, grew louder as it sped up faster and faster. Reacting to the warning, the villagers scrambled for cover.

"What's that noise?" Nea asked.

"It's an air raid siren!" Hale exclaimed. "We must find shelter."

The sound of an aircraft engine droning in the sky could be heard. Hale glanced up into the sky and saw a plane diving toward the main street of the village, "We've got to get Liv off the street, or we are going to lose her!"

Raynar turned and looked at Hale, "Untie her and lead her to safety. I'll take care of the women."

Hale turned and ran toward Liv who was tied to a post in front of the church. As he reached the animal, the noise of the aircraft shifted and became higher pitched. As he worked to unbuckle her from the sleigh, he stole a quick glance over his shoulder. He spotted the approaching plane. Like everything else the Russians owned, the fighter was painted a dull and drab dark green. Each wing on the airplane sported a large red star.

The aircraft was diving straight toward the main street of the village. *I've got to hurry!* The pilot lined up his aircraft perfectly with the main boulevard of Perkjarvi. It almost seemed as if he was trying to land the plane on the road. Hale stole another glance as he began working to untie Liv from the post; he noticed that the edges of the wings would just fit between the structures that lined main street.

As Hale finished with the knot and pulled Liv free of the post, the plane began to fire. Bullets struck the ground a few hundred feet down the street from Hale scattering those still in the street. The young sniper pulled hard on Liv's bridal to get the old horse moving as the line of bullets rapidly approached. As he tugged on Liv's bridal, Hale stole another glance back at the two advancing lines of bullets. Desperate to get out of the way of the advancing line of death, he tried to run as fast as he could toward the edge of the church and safety.

As Hale reached the corner of the structure, the plane sounded as if it was right behind him. The sound of dual machine guns firing, and the roar of the engine created a frightening racket. Desperate to escape, he forgot his injury as he pulled hard on Liv's bridal with his right arm. His injured shoulder screamed in protest as he led the horse into the alleyway between the church and a house. A trail of bullets was stitched into the ground, just missing Liv's hind quarter as Hale pulled the horse to safety.

The sound of the bullets striking so close to her back legs caused Liv to spook and rear up on her hind legs. Hale lost his grip on her bridal as she yanked herself free of his grasp. Losing his balance, he fell to the ground. Time seemed to freeze as he looked up at the bottom of Liv's hooves hovering over him.

Sporadic gunfire echoed through the village as people fired their guns at the departing aircraft. The sound snapped Hale out of his frozen state, and he rolled to the side just as Liv's hooves smashed down upon the snow-covered earth with a loud thump in the spot he had just occupied.

Raynar grabbed her bridal with both of his hands and began whispering into Liv's ear to calm her, "Easy girl, it's ok. You made it, you're safe now."

Liv whinnied in protest as her panic filled eyes bulged. Hale, his shoulder still screaming in protest, came to his feet and joined his father. The two men worked to calm the frightened animal as they whispered soothing words into both of Liv's ears, "You're good now Liv, the plane can't get you here."

Slowly the panic-stricken horse calmed, and the two men relaxed. The sound of a car engine sputtering to life could be heard over the wails of the town's folk injured in the attack. The sound of the car engine increased as the driver accelerated rapidly toward the nearby cover of the forest.

Hale stepped out of the alleyway and looked in the direction the plane had flown in. He was surprised to see the aircraft was drawing closer. It must have turned around and was now returning for another strafing run, "Damn!" Hale exclaimed.

"Language Hale." Raynar barked.

"My language is the least of our worries. The fucking bastard is coming back." Hale gruffly replied.

Raynar, maintaining his grip on Liv's bridal, turned toward the women who were standing up and brushing the snow off their clothes, "Get back down. The plane is returning."

Nea and Jenna nodded. The two women pulled Aina down with them as they laid back down on the freezing ground. Ignoring his family, Hale ran to the sleigh, and pulled out his rifle. As the plane approached, Hale noted that it was a fighter/bomber based on what he had been taught. His eyes focused on the single bomb attached to the undercarriage for a moment. *Why didn't the bastard drop the bomb on us?*

Focusing his mind on the task at hand, he raised up his rifle and took aim at the pilot. The pilot, seeing Hale standing defiantly in the middle of the street with his rifle raised, adjusted his course slightly, so that the bold Finn was lined up in his cross hairs.

Time seemed to slow to a crawl as Hale stood his ground and held his breath. As the young sniper took aim and lined up the iron sights of his rifle on the brown leather skull cap of the pilot's head, a line of bullets fired into the ground began to advance toward him. Hale ignored the danger of the approaching attack and squeezed the trigger. His rifle barked and the stock recoiled, hitting him in his bad shoulder. He choked off a scream as he dove to the side to avoid being hit by the rapidly advancing line of bullets.

As Hale dove into the alleyway and rolled to a stop, his bullet smashed through the canopy of the cockpit. The misshapen lead bullet began tumbling through the air as it struck the forehead of the pilot. The bullet, traveling at greater than the speed of sound, met the pilot's forehead which was traveling at around four hundred kilometers per hour as the plane dove with a dull smack. The bone of the pilot's forehead shattered into pieces at the impact and continued traveling into the pilot's brain at over one thousand kilometers per hour, cleaving the organ in half.

Killed instantly, the pilot slumped forward onto the aircraft's controls, causing the plane to spin out of control. A few moments later a large fireball erupted as the plane struck several trees just outside of town. Raynar, his mouth hanging open exclaimed, "My God Hale you shot the plane down!"

Raynar's sentence was choked off as a large secondary explosion from the crash site rocked the village. *The bomb.* Hale thought.

The villagers stood up and began cheering at the sudden change in fortunes. A moment before they had been cowering in the dirt, now they stood tall and shook their fists at the tower of flames burning in the forest. Hale, exhausted by what had just transpired, sank to his knees.

Nea's warm arms wrapped around him, barely registered in his mind as a fog of numbness descended upon him, "Hale you're a hero, you saved the village!" Nea shouted in excitement.

Seeing the smiling face of the woman he loved, the mother of his child, Hale snapped out of his state and smiled faintly, "Hale what's wrong? Are you hurt?" Asked the worried voice of his mother.

As Nea helped Hale to his feet he said, "I'm just tired mom, really tired."

"Let's get you home then. You'll feel better with a warm meal and some rest." Jenna, his mom said.

The family climbed back into the sleigh, as Raynar worked to fasten Liv back to the sleigh's yoke. Nea, led Hale by the hand, and helped to get him into the sleigh. His mother picked up his rifle, the rifle that they had given him for his thirteenth birthday. The weapon he had just used to kill a man. Overcome by what had happened to her boy, and what had happened to her people she began to weep.

Raynar, noticing his wife's distress, asked, "Jeanna, what's wrong? Are you hurt?"

"Our innocent boy has become a killer of men." Jenna replied, "Soon he will be forced to go back to the front and fight. He might not come back! And God willing he survives; he won't be our boy anymore." Overcome by her grief she sobbed before adding, "I want our family back."

Raynar wrapped his arms around Jenna and held her as she cried, "It will be fine honey. We taught our boy well. He's smart, and resourceful. He'll come back home to us."

Jenna looked up into the kind eyes of her husband and nodded slowly. She pulled out a handkerchief to wipe her nose, the mucus was already freezing to her skin and nodded slowly, "I hope you're right. I pray that you are right."

Hale fell asleep in Nea's arms as the Karhonen family's sleigh made its way over the frozen lands of southern Finland toward their home. Hale was woken with a kiss from Nea when they arrived. It was dark, "Aina can you bring some firewood in so your mom can start the stove?" Raynar asked.

"Yes father." Hale's sister replied.

"I'll get some soup started while your father puts Liv away in the barn." Jenna said.

"I can help my father with Liv." Hale said.

"Nonsense. You're hurt and exhausted. You are going to bed young man. I'll wake you when the food is ready." Jenna said.

Hale turned to Nea and said, "We'll you stay with me love?"

Nea shook her head, "No, I've got to go tell my parents the exciting news about the wedding tomorrow and get a dress ready. You rest now and recover your strength. You'll need it tomorrow night." Nea winked as she said the last few words.

Overhearing the exchange between his son and Nea, Raynar coughed loudly. Nea's cheeks turned a deep crimson as she realized that Hale's father had overheard her, "I'll see you tomorrow then." Hale said.

"Yes, the next time you see me, we'll be getting married!" Nea exclaimed excitedly.

The young couple embraced and kissed, "Be careful in the woods going home." Hale said.

"No worries love. The forest is my home." Nea replied as a wolf howled. The couple held hands and listened to the long and mournful bay of the predator.

Hale quickly found his way to his old bedroom and collapsed on the bed in exhaustion. He didn't bother to take any of his clothing off, and he was asleep a moment after his head hit the pillow. He slept for a few hours until he was awoken to join the family for dinner.

The family quickly fell into old patterns of familiarity as they sat around the kitchen table enjoying a meal together for the first time in months. After the meal, Jenna and Aina worked to clean up. Raynar led Hale into his study. He poured each of them a drink and then raised his glass in a toast, "To my boy Hale. A hero of Finland."

Hale raised his glass of port and gently tapped it against his father's, "I wouldn't know about that hero nonsense. I'm just trying to survive and keep my country safe."

"Boy." Hale's father paused for a moment, "I can't call you that anymore. You proved that to me today. Hale, what I witnessed today was an act of unspeakable bravery. You intentionally put yourself in danger and stood your ground while you lined up that shot. It was the damnedest thing I had ever seen. You saved lives today."

Hale opened his mouth to interrupt the praise from his father. The older Karhonen held up his hand and said, "Let me finish. I raised you to be a good hunter. Trained you how to shoot, but what I witnessed today was just incredible. How did you make that shot?"

Father, I've found that it doesn't really matter whether the enemy is standing still, moving, man, or beast. The techniques you taught me as a boy work. Hold your breath, line up the shot with the two iron sights, and pull the trigger. It sounds so simple, but the Russians don't seem to understand these basic principles. I just hope and pray that many of my fellow Finns had a father such as you. One that taught them to shoot in the manner that you taught me. We will need such men to kill many times their number of Russians for Finland to survive."

The two men embraced, "Thank you son. Your praise means a lot." Raynar said.

Raynar began to tell him of his own time in the army. How he had fought in the Finnish civil war twenty years prior. Hale enjoyed hearing his father's stories of the civil war. The stories that he had never been told as a boy growing up in Raynar's household.

Raynar had never shared the tale of this part of his life

with anyone in the family, not even his wife. For Hale's father, talk of the suffering of war was only suitable between men that had experienced its horrors. Hale had become a man worthy of hearing these tales in his father's eyes.

Despite his interest in the stories, Hale, still exhausted, fell asleep in the overstuffed chair he occupied in his father's study. As the younger Karhonen slept, the older one retrieved Hale's rifle from his childhood bedroom and sat with it in his lap for a time. He ran his fingers over the wood grain of the stock. He frowned slightly as his fingers found the indentation caused by a Russian bullet. Closing his eyes, he remembered back to the day that he had given Hale this weapon. The memory of that delighted boy excited to have his own rifle filled Raynar's mind and he smiled at the memory.

As Hale's father continued to run his fingers along the wooden grain of the rifle, his mind shifted to events earlier in the day. Hale stood his ground, holding this rifle. His boy ignored the approaching danger of the bullets and squeezed the trigger. He had never imagined that Hale would use this gift for anything other than putting food on the family's table. How wrong he had been.

Raynar poured himself another glass of port and took a long sip. A single tear ran down his cheek as he mourned the loss of his boy. Looking up, he saw the form of his son, the man, dozing in the chair across from him. Fighting back more tears, he rose quietly from the chair and fetched his gun cleaning supplies.

Over the next hour, he worked slowly to clean out the grit in the barrel. He took the gun apart, and lovingly cared for each individual part. He expertly assembled it all back together. Then he oiled the metal of the exterior of the weapon, and finally, using wood oil, the stock. Next, he took each of the three clips, and carefully removed the bullets. He cleaned and oiled each of them until the dull metal shined as if it was new again. He was determined to ensure that this weapon would never fail Hale.

Finished, Raynar leaned the rifle against one of the two bookshelves in his study. He looked up at Hale, his son's eyes were open, "How long have you been awake?"

Hale yawned and said, "For a few minutes. You cleaned my rifle?"

"Yes, it looked like it hadn't been done properly in a while." Raynar replied.

"No, it hadn't. I've been moving and fighting non-stop for nearly the last week." Hale said.

"I've told you my stories. Now tell me yours. What's it like fighting the Russians?" Raynar asked.

Hale's father poured them each another drink and then sat back and listened as Hale told him the events of the last week, "It's amazing you managed to survive all of that." Raynar said.

"Many good men weren't as lucky. I don't feel like I am special, that I did anything unusual to live. In this kind of war against the Russians, it seems to be more about luck than anything." Hale said.

Raynar downed the last bit of port in his glass and stood. Hale followed suit. Raynar took a step forward and embraced his son, "Son, I'm proud of you. Of the man you have become. If you don't." Hale's father paused for a moment to collect himself as he fought back tears, "If you don't come back. Know that I am proud of the man that you have become. I will help to raise your child and be there for them as long as God wills it."

Hale looked into his father's eyes. He could see that the older man was fighting back tears as he said the words. Hale, overcome by emotion of the moment, began to weep, "It's all right son. Let it out." Raynar said.

Hale cried in his father's arms for several minutes. Finally, he said, "I hadn't thought yet about the possibility of my child growing up without me. Thank you for your promise father. It will help to ease my heart in the days to come.

Chapter 10

Mid-Afternoon Karelia Isthmus Finland, Village of Perkjarvi, December 6th, 1939

The morning dawned sunny and bitterly cold. The sunlight reflected off the white canopy shrouding the earth causing the Karhonen family to squint as old Liv pulled their sleigh into the village. Arriving at the church, they found Nea's family already there putting up decorations for the ceremony to come.

The two families worked together, to transform the simple chapel into a festive room filled with color. As two o'clock drew near, Hale excused himself. He knocked on the door of Oskar's office, "Come in."

"Hello father, it's almost time. Do you mind if I change in here?" Hale asked.

"Go right ahead. I'm just finishing up some lunch. Would you like some?" Oskar asked.

"No, we ate heartily before leaving the farm this morning. My aunt is working on a fantastic feast back at the farm for our reception later." Hale smiled as he said, "I should probably save some room."

"Indeed, my son, you are wise beyond your years. Never disappoint a woman who has worked hard to fill your belly." Oskar said.

The rotund preacher turned his attention back to his meal. Hale finished dressing in his Sunday best and quietly slipped out of Oskar's office. Looking down at himself he admired the look and feel of his black suit. He closed his eyes for a minute and smiled. Soon he would be joined to Nea forever.

Hale rejoined his family in the main sanctuary. His mother, seeing him in his suit, came and fussed over him to ensure all was perfect, "There, now step back, let me have a good look at you."

Hale dutifully took a step back from his mother, and turned slowly, "How do I look?"

"Like a handsome war hero ready to meet his bride." Jeanna replied.

The clock in the back of the church began playing it's on the hour melody. During the pause between the melody and the hour dong, the sound of a sleigh pulling up outside the church could be heard. As the second dong rang then fell silent, the church door opened.

Everyone inside the church squinted at the sudden change in light. The bright sunlight of the sun streamed directly into the church blinding everyone inside as they looked at the open door. A shadowy figure, they couldn't tell who, stepping into the doorway. Whoever they were paused for several moments taking in the sight of the decorated church.

Finally, the person stepped forward into the sanctuary, it was Nea. She wore a white dress. Sitting on top of her head, catching the rays of sunlight was a golden crown. As Hale met the penetrating gaze of her emerald eyes, she smiled at him. The moment those eyes settled on him he froze. *She's amazing!* Hale was so transfixed by Nea, he froze. He stood there, unable to move, with mouth hanging open at the sight of her. *So beautiful.*

After several long moments he shook off the spell that Nea's appearance had cast upon him. He used his eyes to slowly look Nea up and down amazed at the transformation. The farm girl, his childhood friend, had been transformed into a gorgeous woman. Her red hair was braided and wound around her head in an intricate design. She had found some makeup somewhere. Just enough of it had been applied to accentuate her natural beauty without overwhelming it.

Resting across her shoulders was a wrap crafted from the pelt of a white wolf. The wrap covered up her prominently displayed breasts keeping the exposed skin mostly covered but revealing enough of a hint underneath to set the hearts of every male in the room racing. Hale's eyes continued to fall and settled on her slightly bulging midsection, *My child.*

Hale lowered his eyes further, continuing to take all of her in and trying to commit this moment to memory. The dress accentuated the natural curve of Nea's hips, and then loosened up around her legs creating a bell like shape as the hem of the dress ended a few inches off the floor at ankle level. Hale, ignoring protocol, walked up to Nea and asked, "How did you find a wedding dress so quickly?"

Nea, pleased with the effect she was having on Hale said, "As soon as I knew I was pregnant, we traveled to Viipuri. There is a shop that sells nothing but wedding dresses. You should have seen it, it was incredible."

"Not as incredible as you are now." Hale replied.

Nea's cheeks turned a deep shade of crimson at the compliment.

"You're looking pretty good yourself." Nea said.

"You've seen me in this before in church." Hale said.

"Yes, but now you really fill it out. The army life has certainly agreed with you." Nea said.

Hale opened his mouth to reply but was interrupted by the sound of a muffled belch coming from the other side of the door set in the back of the sanctuary. A moment later, the priest's rotund figure came bursting through the portal.

Seeing the bride standing just inside the doorway at the back of the church he said, "Let's get started. Impi start playing."

The older lady nodded at Father Oskar's command and started playing the piano. Hale quickly strolled down the aisle and took his place at the front of the sanctuary on the right side. Simultaneously, Nea's father joined her by the double doors at the back of the sanctuary. She slipped her arm into the older man's, made eye contact with him, and whispered, "Now."

The pair started taking slow steps down the aisle toward Hale. Raynar, stood just behind Hale, beamed with pride. Jenna, Hale's mother, sat on the left side of the first pew right near Raynar. She began crying as Impi continued to play Canon D, the traditional wedding processional piece.

As Hale watched his bride come down the aisle, the rest of the world seemed to fall away as his vision filled with only Nea. Memories of their time together growing up, began to flash through his mind, Nea as a little girl playing in the mud of the creek beside him. Then as an awkward ten-year-old, running across a meadow. His memory shifted as she became a pre-teen, the earliest hints of the woman she was to become had appeared. She smiled down at him and held up a bug, "Eat this!" She begged.

His mind advanced a few more years to her fifteenth birthday. That was the day he had noticed her as a woman. The day they clumsily shared their first kiss. Finally, his mind focused on the Nea that was coming down the aisle toward him.

The sight of this woman stole his breath and froze the beat of his heart. As the advancing pair reached the last pew, Nea's father released her and sat down beside his wife. Hale's bride took the final few steps on her own. As she reached the front of the church, the couple turned and faced each other.

Father Oskar raised his arms high over the couple and began, "The Grace of our Lord Jesus Christ, the love of God, and the communion of the Holy Spirit be with you all."

The crowd responded in unison, "And also with you."

"We have come together in the presence of God to witness the marriage of Hale and Nea, to surround them with our prayers, and to share in their joy."

Father Oskar took a deep breath and continued, "The scriptures teach us that the bond and covenant of marriage is a gift of God, a holy mystery in which two become one flesh, an image of union of Christ and the church. As Hale and Nea give themselves to each other today, we remember that at Cana in Galilee our Lord Jesus Christ made the wedding feast a sign of God's reign of love."

Father Oskar once again paused for a moment to take a breath. Hale's mind swam in Nea's emerald eyes as Oskar continued, "Let us enter into this celebration confident that, through the Holy Spirit, Christ is present with us now. Also, we pray that this couple may fulfill God's purpose for the whole of their lives."

Hale glanced at Nea nervously. He felt a trickle of sweat begin to run down his back as the weight of the moment hit him. He took a deep breath and smiled at Nea. She returned the smile. He could tell that she was nervous as well. *I think I was less nervous the moment before that first tank fired at me. Why am I feeling this way? I want to marry Nea!* Pulling his mind back into the present, he turned his attention back to Father Oskar.

"Beloved people of God, we have come together in the presence of the almighty to witness and bless the covenant of love and fidelity Hale and Nea are to make with each other."

Father Oskar paused dramatically to let the weight of his words register with the audience before continuing, "The union of two persons in heart, body, and mind is intended by God for the mutual help and comfort given one another in prosperity and adversity; and that their love may be a blessing to all whom they encounter. This solemn covenant is not to be entered into unadvisedly or lightly, but reverently, deliberately, and with commitment to seek God's will in their lives."

Turning to Hale, Father Oskar asked, "Hale, will you have Nea to be your wife, to live together in the covenant of marriage? Will you love her, comfort her, honor and keep her in sickness and health, and forsaking all others, be faithful to her as long as you both shall live?"

Hale swallowed nervously as the priest spoke the words. *Why is this more difficult than facing a platoon of Russians?* Nea smiled nervously at him as he stood in silence for several seconds before saying loudly, "I will."

Turning to Nea, Father Oskar repeated the question. Without hesitation Nea smiled and said, "I will."

Hale took Nea's hands in his as Father Oskar turned to the families sitting in the pews and asked, "Will you the families of Hale and Nea, give your love and blessing to this new family?"

Both families replied in unison, "We will."

"Will all of you, by God's grace, do everything in your power to uphold and care for these two persons in their life together?" Father Oskar asked.

Both families again replied in unison, "We will."

Turning back to Hale, Father Oskar said, "Hale, living in the promise of God, joined in Christ in your baptism; will you give yourself to Nea in love and faithfulness? Will you share your life with her in joy and in sorrow, in health, and in sickness, for richer, for poorer, for better, for worse, and will you be faithful to her as long as you both shall live?

Hale, growing in confidence, said, "I will, with the help of God."

Father Oskar repeated the question to Nea, who replied happily, "I will, with the help of God."

Father Oskar turned from Nea to look at those in attendance and said, "Families, friends, and all those gathered here with Hale and Nea, will you promise to support and care for them in their life together, to sustain and pray for them in times of trouble, to give thanks with them in times of joy, to honor the bonds of their covenant, and to affirm the love of God reflected in their lives?"

Both families replied in unison, "We will, with the help of God."

Father Oskar raised his hands into the air and said, "Eternal God, our creator and redeemer, as you gladdened the wedding at Cana and Galilee by the presence of your Son, so bring joy to this wedding by his presence now. Look in favor upon Hale and Nea and grant that they, rejoicing in all your gifts, may at length celebrate the unending marriage feast with Christ our Lord, one God, now and forever."

Father Oskar placed a hand on Hale and Nea and said, "In the eyes of God I now pronounce you man and wife. Hale, you may kiss your bride."

Hale stepped forward and took Nea into his arms. His lips eagerly sought hers. As their lips met for the first time as husband and wife, a single tear of joy slid down Nea's cheek. Both families stood and cheered as the newlyweds ended their kiss and turned toward them hand in hand. Simultaneously, the dull shrill of the air raid siren began to wail.

The couple looked past the adoring eyes of their families toward the double doors that led to the outside. The faces of the people in the pews turned from joy to horror. Many sprang to their feet with panic in their eyes as the siren continued to wail out its warning of approaching danger. As the siren fell silent a series of dull thumps could be heard coming from the south.

Hale kissed Nea on the lips quickly and said, "I love you!"

Turning to Raynar Hale said, "I'm going to go find out what is going on."

"I'll join you." Raynar replied.

Hale shook his head, "No, get Nea, Mom and Aina to safety. I'll come home as soon as I am able."

Hale's mother objected, "You're hurt, let others handle it."

"I'm more than capable of fighting mother. The village must be protected." Hale replied.

As if to emphasize the situation, the drone of aircraft engines could be heard overhead. As Hale ran down the aisle toward the doors, a whistling sound could be heard outside. He turned his head to see if his family was moving on his word, they weren't. Instead they were still standing where he had left them. A state of shock etched on their faces.

Hale paused, turned back toward his family and yelled, "Get-"

He was cut short by a loud explosion outside. The force of the explosion blew the double doors of the church inward. The shockwave knocked Hale to the ground as the concussion from the detonation expanded.

Hale, uninjured, quickly scrambled to his feet and ran toward the now open doorway, "Hale don't leave us!" Nea screamed.

Hale ignored Nea's plea and emerged onto the street. There was dust, debris, and smoke everywhere as he looked around for the family sleigh. The shattered remains of several sleighs filled his vision. Their horses lay on the ground either slain, or in the throes of agony from the gruesome injuries sustained in the blast. Thanks to their experience with the plane yesterday, Hale's family had pulled their sleigh into the alleyway between buildings.

Hale ran around the corner of the church to his right. There, tied to a power pole, was Liv. Frightened by the explosion, she was trying to pull herself free. Hale ran to the terrified animal and said, "Shhhh it's ok girl your safe."

Hale's words of comfort had an immediate effect on the frightened animal, and she began to calm. Satisfied that Liv would still be around to carry his family to safety, Hale pulled his rifle from the floor of the sleigh. As he emerged from the alleyway, he looked down the main street of the village and spotted a group of Finnish soldiers setting up defenses at the edge of town.

As he ran toward them, he heard something in the air above him shrieking. Looking up, he spotted a Russian fighter/bomber in a steep dive toward the village center. Strapped to the undercarriage of the plunging aircraft was a large bomb.

Suddenly, the bomb was released from the aircraft which pulled up sharply. The bomb, painted a dull gray, whistled through the air as it plummeted toward the hospital. Hale, fearing the worst, stopped his run and watched as the five-hundred-pound instrument of destruction slowly fell toward the roof of the structure the pilot had targeted.

Perfectly aimed, the bomb burst through the center of the red cross painted on the hospital's roof and exploded.

The force of the blast blew out the windows of the building. As flames began to billow out of the broken windows the walls collapsed, and the roof crashed to the ground.

"Oh my God! That was the hospital, you animal!" Hale raged and shook his fist at the retreating aircraft. Already out of range there was nothing he could do.

Hale's attention was drawn to the gunfire that suddenly erupted on the edge of town. As he looked in that direction, he saw two platoons of Finnish soldiers, using overturned wagons as cover, firing into the forest. In addition to the riflemen, two groups of three men each worked quickly to set up heavy weapons. One a machine gun, the other, an anti-tank gun.

The roof of the southernmost building of the village suddenly exploded, *That wasn't a bomb, that was a high explosive tank round. The Russians are here!* Hale turned back toward the church and ran inside.

The sanctuary was in chaos as both families stood around and argued, "Enough!" Hale bellowed.

Everyone in the church stopped and looked at Hale, "The Russians are attacking the village. Dad, get Mom, Aina and Nea into the sleigh and moving toward the farm now! You should be safe there for tonight. Turning to Nea's parents he said, "Do you have transportation?"

Nea's father Tarmo replied, "Our sleigh was parked out front."

"Then you don't have a sleigh anymore." Turning to his father Hale said, "Can you take Nea's family too?"

Hale's father nodded, "Yes, they can ride on the rails."

"Good that's settled. The rest of you make your way out of the village to the north. I don't know how many Russians are out there, but we have maybe two platoons trying to set up a defense on the southside of town. That isn't going to hold the bastards for long, so get moving!"

Ignoring the tidal wave of questions that erupted from his friends and family, Hale turned and ran out of the church. He made his way back to the family sleigh, spent a moment comforting Liv, and then pulled his PPD 34 from the sleigh floor. *I don't have any ammunition for you, but you might come in handy if I can find some.*

Hale left the alleyway and ran toward the south edge of the village. As he ran, he saw the Finnish defenders had finished setting up their heavy weapons. The anti-tank gun, one of the precious few 37mm PstK/36's Finland owned, fired a shot at a target in the forest. A moment later an explosion erupted at the edge of the tree line. *They got one of the bastards!* Hale thought.

As he approached the makeshift barricade of overturned wagons, the defenders had hastily erected in the middle of the street, automatic weapons fire erupted, driving Hale to the ground. He dove to the muddy earth in his Sunday best, ruining the suit. Cursing, at the mud, the cold, and the bullets, he scrambled on all fours until he reached the thin line of soldiers defending Perkjavi.

One of the defenders, a sergeant judging by his stripes, looked down at Hale in disdain, "What good do you think you are going to accomplish boy? You'll only get in the way of the real soldiers trying to save your ass."

Hale glared up at the man and said, "I'm a sniper with Er.P3, I was getting married in the church."

Hearing Hale's retort the sergeant noticed Hale's well

cared for rifle for the first time. He gestured toward the forest and said, "Then by all means snipe. It's not going to do much good, but another man might buy the villagers a few more seconds to escape. We've been ordered by 5th Division headquarters to fight a delaying action here to buy our people a little time before we continue our retreat toward the Mannerheim Line."

Hale opened his mouth to ask another question, but the Sergeant, who had been reloading his rifle, stood and fired a shot. Hale quickly followed suit. He gasped at the sheer number of Soviets charging toward them. Ignoring the bullets snapping around him he carefully took aim and put a bullet in one of the enemy soldiers. Their shots fired; the two men were forced to duck back down as a hail of lead whistled around them.

Both men sat down on the muddy road, their backs to the overturned wagon, "Nice shot. I'm Taisto."

"Hale."

Taisto turned to a group of men working on setting up a heavy machine gun and yelled, "If you ladies don't start firing now, we are fucked."

Heeding Taisto's words, a large man, Hale couldn't see his name tag, grabbed the gun, and set it down on the top of a wagon. Using the overturned cart as a stand, he squeezed the trigger as he moved the gun back and forth.

Hale stole a quick glance over the edge of the wagon he hid behind to choose his next target. The targets were quickly disappearing as the heavy machine gun mowed down row after row of charging Russian soldiers. The air was filled with the sounds of screaming Russians and a mist of blood as they were cut to pieces by the dozens.

Hale quickly ducked back down and started to smile.

He turned to Taisto to share the good news. As he did so, the heavy machine gunner was blown into messy bits as a high explosive tank round, penetrated the overturned wagon they were using as cover, and detonated on top of him. In an instant, the big man was torn to shreds, along with the crew feeding bullets to the gun, and the wagon they used as cover.

Almost immediately the 37mm PstK/36 anti-tank gun barked in response. The round slammed into the Soviet T-28 tank that had fired the shot and penetrated the front armor. A fraction of a second later, the turret of the enemy tank was blown into the sky, as the round found the ammunition bunker inside the tank and detonated it.

Taisto, cursing at the loss of the machine gun, stood up to fire a shot. As soon as his head rose above the protection afforded by the wagon, it exploded into a bloody mess.

"Summer of cunts!" Hale exclaimed as he was covered in blood.

He looked around to take stock of the situation. Nearly half of the defenders had been killed in the last sixty seconds. Gazing through the chaotic scene, the young sniper made eye contact with another man. The man, who shook violently as he worked to reload his rifle, had the two stripes of a Finnish corporal on his epaulettes. Hale took a deep breath and peeked around the edge of the wagon. He would not make the same mistake as the former Sergeant. *I have no desire for my brains to join Taisto's all over the ground.*

Hale's eyes widened as they filled with the sight of hundreds of Russians advancing toward them. The Red Army Soldiers were stepping over the corpses of their comrades recently slain by the efforts of the heavy machine gunner. The corporal, separated from Hale by the crater that used to be the unit's heavy machine gun squad's position, fired a shot, slew a Russian, and yelled, "We can't hold here, retreat further into town!"

The corporal's statement was punctuated by the loud shot from the 37mm PstK/36 anti-tank gun. The projectile slammed into the armor of an advancing T-26 light tank causing it to explode. Flame shot out of the port holes of the tank as it rolled to a stop and the men inside screamed in agony as they boiled alive.

The gun crew worked quickly to prepare the PstK/36 for the withdrawal. As they did so, the remainder of the Finnish survivors stood and fled. Half of them were immediately shot in the back by the tidal wave of dark green advancing toward their collapsing position. Hale, desperate to buy the gun crew the time they needed to pull the precious weapon to safety, looked about for a faster firing weapon.

Miraculously, a PPD 34 magazine, covered in gore and mud lay at his feet, "Where did you come from?" Hale asked.

Placing his rifle on his left shoulder, he drew his PPD 34 from his right shoulder, ejected the empty magazine, and slammed the gory one home. The mess covered magazine, slid into place with a satisfying click. Hale smiled, *Judging by the weight this magazine is full.*

As the gun crew, staying low, began to pull their gun down the muddy street, Hale stood and hosed down the Russians with his PPD 34. Surprised by his attack, hundreds of Russians dove to the ground seeking cover. Two dozen of them would never rise again.

Ammunition expended; Hale ducked back down

behind the wagon. Desperate for another weapon to help stem the tide, he looked around. His eyes landed on the legless torso of a dead Finn nearby. His gray uniform was covered in mud, blood, and guts. Hale ignored the horrific scene. Instead his eyes focused on the two grenades clipped to the man's suspenders, he smiled.

He exposed himself for a moment as he reached over to pull the body close. Gunfire erupted. The bullets smacked into the mud all around him as he hauled the body back under cover. He quickly unclipped the two grenades, pulled the pins, and heaved them in the direction of the Russians.

As soon as they exploded, he stood, put a bullet into a Russian that was too stupid to dive for cover, and ran up the main street of the village northward. As he passed the raging fire that used to be the hospital, he ducked into the alleyway where Liv and the sleigh had been parked, it was empty.

Smiling, his eyes followed the trail caused by the sleigh as it had exited the alleyway to the east and then turned north, *Good, they followed my instructions.*

Hale ejected the clip from his rifle and slammed a new one home. He peeked around the corner of the church. The Russians had reached the barricade and were pouring through the hole created by the tank shell that destroyed the heavy machine gun crew.

He took a deep breath and held it. Taking aim at a Russian he pulled the trigger. Before his first victim could hit the ground, he operated the bolt on his rifle and slew another. He repeated this move over and over until the Russians were able to pinpoint his position. A barrage of bullets slammed into the corner of the church forcing the young sniper to take cover.

His rifle clips and submachine gun magazine empty, he looked around to see if any other Finnish soldiers were about, there were none. *Father, I hope you have a good lead on these jackals, I don't have anything left to buy you more time.*

Hale turned and ran toward the tree line behind the church. As he ran, he noticed the tracks left by the family sleigh as they turned northward and followed the tree line. *Heading right for the road out of town. Godspeed.* Hale thought. As Hale ran, a few Russians caught sight of him, raised their rifles, and fired at the fleeing Finn. They missed.

As he reached the tree line, a thought occurred to him, *There's three bullets in my pocket left from the first clip that I didn't fully use.*

Smiling Hale dug the bullets out of his pocket, along with one of his metal clips. He loaded the three precious bullets into the clip and then slammed it into the open breach of his rifle. With practiced ease, he pulled the clip out of the gun as he felt the three bullets click into place within the gun's internal magazine. *Now I wait for the right opportunity.*

He withdrew into the tree line and waited. As the adrenaline left his body, he began to shiver. The mud and blood covered suit he wore did little to protect him from the oppressive cold of a Finnish December, *I should have taken a moment to grab my coat.*

After what felt like an eternity of shaking in the bitter cold as his body fought against hypothermia, a pair of Russians appeared in the alleyway between the church and a house. The two men appeared to be shirking their responsibility as they lit two cigarettes and began speaking with each other. Hale started to rub his hands together to return feeling to his frozen appendages.

The young sniper crept to the edge of the tree line and looked to his left and right. There were no other Russians in site, *This might work, but I need them to come to me.*

Hale decided to gamble, he set his rifle behind a tree so that the Russians wouldn't be able to see it and stepped out into the open, "Hey Shitheads. I'm freezing, can I come back into the village?"

The two Russians immediately ceased their conversation and turned toward the sound of Hale's voice. Fortunately for Hale, they didn't understand Finnish. The Red Army Soldiers, neither over the age of twenty, raised their rifles. The one on the left barked, "Stoy!"

Hale raised his arms and showed the enemy soldiers his palms, "Whatever you say."

He waited patiently as the two Russians ran toward him, their rifles pointed at his chest. He coyly began stepping back toward the tree line, "Stoy!" The Russian barked again.

Ignoring the order, Hale took a large step back, snatched up his rifle, and put a bullet into the vocal Russian. As he fired, he smiled and said, "Stoy this you swine."

Hale's un-aimed shot crashed into the chest of the man knocking him off his feet. The other soldier stopped running and fired off a shot at Hale as the young sniper dove for cover behind a tree. Rolling back to his feet, he emerged from the protection of the trunk on the other side of it, raised his rifle, and put a bullet right into the shocked open mouth of the remaining Russian.

Wasting no time, Hale ran to the first Russian corpse. He quickly removed the man's dark green greatcoat and red star emblazoned hat. Next, he snatched up the man's pack and ammo satchel, and then turned and ran for the tree line. Finding cover behind a large oak tree, he quickly put the coat and hat on.

Next, he plunged his hands into the ammo satchel. He felt the cold metal of dozens of bullets with his fingertips. Smiling at his good fortune he set about reloading all three of his clips. Finished, he counted the bullets he had left, *Thirty, just enough to load my PPD 34 magazine.*

As Hale worked to place bullets into his submachine gun's gore encrusted magazine, a group of Russians arrived to investigate the gun fire. Seeing the slain corpses of their comrades, the squad's Sergeant immediately began barking orders. The squad quickly fanned out and began advancing toward the tree line, as the Soviet Sergeant bent down to investigate the coatless corpse.

Hale, ignoring the Russians, continued loading the magazine of his PPD 34. Finishing, he stole a quick glance to see where the advancing Russians were. The nearest one, saw Hale, raised his rifle, and put a bullet into the tree, about two inches from Hale's head as he yelled, "Vot." Repeatedly.

Hale exhaled, ejecting a large cloud of steam from his mouth. Snatching up a rock from the ground, he heaved it to his right. The movement and noise of the rock hitting the ground, caused all seven of the advancing Russians to turn and fire in the direction of the rock. Hale emerged from behind the oak in the opposite direction that he had thrown the rock.

Yelling, he hosed down the squad of Russians with his PPD 34. As the last Soviet toppled over, the Sergeant stood and took aim at Hale. His weapon, empty, Hale dove for cover as the Sergeant squeezed the trigger. The rifle roared, sending the bullet into the space that Hale had just occupied a moment before. Like before, he rolled into a crouching position, on the other side of the tree trunk, snatched up his rifle and as he came back to his feet put a shot into the Sergeant's head.

Before the Sergeant's corpse hit the ground, Hale was running toward the nearest Russian body. He snatched up the man's ammo satchel, the three grenades clipped to his belt, and the man's backpack. The sound of whistles and shouts filled the air, as Hale took a moment to remove the man's gloves.

Before any Russians could arrive on the grisly scene of carnage, Hale disappeared into the forest. He ran for ten minutes, trying to put some distance between himself and the Red Army Soldiers he had slain. As he ran, he spotted a fallen log that would afford him good cover while he regrouped. He stopped running and listened for sixty seconds to determine if there was anyone pursuing him. Satisfied there wasn't, he slipped behind the log to hide and went to work.

He started by clipping the three grenades to his own belt, and then checked the ammo satchel. Like the first one, this satchel had at least fifty rounds of 7.62 mm ammunition. *Now I understand why their aim is so bad. I don't think these Russians ever use their ammo.*

He counted out fifty rounds as he removed the bullets one by one from the satchel. Satisfied that he had more than enough, he worked to quickly reload the PPD 34 magazine as the first sounds of the pursuit drew closer. He paused for a moment to listen to the shouting and whistles. *I wonder how many of the bastards they sent after me? Not much sense in hanging around and giving them a chance to find me. Thanks to Stalin's war machine, I'm now nicely armed. Time to head to the farm, collect my family, and lead them to safety behind the Mannerheim line.*

Dressed like a Russian, Hale set off in the direction of his family's farm. *With these clothes I took, I look like a Russian now. I sure hope there aren't any Finnish snipers lurking in these woods.* Hale chuckled out loud at the thought, *Thank God it's getting dark.*

He set a brisk pace, not wanting to waste the remaining hour of daylight. As he ran, his thoughts drifted back to the ceremony earlier in the day, *I never realized Nea could be so beautiful! I'm a lucky man.*

Despite the cold, thoughts of his new wife warmed his nether regions. As he ran, his mind filled with the pleasures of the night to come. He dwelled on these happy thoughts as the shouting Russians, and the kilometers fell away. Once the Sun set, he was forced to slow his pace. As soon as the last of the fading rays of the yellow orb disappeared, the forest was cloaked in a sea of blackness. With no moon on this night, Hale could hardly see his hand if he held it out two feet in front of his eyes. Fortunately for the young sniper, he knew these woods like the back of that same hand.

About a kilometer out, no longer fearing losing his way in the sea of murky darkness, he quickened his pace to a brisk walk. *I'll be home in time for dinner.* He smiled at the thought as his stomach voiced its agreement with a dull growl. An owl hooted to his right, startling him back into the present. He caught a hint of wood smoke smell with his nose and smiled, *Not long now. I wonder what Auntie is making tonight?*

His reverie was shattered by the noise of gunfire as the sounds from several rifles firing nearly simultaneously broke the silence of the forest. *The Russians are here? My God!*

Hale, heedless of the darkness, increased his pace. As

he ran, branches whacked him across the face, and thorns pulled at his clothes. He ignored both and continued moving as quickly as his weary legs would take him toward the sound of the gun fire and home.

Chapter 11

Evening, Karelia Finland, Karhonen Farm, North of the Village of Perkjarvi, December 6th, 1939

Hale continued to run for home as another salvo of gunfire pierced the darkness. A moment later three more shots boomed out. *They returned fire, that means they are still fighting! Who is fighting though? Dad is the only male there, so it should have been one shot not three.*

Hale reached the edge of the farm's clearing. He sighed in relief as his eyes took in the curls of smoke rising from the farmhouse's chimney and a faint yellow glow in the windows. Otherwise the farm was shrouded in darkness. Thank God, *the Soviets haven't stormed the house yet.*

To the north of the house, sat the barn. The large structure was completely dark and showed no signs of life.

Between Hale and the barn lay a small pond, it's smooth surface frozen solid by the bitter cold.

Hale's eyes saw several flashes of light to his left as rifle fire erupted. He could hear the bullets impacting the wooden siding of the house all save one. The one, smashed through glass, and traveled into the house. The occupants of the house, presumably Hale's family, returned fire.

This time there were only two shots fired. *Was someone hit? What happened to the third shooter?* Hale's thoughts began to race with worry, *Dad, Mom, or Nea?*

A few moments later, a third shot rang out, followed by a loud scream, *They got one! I've got to get into this fight, but I need more information, or I'll just get myself killed. Patience Hale, Dad can hang on for a little while longer.*

Hale pulled his rifle off his shoulder, got down on his knees, and began crawling toward the Russian position. To avoid detection, he attempted to use the contours of the terrain as much as possible as he crept forward. The Red Army rifles flashed in the darkness and Hale was momentarily blinded by the spectacle as the enemy squad fired at his home.

Hale's family again returned fire this time with three rifles simultaneously. As silence fell, Hale's ears registered the sound of an approaching truck. He stopped crawling and looked in the direction of the noise. The light from two headlights, mostly covered with tape, blinded him. *Shouldn't have looked right at the lights.* Hale inwardly cursed himself for the mistake.

As his eyes adjusted, he spotted the black form of another truck parked behind where he thought the rifleman was positioned. *They must have radioed for help. I guess the pathetic bastards couldn't handle an old farmer and some women without backup.*

The brakes from the truck squealed as the vehicle lurched to a stop. Immediately a group of men debarked from the rear and began pulling out objects that Hale couldn't make out. As the young Finn watched the Soviets work, he caught the Russian word for mortar. A word he was taught to recognize. It came from one of the riflemen. *Mortar? Oh shit! They are going to destroy the house.*

Hale, acting quickly, pulled his three grenades off his belt, yanked the pins out, and heaved two toward the crew unloading the mortar. The last one he threw towards the group of riflemen deployed against the house. The three grenades exploded in sequence creating a boom, boom, boom, cycle throwing the Russians into chaos.

The first grenade landed at the feet of the mortar crew as they worked to unload the truck. When it exploded, it slew six of the eight men of the squad instantly and sent shrapnel into the faces of the two men in the back of the truck. The second grenade landed on the canopy of the truck. The explosion from this grenade finished the two survivors of the mortar squad. The force of the explosion pushed them violently onto the deck of the truck. Their backs were torn apart by shrapnel and flame as they died almost instantly from the explosion.

The third grenade went off roughly in the center of the line of riflemen arrayed against the house. This grenade instantly blew the legs of the nearest riflemen off and sent shrapnel into the next two closest Russians. A moment after this explosion, the original grenade's blast ruptured the gas tank of the mortar squad's truck, creating a large secondary explosion.

This explosion lifted the rear of the truck into the air and set off a box of mortar rounds still in the bed of the truck. As three mortar rounds cooked off simultaneously the truck vaporized into a massive fireball which killed the driver, sitting up front in the cab.

Hale was blinded by the light and stunned by the concussion of the large blast. He cried out in pain as his ears rang from the detonations. A moment later four more explosions erupted in a rough circle around the surviving Russian riflemen. These grenades had been thrown blindly by the Russians in response to Hale's attack. Fortunately for Hale, they had no idea where he actually was. As a result, none of these grenades landed near him.

They don't know where I am. Hale waited patiently for his ears to stop ringing and the stars in his vision to clear. After about two minutes he was confident that he could see the enemy, should they appear. He scanned the area where he believed the riflemen to be, trying to determine where they were so he could attack. They weren't there.

As Hale's mind asked the question, *Where did they go?* The answer became apparent as three rifle shots erupted from the house. Swiveling his head toward the house, Hale saw one of the four surviving Russians go down. The other two shots missed.

Hale raised his own rifle, took aim, and killed one of the three surviving enemy soldiers. As he operated the bolt on his rifle, one of the men reached the front door of the house, put his shoulder down, crashed into the front door, and smashed his way inside.

As Hale raised his rifle to take aim, the last Russian disappeared through the now open doorway. A moment after the Russians entered the house, a series of gun shots came from inside the structure. Hale ran toward the open doorway fearing the worst as the gunfire abruptly stopped.

As he cleared the threshold and entered the house, he raised his rifle. His father lay on the floor, a pool of blood slowly expanded underneath him. A Russian, standing over his father, heard Hale enter the house. The man began to swivel around and raise his rifle toward the unexpected interloper.

Hale, barely pausing to take aim, put a bullet into the forehead of the man that had shot his father. The Russian collapsed to his knees and fell forward onto Hale's father. Hale took several steps toward his dad as he worked the bolt on his rifle. His father, still alive, groaned in agony.

Hale's eye caught movement off to his right and began to turn toward it. Simultaneously, his mother emerged from another room behind Hale, and shrieked at the sight of her husband bleeding on the floor. Hale, ignoring his mother, turned toward the movement. His heart sank as he saw the second Russian's arm wrapped around Nea. He held a blade with a jagged serrated edge pressed to her neck.

The Soviet barked gruffly, "Bros' pistolet!"

Hale, understanding the man's meaning, slowly nodded as he raised his left hand. He maintained eye contact with the soldier, as he squatted and placed his rifle onto the floor. As he began to stand back up, his mother began weeping, "He's dead!" She wailed.

Ignoring his grief-stricken mother, Hale made eye contact with the Russian. Nervous, the man, a sergeant judging by the two red triangles on his collar, swallowed hard, and tightened the grip of his shaking hand on the knife. He smiled at Hale and pressed it a little into Nea's flesh. The blade penetrated her flesh, causing a single drop of blood to slowly slide down the blade toward the pommel.

Enraged at the sight of his wife being hurt, Hale took a step forward. The Russian held up his left hand which had been gripping Nea around the waist and indicated for Hale to stop. Fuming, the young Finn obeyed.

The Russian, a middle-aged man, revealed several missing teeth as he smiled at Hale, and squeezed Nea's breast through her dress with his left hand. Hale shuddered in rage at the violation of his wife and took another step forward. The Russian responded by pressing the knife a little deeper into Nea's flesh. Nea let out a painful gasp.

Hale again stopped and made eye contact with the man that held his wife hostage, "Ne boleye togo." The Soviet blurted gruffly.

Hale, understanding the meaning of the words, nodded slowly and held his hands up in supplication. The Russian smiled at Hale and began lifting Nea's dress with his left hand. Hale quivered in rage, as he was forced to watch this man violate his wife.

For a moment his consciousness left the scene and he remembered back to the day Nea had worn this dress for the first time. She slowly spun around in front of him modeling the dress and asked, "What do you think?"

Hale took in the bright red dress, his eyes focused on the white flowers that dotted the surface and nodded in appreciation, "It's beautiful. Especially on you."

Nea smiled. Hale's thoughts jolted back into the present. The man that held his wife at knife point had gotten his hand all the way up under her dress and reached toward her crotch. She let out a gasp, as rough fingers pulled at her underwear.

Helpless to resist, she remained perfectly still, fearing that the knife would dig deeper into her neck if she resisted. The Russian, growing frustrated with her dress, roared, "Snimi seychas devochka!"

Understanding the brute's meaning, Nea reached over her shoulder with her free left hand and unfastened the clasp of her dress. The Soviet loosened his grip, and allowed the dress to fall away. Underneath, Nea was wearing a lacey and very provocative piece of lingerie.

The white lace teddy was held to her body by two thin straps of fabric that rested on her shoulders. The silky material expanded to partially cover her breasts leaving most of her cleavage visible. The garment extended to cover her body below her breasts, ending in a hem of white lace material crafted to look like flowers at her mid-thigh.

The Russian smiled as he took in an eyeful of the provocative garment that Nea was wearing. Excited, he began to breathe hard. Nea nearly retched at the smell of his foul breath. His breath reeked of rotting cabbage and vodka. She made eye contact with Hale and begged with her eyes, *Do something.*

Hale, fearful that any move on his part would result in Nea's death. Stood completely still. His vision turned red as his blood boiled over the sight of his wife being violated. The Russian, enjoying Hale's reaction, ran his free left hand up and down Nea's body. He held his hand over her crotch and paused dramatically to look up at Hale. Smiling, he began rubbing it.

Nea let out a gasp of surprise as calloused fingers rubbed against the soft folds of her skin. The Soviet paused his efforts, and again, and looked up at Hale. This caused the young Finn, already quivering with rage, to take a step forward. The man held up the index finger of his left hand and moved it from side to side as if to warn Hale no you don't as his eyes settled on the knife, he held at Nea's throat.

Seeing the danger to his beautiful wife, Hale froze again. Satisfied, the man removed his fingers from Nea's crotch. He then slid the left strap of her teddy off, and slowly moved his left hand over to the right strap. He made a dramatic show of slowly pulling it off her shoulder. All the while keeping an eye on Hale.

Seeing that the Finn was cooperating, he smiled at him, and yanked hard on the lingerie. The garment fell away, revealing Nea's pale perky breasts. Seeing his wife's body exposed to this vulgar barbarian, Hale barely managed to contain the urge to charge down the hall and rip this man apart with his bare hands. Quaking with rage, he somehow managed to remain where he was.

The Russian, slowly ran his free hand up and down Nea's torso, pausing over each breast to squeeze them hard. Nea gasped out in pain. Hale, enraged, smashed his fist against a wall of the hallway. The plaster buckled from the blow leaving a large hole in the wall.

The Soviet Sergeant chuckled loudly at Hale's frustration. He stopped for a minute and simply watched as Hale's gaze remained locked with the Russian's eyes. Satisfied that Hale wasn't about to do anything rash; he moved his left hand down to Nea's panties.

With a tug from the Russian's fingers, the garment slid down her legs and landed on the top of her feet. Hale's wife was now completely nude. The Russian took a moment to look down at her body and whistled appreciatively. Enraged at his impotency, Hale smashed his left fist into the hallway wall creating another hole across the hall from the first.

The Soviet chuckling at Hale, dropped his free hand to Nea's crotch and began to rub her sex with his fingers. She gasped in surprise, then clamped her mouth shut to remain silent. She didn't want this monster to get any pleasure out of his actions. When this failed to elicit a reaction out of Nea, or Hale, he removed his hand from her crotch.

This time, instead of touching Nea, he reached behind her and unbuckled the belt of his trousers. Hale, unable to stand it, took a step forward. Before he had a chance to take a second, the Soviet Sergeant pressed the blade deeper into Nea's flesh. She let out a surprised yelp, and then clamped her mouth shut, trying to hold in the pain.

Hale, seeing the blood, now flowing freely from his wife's neck, took a step back and raised his hands up in supplication. Satisfied that Hale wasn't going to try anything further; the Russian removed his trousers. He then moved a little to Nea's side so that Hale could see how excited he was at the prospect of having his wife.

The Russian, then pushed Nea's torso forward, so he

could position himself behind her. Careful, to maintain his hold on the knife, he looked up and met Hale's gaze as he tried to push into her. Instead of Nea screaming at the violation, the Soviet Sergeant suddenly cried out in painful surprise.

He pushed Nea forward toward Hale, as he turned and swung the knife at something behind him, his knees gave out and he toppled to the ground in a heap. Standing behind him was Hale's sister Aina. She grasped the pommel of their Grandfather's pukko blade. The metal of the blade was covered in the Russian's blood.

Ignoring everyone, the little girl repeatedly plunged the blade into the quivering corpse of the Russian as Hale and Nea embraced. Nea sobbed uncontrollably as Hale stroked her hair and whispered into her ear, "It's all right. You're safe now."

As Hale whispered the words, his eyes rested on the sight of his sister, repeatedly plunging his Grandfather's blade into the bleeding mess the Russian had become, "Aina it's ok now, you saved Nea, you saved us all. Please stop doing that, the bad man is dead."

Meeting Hale's gaze Aina burst into tears and dropped the knife. Hale motioned with his right hand for the girl to come to him. She stood and ran down the hall wrapping her arms around Hale and Nea, "It's over now. You're both going to be fine."

As soon as Hale spoke the words, a fresh round of wailing erupted from his mother. Turning in her direction, Hale gestured for her to come and said, "Mom, you can't help him anymore. Please come here, Aina needs you."

Jenna shook her head no, at Hale's suggestion, wrapped her arms around the body of her husband and sobbed. Her entire body shook as the grief flowed out in waves. In response to Jeanna's distress, Aina ran to her mother. Seeing the corpse of her father for the first time, the young girl wrapped bloody hands around her mom as they both trembled with overwhelming grief.

Looking into Nea's eyes Hale asked, "Are you ok?"

"I think so. Oh Hale, I thought he was going to rape me." Her voice trailed off as she began to cry again.

Hale continued to stroke Nea's hair as she wept. The blood from her neck wound formed rivulets as it traveled down her body between her breasts. Noticing that his wife was still bleeding Hale said, "Let me get you a towel. We need to stop the bleeding."

Nea looked down at the wound in her neck and nodded dully. Hale quickly located a dish towel in the kitchen and returned, "Here use this to stop the bleeding."

Nea nodded dully and mumbled, "Thanks."

Hale hugged Nea reassuringly and said, "Are you good to be alone for a few moments? I need to go check on my mom and to take care." Hale's voice wavered and tears began to slide down his cheeks as he said, "To take care of Dad."

Nea placed her left hand on Hale's cheek and said, "Go to your mom. I'll be fine. She needs you right now more than I do."

Hale nodded as Nea gave him a reassuring smile. He wrapped his mother and Aina into an embrace. Holding them for a time, he joined in their mourning, "Mom, we've got to take care of him now. More Russians will come soon to see what happened to the first group."

Jenna looked into Hale's eyes and said, "We'll bring him with us?"

Hale shook his head, "No mom, we can't."

"We can load him in the sleigh." Jenna replied.

"The sleigh can only be used on roads. The roads are crawling with the Russians. If we try to use them, we'll just end up dead." Hale replied.

"Then we can drag him on the sleigh Aina's uses to play with." Jenna replied sharply.

Hale signed and used his hand to gently prompt his mother to look at him, "Mom, we will need to move quickly. I've got to lead us past the Russians to the Mannerheim Line, so that you, Aina, and Nea will be safe. I fear I won't be able to do that if we bring Father."

"Then what do we do with him? We can't just leave him here." Jenna's voice trembled and she fought back a sob as she added, "We can't leave him here, like this." Her voice trailed off as she said the last sentence.

Hale pondered the question for a minute and said, "The ground is frozen solid, so I can't dig him a hole, not quickly enough."

"Then we must bring him." Hale's mother snapped.

Hale held up a hand, "There is another possibility. There might be a crater in the ground, from the truck explosion. Let me go check, we may be able to bury him there, and then come back for him later."

Jeanna nodded, "You go do that, I'll wrap him in a blanket. You're right of course. We must flee so that Aina, and your baby can have a future." She paused for a moment and tearfully added, "Oh Hale, he was so proud of you. So happy that he was going to be a Grandfather. He would have been a great one you know."

Hale nodded, "The best."

Hale held her hand and gently squeezed it before breaking the contact and turning to leave. He looked over at Nea who was watching them through dull eyes. She held the kitchen towel Hale had given her against her wound, "Love will you be ok for a short time? I need to find a place to put my father to rest."

Nea nodded dully, "Good." Hale wrapped his arms around her, looked into her eyes, and said, "Can you help Mom and Aina get ready for the journey? Everyone needs to dress warmly." He paused for a moment and looked down at her nakedness. If you don't have anything warm enough for the journey, I'm sure my mom can find something for you to wear."

Nea gave Hale a faint smile and said, "Tramping through the woods, after nearly being raped and butchered is not how I envisioned our wedding night together."

Hale managed a faint laugh in response to Nea's levity, "Nor I."

Epilogue

Early Morning, Karelia Isthmus, Finland, Karhonen Farm, North of the Village of Perkjarvi, December 7th, 1939

A Gaz-MM truck screeched to a halt. A man opened the passenger side door from the inside and lowered himself to the ground. Taking a deep breath, he put his hand on his hips and looked around at the scene. Behind him, a squad of soldiers disembarked from the rear of the truck and fanned out to secure the area.

The man pulled a cigarette from a silver chrome plated case he kept in his pocket and lit it with a match. The light from the match revealed three red squares on his collar. The Commissar took a deep drag off the cigarette. He savored the taste of the tobacco and slowly exhaled into the frigid cold. Turning to the driver who had just joined him he said, "He was here."

"The sniper?" The driver asked.

The Commissar slowly nodded, "Yes the sniper. Who else could have lured two of our men to their deaths, stripped them of their gear, and made his way through the countryside to kill two more squads of our men?"

A Sergeant ran to the Commissar and saluted, "Report."

The Sergeant swallowed nervously, "Sir, it looks like some kind of fight took place here."

"Wow, you're a genius. Care to elaborate?" The Commissar snapped back.

The Sergeant's eyes narrowed, "Sir, there are two squads of our soldiers here dead. It appears that a squad of riflemen mainly died facing the house, so the Finn's must have been holed up there."

"What about the mortar squad?" The Commissar asked.

"That's a separate matter." The Sergeant replied.

"How so?" The Commissar asked.

"It looks like they were engaged by a separate force. Whatever that force had, caused the truck, and the mortar rounds they had with them to explode. I'm afraid there isn't much left of the squad. One thing was curious."

"Curious? How?" The Commissar demanded.

It appears that the spot of the initial explosion has been filled back in. Why would the Finns do that?" The Sergeant asked.

The Commissar shrugged his shoulders, "Who knows why these people do what they fucking do. Maybe they had someone to bury. With the soil frozen solid, it would have been the only way. At least we killed one of the fuckers."

"In exchange for sixteen of ours." The Sergeant replied.

The Commissar glared at the Sergeant for a moment and then asked, "What about the house?"

"We found the two riflemen that didn't die with the rest of their squad inside. One had been shot; the other had been stabbed dozens of times." The Sergeant stifled a shiver as he said the last few words and then continued, "One of them had his pants down around his ankles."

"Which one?" Inquired the Commissar.

"The one that had been stabbed." The Sergeant replied.

"Interesting. Anything else?" The Commissar asked.

The Sergeant nodded, "There was a pool of blood on the kitchen floor that didn't appear to belong to either of our slain soldiers."

"That's where the Fin buried in the crater must have died." The Commissar paused and looked around at the chaotic scene, "I bet he was the one out here. The one that destroyed the mortar squad and killed most of the riflemen."

"Who, Sir?" The Sergeant inquired.

"Hale Karhonen!" The Commissar snapped. Turning to face the Sergeant, his eyes narrowed as he barked, "Anything else?"

The Sergeant's shoulders slumped, and he involuntarily took a step back from this enraged officer, "Yes, Sir. We found a set of tracks at the edge of the clearing over there. They lead into the forest. One of my men followed them for a short time. He said that they turn north about three hundred meters into the woods."

"They're making for the Mannerheim line. Call headquarters, we need a dog team to track the bastard, and at least three more squads. He paused for a moment, put his hands on his hips, took a long look around him at the carnage and added, "Clearly two squads aren't enough."

"No, Sir." The Sergeant agreed.

"Prioritize the dogs so we can run the son of a bitch down." The Sergeant turned to leave when the Commissar added, "Oh, and one more thing, cancel Pekka's execution. He may be of further use to us."

"Yes, Sir."

James Mullins

Afterword

I hope you enjoyed The Winter Sniper. Getting to know Hale over the last year has been a great experience. I hope you have enjoyed the journey as much as I have and I look forward to seeing you again for the continuation of the tale in the second novel of the series Against the Commissar.

From Hale's perspective, this book covered the first eight days of the Soviet invasion of Finland. The Winter War, as the conflict between Finland and the Soviet Union came to be known, lasted four months from November 30th 1939 to March 13th of 1940. This leaves plenty more of the war to write about!

The idea for the story first occurred to me in 2018 when I was in Barnes and Noble waiting for my better half to pick out some books. Being an avid book reader myself, and a writer one would think that having to wait in Barnes and Noble wasn't such a bad thing, right? Well yeah, but thanks to space constraints with my residence I can't buy physical books anymore. It was like being a candy addict surrounded by candy you couldn't sample, because you were on a diet.

Determined to make the best of the situation I found myself wandering, as I always do, to the section on military history. I let my eyes scan the rows of books trying to stifle a yawn, medieval books, done that, Ancient Rome, I could probably write my own book on that subject, World War II, yawn. What history nerd hasn't read eight million books about the biggest conflict in history? Then it happened, my eyes landed on Osprey's Finland at War and my mind said, *Hello this is new!*

I picked the book up, found a seat, and started reading it. I got about twenty pages in before I was collected by my wife as it was time to go. Fast forward to November of

2018, I found myself in Barnes and Nobles once again, this time waiting on my parents who I was visiting for the Thanksgiving Holiday. Rinse and repeat, guess where I ended up and continued where I left off? You got it, Finland at War.

At the time, I had just finished writing Book 3 in the Byzantium Infected Series Emperor's Errand. I was on a writing break, while my editor did his thing to make it a better book. By the time my parents collected me to leave, I was hooked. During my break from hungry zombies bent on making a meal out of the Medieval Roman Empire, I decided to write a short story about Finland's Winter War.

I wrote my short story and put it up on a popular E-Book seller for free. That story became chapter one of this book. The results were pretty astonishing. I received more likes and emails for that one short story than I had on all of the short stories combined that I had published on that site set in the Byzantium Infected Universe.

Since I had so much fun doing the research and writing the short story, the choice became clear. It was time to write a full-length novel! The result of that thought is the story you just completed.

Thank you very much for purchasing and reading this novel. I really appreciate you! Could I ask for a favor? I need your help to spread the word to other readers. If you enjoyed the story, I would very much appreciate it, if you would return to Amazon or stop by Good Reads and leave an honest review. Even if you just click one of the stars, every little bit helps. It is the word-of-mouth testimony from readers like you, that is the life blood of independent authors such as myself. Let me extend a personal thank you in advance for your review. I appreciate it, thank you!

If you enjoyed my style of writing and have an interest

in the 7th Century Zombie Apocalypse check out my Byzantium Infected Series. This series follows the adventures of three Roman Infantrymen Athos, Baltazar, and Constan as they navigate their changed world through four novels: Scourge of Byzantium, Damascus of the Damned, Emperor's Errand Part I, and Emperor's Errand Part II. Following the About the Author section I have included two chapters from the first novel in the series Scourge of Byzantium. All four of these novels are available for Amazon Kindle, and Print.

If you want to keep abreast of the latest developments in the Winter Sniper Universe and my other projects follow me on Facebook and Twitter.

You can find me on facebook at:
https://www.facebook.com/James-Mullins-174236536279317/

And Twitter at: https://twitter.com/JMullinsAuthor

If you want to drop me a direct line, I'd love to hear what you think about the story, or whatever else is on your mind. Feedback is greatly appreciated. You can email me directly at jamesmullinsauthor@yahoo.com

Thanks for reading!

About the Author

James Mullins holds three college degrees, a Masters and Bachelors in Business Administration and an Associates Acquisition and Contract Management. He lives with his beautifully intelligent Wife Anna and ten pounds of tenaciousness and fury Catalina the Cat (she keeps us in line) and the newest addition to the family TBD the kitten. Hopefully when you return for book two in the series he will have a name!

James has had a diverse employment history. He got his start as an Avionics Attack System Specialist for the United States Air Force's 71st Fighter Squadron, known as the Ironmen. During several tours of duty in the Middle East, James came to appreciate the beauty and harshness of the desert. Next, he built upon his problem-solving skills as a Pest Control Department Manager for Patriot Pest Control. During this time, he happily slew millions of bugs for the betterment of humankind, or at least making the lives of many a little less gross.

Today, he works for a major defense contractor in the United States. He spends his days helping to keep the purchasing community on the straight and narrow, so that his co-workers can continue to build good ships. All his life he has had a passion for history with diverse interests in Rome, Byzantium, the Middle Ages, and the American Civil War. The Winter Sniper is his fifth novel.

Printed in Great Britain
by Amazon

63971823R00163